MURDER ENDS THE SONG

ALFRED MEYERS

COACHWHIP PUBLICATIONS
Greenville, Ohio

Murder Ends the Song, by Alfred Meyers
© 2015 Coachwhip Publications

First published 1941.
No claims made on public domain material.

CoachwhipBooks.com

ISBN 1-61646-298-1
ISBN-13 978-1-61646-298-7

Dearest Death: Alfred Louis Meyers and *Murder Ends the Song* (1941)

Curtis Evans

IN 1980 NGAIO MARSH (1895-1982) published her penultimate detective novel, *Photo-Finish* (1980), a mystery set in the opera world. Between the plots of *Photo-Finish* and Alfred Louis Meyers' *Murder Ends the Song* (1941), another opera mystery, there are some striking similarities. Whether Marsh ever read Meyers' novel I do not know, but fans of Marsh certainly should do so, now that Meyers' mystery has been reprinted, after nearly seventy-five years. Like Marsh, Meyers in *Murder Ends the Song* shows considerable sophistication in his depiction of an opera milieu, yet he surpasses the Crime Queen in fashioning a classic detective novel puzzle, teasingly clued and genuinely baffling.

Alfred Louis Meyers (1906-1963) was a great opera buff, without a doubt. At Notre Dame University, where he received a B.A. and an M.A. in English (his 1928 thesis was titled "An American Paradox"), Meyers was a prominent member of the Glee Club; and in 1937 he sang in the chorus of the San Francisco Opera, having settled in the City by the Bay after the death of his father, a bank cashier in La Grande, a small city in northeastern Oregon. The son, the author bio on the dust jacket of *Murder Ends the Song* explains, had worked "off and on in his father's bank," all the while "singing in any chorus that would use his talents."

In *Murder Ends the Song*, published at the tail end of the Golden Age of the detective novel, Meyers chronicles the slaying of Marina Grazie, an imperious but past-her-prime coloratura soprano—the sort who trills impossibly high notes in bel canto operas—attempting a comeback of sorts in Portland, Oregon. Several times in the novel Meyers mentions the opera singer Luisa Tetrazzini (1871-1940), one of the great adepts of this showy art form. Meyers' Marina Grazie is to an extent modeled after Tetrazzini, who died at the age of 68 the year Meyers was composing his mystery. In 1910, when Meyers was but a child, the diva performed a celebrated outdoor concert in San Francisco, a city she loved, just four years after the infamous earthquake. Five years earlier Tetrazzini had made her U.S. debut at San Francisco's Tivoli Theater, in the role of Gilda in Verdi's *Rigoletto*. At the conclusion of her performance of the renowned aria "Caro nome" ("dearest name"), journalist Samuel Dickson reported at the time, "there was a breathless pause, and then [the audience] went mad. . . . Men stood on the seats of their chairs and threw their hats in the air; women tore flowers from their dresses and threw them on the stage. And when that mad pandemonium had finally stilled. . . . Tetrazzini sang the 'Caro nome' again."[1] This renowned aria plays a pivotal role in *Murder Ends the Song*: in the novel readers will find provided a diagram of a page of the sheet music, as well as an illustration of the aria's title, found scrawled in blood on the mirror in Grazie's dressing room.

Along with Tony Graine, the tenor currently performing with Grazie in her attempted West Coast comeback, Tony's accompanist and bosom buddy, Walter Sands ("Sandy"), and a caricatured caretaking couple, Mr. and Mrs. Tait, Marina Grazie and her entourage, composed of her niece, her doctor, her accompanist, her companion-secretary and her chauffeur, find themselves stranded in the isolated, hulking old barn of a country mansion

---

[1] Leta E. Miller, *Music and Politics in San Francisco: From the 1906 Quake to the Second World War* (Berkeley, CA and Los Angeles: University of California Press, 2012), 141. The American pasta dish tetrazzini is said to have been created in the diva's honor around this time, by Ernest Arbogast, chef of San Francisco's Palace Hotel.

known as Lucifer's Pride, built many years previously along the Columbia River Gorge by an eccentric millionaire, wheat king Lucifer Bolliver, as a would-be wedding present for Grazie. (Sadly for Bolliver, she broke off the engagement, keeping the diamond.) The mansion can only be reached by a ferry boat, which most unfortunately has been obliterated in an ice storm. The much-hated Marina soon meets her demise at Lucifer's Pride, by means of a knitting needle stabbed into the base of her skull (a method employed a few years previously in an English detective novel). This brutal act commences a twenty-four-hour nightmare for those individuals trapped in Lucifer's Pride. (Here similarities with the real-life coloratura soprano Luisa Tetrazzini end, by the way, for Tetrazzini seems to have been generally beloved.)

Two more deaths follow before Tony Graine, who has turned amateur detective, cracks the case. Along the way, the reader is provided with three illustrations, a floor plan, a list of documents and, near the end of the tale, a tabulation of clues. Alfred Meyers was a good sportsman, not afraid to "play the game" fairly with his readers, and the result is a most enjoyable classic mystery, composed in the manner of the great Ellery Queen. Moreover, Meyers' novel has a surprisingly poignant ending. Essentially with *Murder Ends the Song* Meyers looks back to the past in devising a classical style puzzle, but also ahead to the future in endowing his resolution with emotional resonance. It is a shame that this fine detective novel was so long forgotten, but this neglect perhaps should not be surprising, given that the book until now was never reprinted in paperback—despite good notices in the *New York Times Book Review* and the *Saturday Review*—and that its publisher, Reynal & Hitchcock, was not, to my knowledge, much associated with the mystery genre.

Despite apparently having only published this one novel, Meyers, according to Jeffrey Marks' *Anthony Boucher: A Bibliobiography,* in 1947 was elected the first Treasurer of the Northern California chapter of the Mystery Writers of America. (The distinguished Lenore Glen Offord was elected Secretary and the eminent Anthony Boucher Vice President, which raises the question, who the heck was the President?) The same year Meyers also wrote one of the chapters in the true crime anthology *San Francisco Murders*. (Other contributors were Boucher, Offord and Hildergarde Teilhet.) What Meyers did after this I do not know, although he was still living in San Francisco in 1958, five years before his untimely death in 1963.

It turns out that Alfred Louis Meyers is connected to my family by marriage, if one goes back quite far. Alice Palmer, a sister of Meyer's six great grandfather John Palmer (1667-1739), was the third wife of my eight great grandfather Richard Buffington (1654-1748). Like Raymond Chandler, whose family is also related to mine by marriage, our ancestors go back to Chester County, Pennsylvania at the time of William Penn. Additionally, I also have discovered interesting details concerning Meyers' more immediate family background. His maternal ancestors, the Palmers and the Newlins, though originally Pennsylvania Quakers, moved out to Oregon from Iowa in the early 1870s and converted to Catholicism. Meyers' mother, Mildred Lee Newlin (in memory of whom *Murder Ends the Song* is dedicated), married a Frederick Louis Meyers, a Catholic originally from Toronto, who moved to La Grande, Oregon in the 1890s, after he graduated from the University of Ottawa. In La Grande he started as an office boy in the La Grande National Bank, eventually becoming Cashier.

In 1922-23, when Frederick's and Mildred's son Alfred was a high school student, the La Grande chapter (klavern) of the militantly anti-Catholic Ku Klux Klan mounted a pressure campaign to secure Frederick Meyers' dismissal as Cashier of the La Grande National Bank. This KKK campaign failed, but the La Grande klavern did succeed in getting Evalyn Rohan Newlin, the wife of Mildred Newlin Meyer's brother Chester Peter Newlin, fired from her job as a public schoolteacher, on the grounds that she sent her children to a Catholic school.

All the Meyers children attended this Catholic school, Sacred Heart Academy, themselves. In 1997, Alfred's sister Margaret, a member of the Society of the Sisters of the Holy Names of Jesus and Mary, recalled that their parents kept these unpleasant details from the children, though she added that for several years in the 1920s the La Grande klavern burned crosses "halfway up Table Mountain, a steep hillside directly above our residential area in La Grande." She also remembered seeing "Klan members, their identity concealed under full regalia, riding horseback about our streets in broad daylight."[2]

Happily, at the Catholic University of Notre Dame, where he received his B.A. and M.A. degrees in the 1920s, Alfred Meyers found a much more supportive and stimulating environment. He also was able to indulge his great passion for singing when he became a member of the prestigious Notre Dame Glee Club. It was this passion that gave life to his single detective novel, *Murders Ends the Song*, a superlative example of the classic form.

---

[2] On the harassment of the Meyers family by the La Grange Ku Klux Klan, see David A. Horowitz, ed., *Inside the Klavern: The Secret History of a Ku Klux Klan of the 1920s* (Carbondale: Southern Illinois University, 1990) and Sister Margaret Meyers, "The Ku Klux Klan in La Grande, Oregon, 1918-1924," *American Catholic History Classroom*, at http://cuomeka.wrlc.org/exhibits/show/osc/documents/osc-doc9.

To My Mother

1

I HAVE ONLY THREE AVERSIONS: boiled cabbage, scrambled brains, and coloratura sopranos. Of the three I think the last the most noxious. Once, starving, I choked down cabbage and brains. At the same meal, too. I can't say I enjoyed them but I did get them down the hatch.

I have yet to hear a coloratura who has not bored me to the point of committing mayhem. From Tetrazzini right down the line through Galli-Curci and Toti dal Monte to Lily Pons, they have impressed me as being about as satisfying aesthetically as a mouthful of rancid lard to a starving man.

At the time I first heard Marina Grazie, Galli-Curci had passed her prime; Lily Pons had not yet electrified New York with her vocal lightning; and Marina, sharing honors with Jeritza and Bori, was queening it at the Metropolitan. She had the coloratura field to herself: *Lucia*, Mozart's *Magic Flute* (which had been revived for her that year), *Rigoletto*, and Filina to Bori's Mignon in the Ambroise Thomas atrocity.

The afternoon I attended she was singing *Lucia*—singing it like a nightingale on a sloe-gin jag. Technically she was, I suppose, in fine enough form. Cascades of tone tumbled from her throat in profusion, bombarding the ears like spurts from a machine-gun; cadenzas and trills sparked and spattered like hails of silver bullets. It was something like a vocal Fourth of July fireworks display. The audience sat paralyzed until, at the conclusion of the Mad Scene, they too went mad. Egged on by Marina's notoriously well-paid claque, they sent up such a bedlam of applause and bravas and stamping of feet that at last the curtains were closed for a moment while the frenzied ecstatics regained their reason.

It was a good show. But it left me completely cold. All I could see was a heaving bosom under a befrilled white nightgown. This was no lovely child, no anguished, tortured Lucy; it was only a hefty meal-sack of a woman flinging out a meaningless burble of sound the sole appeal of which was to the box-office, not the heart. The voice? An hysterical meadowlark could have done as much.

Prejudiced? Unimaginative? That may be. It is, however, my opinion and I choose to be stuck with it. I repeat: I dislike coloraturas, and from the first time I heard it, I disliked Marina's particular brand.

You are, therefore, to imagine my irritation when, the morning after I had sung a smashing Don José in Portland, she was the cause of my being awakened by a telephone call.

It was seven thirty. I was dreaming that Mr. Edward Johnson was pointing to a dotted line and saying: "New York demands your immediate appearance at the Metropolitan. In two weeks you sing Pelléas to Miss Bori's Mélisande." (Someday I shall sing Pelléas at the Met. but not, alas, with Lucrezia, who retired at the close of the 1935-36 season.) I was just reaching for the pen when the phone clattered.

Jerked into wakefulness, I shouted for Sandy and closed my eyes again. But the pen was gone, and Johnson with it.

The phone shrilled on.

I rolled over, cursing. Across the room Sandy had the covers pulled over his head. For five minutes I lay there and exhausted my repertoire of profanity, which is, incidentally, larger than my operatic one. Sandy sprawled on.

At last I gave up. Dragging myself out of bed, I emptied the carafe of water over Sandy and groped my way to the clanging fiend on the writing desk.

The receiver was sizzling.

"Damn you, Graine," came Nero's gentle greeting. "I've been ringing for twenty minutes. Pile into your clothes and hop down here. We're due at the airport in half an hour."

You don't know Nero, do you? His real name is Grady Mawson and he is business manager of the Monte Calvo Company. The trouble is, he fancies himself as a sort of bastard offspring of Messalina and the head of the Russian Ogpu. I've often thought he might be fairly tolerable if someone only slapped his ears down to fairly human size. But no one ever has. You see, Nero also handles the publicity and we opera singers are usually canny enough to kiss the hand that smears butter on our bread.

This, though, was one time when I felt that unbuttered bread might be palatable. I let him have it. With both barrels.

I told him that Portland would never hear a better Don José than the one I had sung the night before. I suggested that if last night's *Carmen* was a success it was due solely to my efforts since his so-called mezzo had sung Mérimée's whoring gypsy wench with all the abandon of a nun intoning Gregorian chant in the cloister chapel. I reminded him that I was to sing the Duke in *Rigoletto* Saturday afternoon but hinted that by that time I would probably have been jailed for murdering a nitwit manager who telephoned his artists in the middle of the night. Finally I told him that I needed sleep and that, by the gods of Valhalla, I was going to have it if I had to tear out the telephone and ram it down his yapping managerial gullet. I added that, by God, I'd have him know he couldn't swear at me.

In short, I told him.

He was floored. The wire brought me only the sound of his choked gurgling as he struggled for words and breath. But no floor is adhesive enough to hold Nero long. He spluttered. He clamored. He raved. He threatened me with everything from the ordeal by fire to the curse of the Witch of Endor.

I laughed.

At last he turned to pleading. "But, damn it, Graine, La Grazie's arriving to sing Gilda with you on Saturday. If we aren't there to meet her, she'll pull the airport down."

From the way he said "Grazie" you would have thought he had cornered Lily Pons herself, arranged her on a platter, and ordered her served up with a garnish of water-cress and lemon jelly. Well, I wasn't having any.

"I don't care if it's the Second Coming," I shouted. "You've known about it ever since San Francisco. Why didn't you fix up your triumphal reception then? I'll be damned if I drag myself out in the small hours to throw palm branches in front of a broken-down old operatic war-horse."

A bed creaked behind me. I turned. Sandy was calmly transferring his cadaverous length from his drenched cot into mine. Nero bellowed that he had told Sandy the night before that I was expected to attend the reception and that, by God, I'd be there or I'd have a wire from Gaul in New York canceling my contract.

Someone in the next room banged on the wall. "Pipe down in there. What do you think this is—the zoo?"

I gave up. I might have known better than to start anything with Nero. Faced with no bed, no contract, and certainly no consideration, I gave up.

"Very well," I said with dignity. "I shall meet you in the lobby in ten minutes. But don't think you've heard the end of this. I—"

"Cut that! You be down here in five minutes or I'll plant a kick on somebody's rear end."

The receiver was slammed in my ear.

I dressed in record time. As I was ready to leave I paused beside the bed where Sandy was ostentatiously snoring. "So you knew about this yesterday, you filthy double-crosser," I whispered into his too-sleeping ear.

His hand moved on the pillow until his thumb came in contact with his nose.

That was the final touch. "We'll have this out later," I promised, and tipped the bed over. Vaguely soothed by the muffled yells that issued from the quaking mass on the floor, I went down to meet Nero.

Meet Nero!

That sounds innocuous enough. Yet I know now that I was taking the first steps on a journey that was to bring me, eventually, face to face with blood and terror and death.

Meet Nero.

My God!

2

IT WAS A FOUL DAY. The dirty February sky was wide open, pouring down sheets of half-frozen water. Office workers skittered down the glazed sidewalks, clutching at buildings and each other in a frantic effort to maintain traction. Everything was obscured by a veil of fog that forced its way even through the closed windows of our taxi, rasping the throat, stinging the eyes. It was cold as hell.

"The City of Roses," I grumbled, tugging my muffler tighter around my throat.

"Even a rosebush has to take time out," Nero said blithely. He had won his point and could afford good humor. "Anyway, what do you care? The town's breaking its g-string to hear you."

I shrugged. It was eight o'clock! I was still half asleep and furious, into the bargain. I didn't feel like arguing.

"And if," he went on gaily, "they're packing in now, what'll they do when you two team up? Grazie's got a following out here on the Coast that'd jam Madison Square Garden. Star on three radio programs."

"It seems to me," I remarked icily, "that Mae West has appeared on the radio, too. Why not sign her up to sing *Butterfly?*"

"That's an idea." He snapped his fingers. "A novelty."

That should give you a fair idea of the way Nero's mind worked. I groaned. "And there's one thing more," I said presently. "If there's any slapping done, I don't intend to be in the receiving line."

While I was dressing I had remembered the performance at the Metropolitan just before Grazie took her run-out when she hauled off and whaled Caroni, the tenor, till the gallery echoed. She said afterwards that Caroni had sung flat. Caroni, always the gentleman, countered that Marina's vocal utterance could scarcely be called singing, flat or otherwise. That row was, as I recall it, the only interesting phase of that whole Metropolitan season. I did not, however, intend to have it repeated for the edification of the Pacific Coast.

"She'll behave," Nero said indifferently. "It's in her contract in black and white. Anyway, she wouldn't bother making trouble with small-fry like you."

How do you like that? After all, I've been at the game only two years and I know I'm no Gigli. But I do have a clipping from the San Francisco *Chronicle* admitting that my Des Grieux in *Manon* is finer than Schipa's.

"If she's so goddam good," I exploded, "why is she singing with this one-horse outfit? With all her radio programs, I shouldn't think she'd bother with the chicken feed you and Gaul dish out."

He smiled. "Throw no sour grapes at the radio, little boy; you'll get your cut some day."

(He knew as well as I why Marina Grazie had signed with the Monte Calvo Company. The plain truth was that she had attempted a bluff and the bluff had been called. Accustomed as she was to a clear field at the Met, she had gone into a pet in 1931, during Lily Pons's first season in New York. She who had had her own sweet way for fifteen years now found the public engrossed in a streamlined singer who managed to look within forty years and three hundred pounds of the part she was singing. She couldn't take it. Thinking, no doubt, that Gatti-Casazza would track her down, brandishing a contract as fat as she was, she ran out. Holed in in San Francisco. And waited. And waited. *And waited.* Gatti, annoyed at the publicity over the Caroni slapping, was content to let her go. Two years later "The Great Grazie" appeared as guest artist on the Conch Oil program. She had never gotten a look-in at the Met. since.)

"She's tired of sulking," I went on, "and she's trying to make a comeback. But you'll find out she's the lousiest thing you've ever tried to handle."

Murder Ends the Song

That remark went home. A shadow passed over Nero's face. He recovered himself instantly, however, and laid a paternal hand on my knee.

"You're a big boy now, Tony. Time to grow up and forget these petty jealousies. You singers are all alike. I tell you—"

"You'll tell me nothing. I'm with this claptrap company to make a name for myself. Well, I'm doing it. Read the papers and see for yourself. And I'll be damned if I'll be made a fool of before two thousand people. I've got my career to think of."

"You knew she was appearing out here when you signed up," he pointed out.

But I was past reasoning. My position was the result solely of merit and value of performances given. I had asked no favors; I had earned everything I had received. I don't think I could be blamed for resenting this fanfare over a woman who, as far as this country was concerned, had been artistically dead for years, who was being added to the company solely for the box-office value of a name that should have been allowed to remain decently interred, and who would undoubtedly attempt to rule the roost with the high and mighty hand of an old-school prima donna.

Yes, I'll admit I was good and furious, angry to the point of indiscretion. As proof of it, consider my next remark:

"All right, I'll sing your goddam Duke with her on Saturday but I'm warning you—if she pulls one boner, if she starts up-staging me once, I swear I'll—I'll murder her."

People often say things like that without meaning a thing. That remark was important only because it was the first time that the word "murder" was mentioned in connection with Grazie. But it was not the last. During the days to follow murder was to stalk us like a nightmare, lurking in dark, silent, cold rooms, haunting us by day and night.

I have admitted frankly my dislike of Marina. But I insist I could not carry dislike, however virulent, to the point of actual violence, of murder.

Yet someone did.

Someone did just that.

3

AT EIGHT FORTY-FIVE the congregation had assembled at Swan Island Airport for morning worship: news reporters, camera men, male interviewers and sob-sisters, a reception committee from the Hotel Olympia, a delegation from the City Hall headed by His Honor, the Mayor, sightseers and hangers-on drawn by the aura of impending excitement.

An affable young reporter named Hank, who had given me a front page story in the *Oregonian* on my arrival, hailed me. He was holding one of the press-sheets Nero had sent around to all the papers.

"Quite a party the Madame's dragging along," he remarked, adding bitterly, "I suppose I'll have to call it an entourage."

I hadn't known who would be in the Grazie party and asked if I might see the list. Hank handed it over. It read:

> "The following are the members of Madame Grazie's party:
> Dr. Beale Thorndyke, physician
> Mr. Julian Porter, accompanist
> Miss Ambrosia Swisshome, companion-secretary
> Miss Elena Grazie, Madame Grazie's niece
> Mr. James Paris, pilot and chauffeur
> Madame Grazie and all members of her party will be guests of the Hotel Olympia during the Portland visit. On Tuesday next Madame Grazie will

pay a visit to Lucifer's Pride. (This fact may be used for publicity but the trip will be private.)"

Hank said, "Know anything about this Lucifer's Pride angle?"

I said I was under the impression that Lucifer had been cured of that sin a long while ago and Hank said he didn't think that was funny enough for the radio, so I simply said I didn't have the vaguest idea and cared even less.

Hank looked at his watch. "Eight fifty. What's holding up the procession? I've got a ten o'clock deadline. Is she coming or is she coming?"

"Keep your pants on, laddie." That was Nero from over my shoulder. "You'll get a story that is a story. Be sure and pump her on the Lucifer's Pride angle."

A faint humming struck through the buzz of conversation. Every head swiveled back and jaws dropped as eyes attempted to pierce the grey murk. The humming grew until, like the fog, it seemed to smother you. Then, like Wotan's raven winging from Valhalla, a plane glided out of the clammy heavens and taxied to rest a short twenty paces from us. The motor stuttered and died.

The mob of groundlings pressed forward, cameramen holding their machines over their heads to keep them out of the crush. Nero cleared his throat imperatively. As at a signal the crowd parted and banked in respectful rows on either side of a passageway through which we marched majestically up to the plane. I could almost hear the pompous strains of the "Triumphal March"; one missed the Ethiopian slaves in chains and brown union suits before Rhadames' chariot.

"Will she eat this up!" Nero whispered as we halted beside the Mayor.

"Hollywood," I jeered.

"That's why she'll love it. Now watch. This'll be a swell sample of a lost art. You're about to see what used to be called 'the grand entrance'."

It was more like the unveiling of a monument.

A short flight of metal steps was wheeled up to the door, which was then flung open dramatically by a stewardess who came smartly to attention. The pilot—a good-looking, youngish chap—hopped out and cleared the way for the first emergence.

It was a tall, bony woman with cropped iron-grey hair and a mouth like a wrinkled prune. A huge cretonne bag hung from one arm, dribbling lengths of knitting in various stages of construction. She marched grimly down the steps, jabbed a reporter in the ribs with a knitting needle, smiled with malicious amusement at his surprised howl of pain, and rooted herself at the foot of the stairs. Her sharp eyes swept us with inquisitive dislike.

"That," Nero muttered, "should be Miss Swisshome. And its name, by all the gods of irony, is Ambrosia."

Next came a young man of about thirty, muscular and chunky. Unlike the woman, he seemed unaware of the crowd. His slumberous, strangely Oriental eyes noted and dismissed. He was smartly dressed in the Hollywood fashion. His face was burned mahogany, but I suspected sun-lamp rather than Sol since there seemed to me a definite hot-house quality about his careless elegance.

"The doctor?" Nero whispered.

"My guess is the accompanying Porter. I don't like him. Looks like a well-fattened stoat."

"Check," he agreed, not knowing what a stoat was but liking the uncomplimentary sound of the word.

The man following was obviously the physician. Older than the accompanist, he was also taller and he was lithe where Porter was bulky. His trimmed, spruce look implied hours with tennis racquet, medicine ball, and golf clubs. He was, I should say, around thirty-six or seven. I liked him as much as I disliked the pianist.

The next arrival brought the reporters to vibrant life. The younger ones nervously straightened their ties and rearranged their sodden hats. The older ones contented themselves with a mental preening and a reminiscent brightening of the eyes.

The cause of it all was a girl. She was smartly dressed in furs and she was lovely and dark-eyed. There was, however, a defiant, almost unhappy urgency in her face. She shot a lightning glance at the crowd, then looked down fixedly at the steps as she started to descend.

I might have missed what followed if I hadn't suddenly become conscious of a definite sparking in the air as though a current of electricity had been shot through us.

The girl had paused on the second step and was staring wide-eyed at the tableau confronting her. The doctor and the accompanist had stepped forward at the same moment to assist her. But something had distracted them. There they stood, facing each other, tense, almost ready to spring at each other's throat. Porter's lips were moving. I could not hear what he said but the doctor could. The latter's face went white and the muscles of his jaw jerked. The watching crowd was hushed.

"Beale! Julian!" The girl's words came in an agonized stage whisper. She thrust out her small gloved hands as though to separate them.

"Please!"

Instantly it was as though nothing had happened. The men glanced towards her and stepped back submissively. The girl continued on down without assistance. She linked her arm through Miss Swisshome's and I saw her sag with weariness against the elder woman.

It was all over and I could scarcely believe I had seen anything. Later on, though, I was to remember that scene. It would find its proper niche in the horrible scheme of things that was being laid out for us.

After that excitement there was a pause.

Inside the plane nothing moved. Outside, all eyes were fixed on the door. There was silence. The quiet deepened until even I was caught in the spell. I found normal breathing difficult. Beside me, Hank and Nero were almost gasping.

The silence spun itself out, coiled like a rope around us. Someone sighed. It was like a pistol shot.

"My God," I thought, "the old harridan certainly knows her timing. Talk about an effect!"

Just as the tension reached its utmost—when another moment's delay would have snapped it into anti-climax—La Grazie stood before us. One moment the doorway was empty; the next, miraculously, it was full of prima donna.

She looked every inch the *grande dame*. Swathed from throat to toes in rippling mink, a mink turban pulled low over one eye, she stood surveying us, a queen dispassionately observing a gathering of her subjects. A Pekinese cradled in one of her arms yapped fitfully. In the crook of the other she carried a large leather case with ostentatious locks. Her chin lifted high, her one visible dark eye keen and penetrating, she simply stood.

And we accepted her. My reason told me that this was simply a dumpy, shapeless woman; that the collar of her coat thrown back would reveal a fat, wrinkled neck; that with the coat removed she would stand, an obese old woman tottering on tiny ankles and spike heels. My reason told me all that, but my sensibilities were caught by the sheer majesty of her poise. I, like the others, was englamoured. Unashamedly entrapped.

What is glamour? I have never known. I can only recognize it when I come in contact with it. Farrar had more of it in one little finger than a dozen of our modern Butterflys and Toscas combined. Mary Garden accomplished more with one twitch of Carmen's shawl than all the singers who have followed her. Eames, Sembrich, Melba, Calvé—the whole list of twenty years ago—they were able to imbue even their public bickering with a strange dramatic dignity. Like demigods they managed, by some witchcraft, to robe themselves in an almost eerie awesomeness.

Of course, public taste is largely responsible. In olden days, readers were titillated by the news that Farrar had slapped the face of the Crown Prince of Germany. Now the public professes to display fascinated interest in the fact that Tiara Rosbloom does her own marketing with a vegetable basket swinging from one arm.

I think it's a damned shame. Although of the new school, still I love the old figures with their stilted stage deportment, their ranting delivery, their sweeping gestures, their *Sturm and Drang*. However much we younger ones may sneer at our elders, we must admit they possessed something sadly lacking in our generation. (Always excepting the magnificent Kirsten Flagstad who, one reads, can knit up to her entrance for Brünnhilde's Immolation Threnody in *Götterdämmerung* and still outglamour the combined efforts of Nordica, Ternina, and Lilli Lehmann.)

Because I feel as I do and because I realize that the operatic stage has lost something very definite in the waning of glamour, I was forced, grudgingly, to admire Marina at that moment. She was demonstrating beyond the shadow of a doubt that even if her voice were only a shattered wreck and her figure gone utterly, she was still in full possession of her grand manner.

She stood, I say—and then chose to break the spell. She smiled, bowed, accepted the hand which Thorndyke extended, and swept down the steps.

Nero advanced, nudging the Mayor forward. "Dear lady," he said grandly, "may I present His Honor, the Mayor of Portland?"

Even His Honor succumbed to her manner, bending over the pudgy outstretched hand, managing a kind of courtly grace. Marina smiled graciously and listened to the short speech of welcome. At the conclusion, inundated by a torrent of roses, she turned on the charm with a vengeance. Standing on tiptoe to make sure of the correct camera angle, she leaned forward and kissed His Honor enthusiastically, holding the pose while the cameras clicked.

"Told you she knows the ropes," Nero muttered to me. "Portland eats that up. Mary Garden kissed the mayor fifteen years ago and the town hasn't gotten over it yet."

I was presented next. I bowed, murmured.

"Ah, yes," she cooed. "You are the young man to sing opposite me tomorrow afternoon. I tell you this: we shall give this so lovely city such singing as they have never heard."

I didn't doubt that, but I only gulped and nodded. I could straighten out that "opposite me" with Nero later.

Then the newspaper people swooped down. Madame stood her ground, parrying the questions with tact, charm, and even wit. I observed that she said nothing definite but said it with such grace and good humor that it sounded somewhat like a "Fireside Chat." I was amazed at her English. I had become so accustomed to the stumbling illiteracies of the Monte Calvo singers that I was astounded at her fluency and precision.

The act progressed nicely. The reporters were frantically taking down Madame's enthusiastic description of the priceless jewels in the case under her arm when Hank asked a question.

"But about this trip to Lucifer's Pride, Madame? Is there any particular reason for it?"

Jewels forgotten, every head snapped up. Pencils poised motionless.

Madame stiffened. The Peke yelped with pain and struggled within the angle of her arm.

"What is this about Lucifer's Pride?" she demanded, all charm gone. She was icy. Hard as granite. "Who has said anything about it?"

Half a dozen of Nero's press-sheets were thrust at her. Flinging the squeaking Peke at Ambrosia Swisshome, she snatched one of the papers. She read it, her visible eye blazing. She looked up, transfixing us.

"Who," she thundered, "who is responsible for this?"

Nero went white.

A girl reporter found a thin voice: "Mr. Mawson passed them out to us."

Madame whirled.

"So! You dolt! Idiot! You fool! How dare you give out information without consulting me? I wrote that no word of this must be made public. I gave orders that no word was to creep out. And what do I find? I ask you: what do I find? Every newspaper in the city has been told. God in heaven, may I not have one moment's privacy!"

She was Wagnerian in her wrath. Nero squirmed under the blaze of her words. His face was red, his lips white with the violence of his effort to hold his tongue. I hadn't enjoyed anything so much in months.

Then Madame caught herself. Suddenly aware of the circle of reportorial eyes, she cast off the outraged Brünnhilde and forced herself into superficial calm.

"Ladies and gentlemen," she said coldly, "I beg you, forgive my—my little temperament. You understand? My visit to Lucifer's Pride is personal, a devoted pilgrimage to the shrine of one who was very kind to me. I beg it that you forgive me."

She stooped, swept up the Peke.

"Doctor! Julian! All of you, we leave now. Your Honor"—drawing the Mayor into her entourage— "you will please to escort me to my car."

Grandly she swept through the crowd, the reporters backing off like spanked children. A few paces away she turned and called back:

"Signor Graine, there will be no rehearsal. Our performance is two-thirty tomorrow. I shall give you luncheon in my suite at twelve sharp. Good day."

She shot a poisonous glance at Nero, uttered the one word, "Worm!" and was gone.

I turned to Nero. "And that, my dear fellow, is known as telling the manager. Shall I get iodine and splints?"

He was in no mood for pleasantries. In fact, he was boiling, not so much because of what she had said as because she had said it before all the newspapers in Portland.

"The dirty bitch," he said, raging. "She can't talk to me like that."

"Ah, but she has," I reminded him.

"Nobody can. I'll wire Gaul. I'll have her contract cancelled. I'll—for two damned red cents I'll go to her hotel and cut her throat." His fist clenched. "I'll murder that dirty bitch."

And there is the second time. Murder again! When the time came, however, Nero was safe. Marina's throat was not cut, and Nero has not seen Lucifer's Pride to this day.

But the fact remains that Marina had a gift for inspiring impulses to violence. First my threat. Then Nero's.

And we were not alone.

There were others.

4

SATURDAY WAS ANOTHER FOUL DAY. The rain and sleet had turned to snow. At ten in the morning it was so dark that I had to turn on the lights to dress. I had a headache, brought on by those operatic Siamese twins, *Cavalleria* and *Pagliacci*, which had been sung so badly the night before that I had a sour taste in my mouth just from listening to them. And to cap the climax, Sandy was gone.

His real name was Walter Sands but I never called him anything but Sandy. He had answered my advertisement in New York for a secretary-accompanist when, just before I joined the Monte Calvo Company for the tour, my former accompanist decided to get married and maintain a family instead of my morale. He was a lank, dank, cadaverous-looking chap, badly dressed and just recovering from a throat ailment that left him practically voiceless. Why I took him on, I don't know. He didn't look like anything human and he sounded like two strips of canvas rubbed together.

But I decided to try him out. And he was a success. As a secretary he was lousy; as an accompanist, fair; as a congenial spirit, he was a jewel. Caustic when I was feeling bitter, prankish when I felt the need of horse-play, sober when I felt arty and uplifted, gay when I was stimulated, sympathetic when I was low, he had the gift of anticipating my mood and of pitching his own at a coincidental level instantaneously. I thought of him as an emotional nickel-in-the-slot phonograph: "Insert your coin and select your record."

That was why I needed him that morning. I felt low as a slug. Furthermore, I needed to smooth out a couple of A flats in the

Questa o quella and *Par mi veder le lagrime* for the afternoon's *Rigoletto*. And, damn it, he wasn't there.

I looked in the closets, under the bed, in the bathroom—and then decided to indulge in a little temperament of my own. I stamped around a bit and broke a vase. I felt better. (Why is the crash of broken pottery so soul-satisfying? Catharsis, I suppose.) I went down to the dining room for breakfast, stamping along in high dudgeon, feeling martyred and long-suffering. I would—I vowed—tear off his arm and beat him with it. And then I'd kick him out to fend for himself, shoot him back to the streets of New York where I'd picked him up, half-starved, white as a ghost, and rail-thin. I'd show him.

"Hi, there. Whadya hear from the mob?"

And there he was, sprawling his bony length in a chair beside the public stenographer's desk. He waved a long hand in greeting and started to grin. But catching sight, I suppose, of my own dour face, he wiped off the smile and put on a scowl that would have done credit to Mussolini.

"Where the hell have you been, Tony?" he growled. "I've been sitting here for hours. Don't you ever get up?"

And there you have Sandy. The man was a genius at stealing my thunder. After all, you can't quarrel with yourself—and Sandy was mirroring me. I said nothing. So he followed me in and we demolished eggs and toast in silence. By that time I felt better. He sensed it.

"Talked to Nero yet this morning?" he began.

"I've talked to no one."

He ignored my ill humor. "You ought to see the papers. So he said he'd murder La Grazie. You know, in a hand-to-hand encounter I'd place my bet on the Madame any day. If he tried any stabbing, she'd grab the knife and cut out his craw. She's dynamite."

"You know her?"

He shrugged. "Seen her on the stage. La Scala, years ago. Didn't I read somewhere that she drinks blood?"

I choked on my coffee. "Blood! Good God!"

"Couldn't swear to it, of course; but I'm sure I saw it. Probably publicity." He pulled a paper from his pocket. "Speaking of publicity, have you read any of the stories our friends of the press have oozed out?"

I said I hadn't.

"Well, you should. You're rather in the shade this morning, my boy. Nothing but Grazie from page one to fourteen. By the way, do you know what's in that treasure chest she was lugging around?"

"I heard her telling the reporters about her jewels," I said.

"Ah, but what jewels." His harsh whisper became almost a croak. "Trophies of every chase she's ever been on. Including a little trinket called the Lucifer diamond."

He paused expectantly. I disappointed him. I had read of the stone in the evening papers before going to bed and at the moment my mind was on other things, notably the A flats in those arias. I said, "Well, well", and pushed back my chair.

"And furthermore," he persisted, following me out of the dining room, "sobsister Gretchen Galbraith of the *Journal* says she bets Madame will wear the thing when she goes to Lucifer's Pride."

"I don't care if she wears it in her bathtub," I snorted. I was getting a little fed up on Lucifer.

"Did you see the picture of Lucifer's Pride?"

He thrust the paper under my nose. I gave it a glance. It looked like a barn. I wasn't interested and told him so. For a wonder, he shut up.

In the room I took of my coat and tackled those A flats. By the time they were smoothed out and Sandy had husked away what little voice he had doing Gilda's part in the *Che m'ami* duet, it was almost noon.

I changed my clothes while Sandy fiddled away at the piano. As I was leaving he shot one more consoling bolt:

"I'll meet you at the Auditorium in time to help you dress. That is, if you're still in one piece. After the way she chewed up Nero, I'll bet she's still out for blood."

Truer word was never spoken. Only, as it happened, it was not my blood.

I took the elevator down to the sixth floor. The boy pointed out Marina's suite. Just as I raised my hand to knock I became aware of a furious altercation inside.

Murder Ends the Song

(I might as well admit here and now that I'm hopelessly, psychopathically curious by nature. I never hesitate to eavesdrop when there is something interesting to be heard. Deplorable? Yes, of course. But during my short career I have discovered in that way many interesting and helpful bits.)

So I stood. And listened.

The combatants were Madame Grazie and, I gathered, Ambrosia Swisshome. Madame was throaty and fairly calm. Miss Swisshome was shrill and quivering with anger. She was speaking at the moment.

"I won't tolerate it, Marina. I will not be treated so."

"You will tolerate anything I choose to do, Ambrosia. And furthermore you will be treated any way I please."

"But it's monstrous. That's what it is. Monstrous! After all I've done for you, after the way I've made a slave of myself. I didn't know such black-hearted ingratitude existed. I—"

"Ambrosia!" Madame cut her off. "I am not accustomed to being addressed in that tone. Please remember what you are."

"As though you'd ever let me forget! Well, if it comes to the worst, I can always remember a few things myself. And I—"

Again the voice was cut off. There was a sound, like a bare hand slapping bare flesh. An agonized cry was followed by weeping.

Marina's voice sliced out words:

"That will teach you, Ambrosia, that there are certain things it is not good to talk about. I am sorry you provoked me—and before my performance, too. Now go to your room and stay there until I tell you you may leave. Signor Graine will be arriving and I wish to be calm."

Miss Swisshome answered. I have at various times heard voices expressing practically all of the primitive emotions. This, though, was the first time I had ever heard living hate. The words were clipped from the cloth of malice and drenched in bile. Venom dripped from every syllable.

"I'll go, Marina, but I'll never forget this. To my dying day I'll remember. And whenever I remember I'll long to put my hands around your throat and crush them together."

Footsteps approached the door. I backed away. "I'm going now. And I say from the bottom of my heart: God damn you and your performance, Marina. Have a pleasant luncheon."

With these words the door was flung open and Miss Swisshome appeared. I would never have recognized the prim, grim spinster who had stepped from the plane the day before. Her iron-grey hair was in disarray; it straggled in ragged shocks around her face. Her eyes were swollen and red; there was no glitter in their dead depths. In the instant of her appearance I saw the outline of a palm and fingers darkening in dull crimson across her mouth and cheek.

I could do nothing but bow and wish her good-morning. She shot me one swift, startled glance, raised her hand to cover her mouth, and sped to the elevator.

I knocked.

"*Entrez!*" Madame carolled.

I looked around. The hall was empty.

5

MADAME WAS WAITING FOR ME. Robed in crimson velvet, girdled with gold, she posed, arms flung wide, eyes shining. I thought of Isolde rushing to Kareol, and waited for those ecstatic words, "*Tristan! Geliebter!*" which never fail to prickle the nape of my neck.

Instead: "Signor Graine! At last."

I kissed her hand and murmured the usual formal phrases, all in the best tradition. She disposed of my things and motioning me to a place beside her, sank down on a divan, the folds of her gown falling into sculptured lines like one of Max Reinhardt's rubberized costumes.

"Luncheon will be toast, tea, and a—how do you say?—coddled egg. I allow myself no more before singing. You like?" She handed me a packet of throat lozenges.

I was dumb with admiration. The scene I had just overheard had left no trace; she was calm as though she had walked through gardens. And here we sat, sucking throat lozenges and chatting of—how do you say?—coddled eggs. It was amazing.

I assured her that her menu was exactly what I always chose before a performance. She linked her fat fingers around one chubby knee and surveyed me.

"So! You are very young, Signor Graine. I heard your Des Grieux in San Francisco. You were good. Very good. A little lacking in temperament, perhaps. Do you sweat?"

"Sweat?" I gaped.

She nodded emphatically. "Everyone with temperament sweats. You should see my underwear after a concert. You could wring it out. But you do have charm. And the voice."

I gulped and blushed. "Madame, you overwhelm me."

"Nonsense," she said sharply. "And you must learn to control that face of yours. An artist never blushes. He accepts, graciously, with assurance."

I refrained from informing her that my blush was one of my best stocks-in-trade; that it brought me more publicity than my *bel canto*. "Mr. Graine blushed like a boy," the sobsisters wrote; and their female readers thought . . . but never mind that.

I discarded the blush and looked austere, nodded with what I hoped was graciousness. "Better?"

"Much." Her little eyes twinkled. She liked the act. "And now about the performance. How is your conductor—what is his name?—Perelli?"

I chose my words. "A trifle impressed by the grandeur of Italian opera, I fancy. He regrets the passing of each note."

"Then I shan't like him. My Gilda is *con brio* . . . a delicate young girl in the first ecstasy of passion."

I strangled on my lozenge. Marina, with her squat body, short fat arms, and full-moon face smothered in lavender powder and orange rouge, looked as much like a delicate maiden as did Marie Dressler in *Anna Christie*. The only young things about her were her ridiculously tiny ankles and feet.

When I had controlled myself. I said: "That, of course, can be arranged. Perelli is accustomed to artistic whims."

Which was a mistake.

"Whim! Whim! What is this whim?" She struggled to her feet, got her balance and flung out her arms in dramatic explosion. "My Gilda is no whim. I have sung her under Toscanini, Panizza, Monteux, Pelletier, Bruno Walter . . . all of them. She is a creation, a *tour de force*. The Metropolitan, La Scala, Covent Garden, The Colon, L'Opera, Chicago, Madrid, Dresden—they have all acclaimed her . . . thrown roses at her feet. And you say, whim!"

Abruptly she folded her arms, fell down into her seat again, and smiled. She patted my knee. "Ah, this afternoon you shall hear Gilda as you have never heard her before."

I didn't doubt that.

The fat fingers tightened on my knee. "But now we talk of other things. I weary of myself. Have you been presented to my niece? My party?"

"I rather hoped I might meet them at luncheon today. Your niece is charming."

Did a shadow of annoyance cross her face? Did a cloud obscure the full moon? It was gone before I could be certain.

"Elena is a dear girl." The hand, I noticed, was abruptly withdrawn. "As for luncheon, I excused them all. They will lunch after we leave for the opera house. I have suggested they remain in their rooms in case I need them."

I could imagine what a suggestion of Marina's might mean. A royal command could be no more dogmatic. Even though Ambrosia Swisshome had taken the elevator down, I rather fancied she had returned by this time and like the others, was following Madame's suggestion. I thought of Sandy's lot as my accompanist in contrast to the life led by these galley-slaves. He came and went almost as he pleased. Because I treated him as a friend he responded with friendship. We had been together for six months and had never had a serious disagreement.

But these poor minions of Marina's could not know what freedom was. I felt a little sorry for them, could understand their grave faces and rebellious, defiant manner.

"I understand," I said. "Your nerves."

The hand fastened on my thigh. "But you are *simpático!* You are—"

What else I was, I was never to know, for lunch arrived at that moment and Madame broke off to order the waiter around a little. After ten minutes the simple arrangements were completed to her satisfaction and the waiter backed out, red-faced and perspiring. The look he flung at Marina was not kindly.

We nibbled toast, sipped tea. For want of something else to say, I asked idly, "Are you still going to Lucifer's Pride?"

She lowered the fragment of toast she had been about to bite. "What do you know about Lucifer's Pride?" Her beady eyes transfixed me.

"There was a great deal in the papers which I didn't read. I saw the picture. It looks like a barn."

Surprisingly she beamed. "It does, doesn't it. That's why I refused to live in it."

"You refused—" I began, and then stopped. One of the few things I did read about the place was that old Lucifer Bollman had begun it for a prospective bride who had persisted in remaining only prospective.

"But you must not tell the papers it was I." She held up an arch forefinger. "It is our little secret. Imagine! Lucifer, the old fool, wished to imprison me in that—that barn. Conceive of it!"

I tried and admitted I couldn't.

She laughed. "But he was—how do you say—a good sport about it. Imagine! He called it his aborted child. Amusing?"

"Frightfully," I said.

"I thought so. And so, after all these years, I go to see Lucifer's child. And, I suppose, mine also. Isn't it? I have always had a fancy to see it, but never have I gone. Now that I am here, I shall. And that is that."

"Definitely that," I said. "A pity Mr. Bollman is not alive to make the trip with you."

She sighed dramatically. "Poor boring old man. He died of a broken heart, you know. Some papers called me a *femme fatale*. Sweet?"

I allowed as how sweet was definitely the word. "It does sound interesting," I went on. "Perhaps I shall drive out some afternoon next week."

She hesitated, then raised her cup to her lips, shooting me a strange, level look over the rim.

"Perhaps that may not be necessary," she murmured cryptically. She lowered the cup. "You have heard perhaps that his ghost roams the place?"

I shook my head.

"But yes. He hunts for me." She trilled with laughter. "Strange, Anthony—I may call you that?—if he were to find me."

"Very strange," I said. "He must be lonely."

Why did I say that, I wonder. I had no way of knowing then that soon, very soon, old Bollman's ghost would be joined by another.

And yet another.

6

AT ONE O'CLOCK, our luncheon over, we arose to go. Smoothing out the folds of her gown with quick, nervous strokes of her jeweled fingers, Madame said she must rest for at least forty-five minutes before the performance and she hoped that the couch she had ordered for that purpose had been placed in her dressing room. Elena, she told me, had gone to the Auditorium that morning and unpacked her wardrobe. Everything would go splendidly. I was not to worry. I would drive to the opera house with her. She would be ready in one moment.

As she turned to leave the room there came a discreet tap at the door. Madame stiffened, her lips tightening.

"I told them distinctly—but no, they would not dare to disobey me." She swept to the door.

I hoped for the sake of everyone that the intruder was not one of her party. I had witnessed enough scenes for one day. Miss Swisshome's Waterloo had sated me with melodrama. I wanted no more of it.

It was only a hotel page, however. "Letter for Madame Grazie," he said and thrust it at her. His voice broke, shooting up to stratospheric heights as he spoke the name. He gulped and fled.

Madame turned. "What an odd young man! Did you see how he ran away?"

"He was frightened."

"What nonsense," she said, but she was pleased. "I do wish my public would not look on me as if I were something supernatural."

I stifled the impulse to remind her that an artist accepts, graciously, with assurance.

She gazed at the letter. "How strange. The address is typewritten. Probably some women's club wishing me to sing for them. Or lecture. Of course, I shall refuse."

"Why not turn it over to your secretary?"

"Ambrosia?" She shook her head. "No, I do not wish to see her until after the performance."

She tore open the envelope and drew out a single sheet of folded paper. I suppose it was habit that made her cock the envelope into a hat and stare into the exposed interior. I knew she was hoping to discover a cheque. Women's club or not, I had the feeling that Marina would have crawled on her fat hands and knees over live coals for any fee, large or small.

Satisfied—and disappointed—at last that the note was unaccompanied, she fished around on her bosom for her eyeglass and fell to studying the note, holding it carefully to the light.

It was then that a most amazing thing occurred.

Marina shriveled.

That is the only word I can find to describe the transformation that took place before my eyes. What little natural color she had in her face was drained off, leaving a staring paper-white mask with two horrid purple patches over her cheek bones and the orange-crimson gash of her lips. Her ample nose became pinched. She tottered on her spindling ankles like a crone who finds that maintaining her balance is an insuperable difficulty. She was an old woman. She looked eighty.

She gave a strangled cry. The note wadded in her shaking fingers, she stumbled to the divan and fell on it. Huddling down into the cushions, she began to laugh. Hideous, stifled laughter that shook the whole great body. Tears ran down her cheeks. She stared straight ahead.

I tried to think of something to do. Tags of half-remembered remedies scurried through my mind: burnt feathers—wrapping in a rug—a key on the back of the neck—a roll on a barrel: I dismissed them all. Water, I thought. But there was none.

In desperation—anything to stop that ghastly sound—I slapped her. Hard. The imprint of my fingers stood out on the powdered purple and white of her cheek. I remember thinking: where have I seen something like that? Then I recalled Ambrosia Swisshome's face with the weal across her lips and cheek.

The blow had its effect. Marina gasped. For a moment there was no sound. The suspended silence was murderous. Her bosom expanded; her hands, fingers spread and rigid, thrust themselves out before her. Her whole body arched forward; then, like a punctured balloon, it collapsed. She wept brokenly.

I spoke to her, shook her. There was no recognition in her eyes. Her face was a ruin. Rivulets of tears streaked the powder-encrusted cheeks with a silt of mascara and rouge. Gone was the great lady. Before me sagged a quivering lump of exhaustion. And fear.

Oh, yes, there was fear. It was obvious in the way she crouched back in the corner, the involuntary straining away from me. And I wondered, helplessly, what could have been in that note, the corner of which I could see protruding from under her thigh.

How long I stood there I do not know. It was Marina who finally gave me my cue.

"Beale," she moaned. "Get. Beale. Oh, my God."

I cursed myself for not having thought of Thorndyke before. A doctor was what she needed. I started for the door.

"No," she screamed. "Don't leave me. I must not be alone. I am afraid. Oh, God, do not leave me."

The situation was intolerable. I shut my ears to her pleading and ran on out into the hall. There was no one in sight and I had no idea which room was which. Blindly I flung open the first door I came to. There were piles of music, opera scores and manuscripts littering every flat inch of space.

"Porter! Julian Porter," I called.

The room was empty.

The next room was, I think, Thorndyke's. At least I saw a doctor's handbag on the writing desk and beside it a hypodermic needle. But there was no trace of the doctor.

I could still hear Marina crying and the sound was maddening. I began frantically to throw open doors right and left. One of them disclosed a cretonne bag disgorging knitting and many steel needles. But no occupant. So Ambrosia had not gone to her room!

I raced on to the adjoining room. Lying on the bed was the fur coat Elena Grazie had worn at the airport. But there was no Elena.

I came back into the hall. The whole party was accounted for. Or rather, not accounted for. Not one of them was in his room. Yet Marina had said: "They would not dare to disobey me."

But they had. Why, suddenly, did they dare? And where had they gone?

7

Leaving the hotel I banged squarely into Sandy. The impact knocked us both breathless. We clasped our middles and glared at each other. Sandy was the first to get his breath.

"Why the hell don't you watch where you're going?" he growled. "And where have you been? Perelli's tearing his hair and the cast is walking circles around him."

"Didn't you tell him I'd be there?"

"Yeah, but he's beginning to disbelieve me. Where's the Madame?"

I steered him across the sidewalk and into a cab. On the way to the Auditorium I recounted the happenings of the past hour. He sat like a goop, mercifully keeping his mouth shut until I had finished. Then he fingered his bony chin with bony fingers.

"Keeryst," he said. "And the gallery already climbing into their seats. What'll Nero say?"

"I'd rather not think of it."

"You'll have to soon enough. Where were the rest of 'em? Did you try to find out where the letter came from?"

"Naturally," I said stiffly. "After the doctor came I went down for a chat with the desk-clerk. He said he went into the office to speak to the cashier. When he came back he noticed the letter lying on the counter with a dime on it. He said he just called a bellboy, gave him the dime, and told him to take the letter to Madame Grazie."

"And he didn't have any idea who left it?"

"Not the faintest."

"It might have been one of that rummy crew the Madame has in tow," he said. "Had they been around?"

"Give me credit for some brains. The clerk said they'd all been at the desk within the half-hour." "All?"

"All. Miss Swisshome wanted writing paper. The niece and the doctor stopped to leave word they'd be in the dining room if anyone called. A couple of minutes later Porter came by to find out where the other two were."

Sandy counted on his fingers. "That isn't all. You've forgotten the chauffeur. But I suppose he was in the office kissing the cashier."

"Sorry to disappoint you. No osculation. But Paris did stop by to find out when Madame wanted the car."

"My God." Sandy wiped his brow. "All present and accounted for. But that procession covered a good bit of time. They couldn't all have left it."

"Oh, yes they could. I asked. The clerk said it might have been there some time without his seeing it. The passengers from the one o'clock train from Chicago were arriving in a body; the fellow was so busy he didn't notice anything in particular."

Sandy sighed. "Well, I give up. Boy, will the scalps fly when Madame gets on her feet again! She'll tear that crowd down and dance on the ruins." He paused. "But what about this afternoon?"

It was my turn to sigh. "Strentoni, I suppose."

Strentoni was a coloratura we had picked up in San Francisco. She was healthy and rather beautiful, but that was all. I suspected more than friendship between her and Perelli. If it were true, I'll admit he could pick them. Friends, not singers.

"Good old Angela," Sandy croaked. "Think you can handle her?"

I snapped my fingers. "I'm not worrying. I can sing the Duke backwards, forwards, or sprawling flat on my belly, à la Jeritza's *Vissi d'arte*."

The taxi pulled up at the stage entrance. Snow was falling heavily. It was cold as hell. We dashed up the alleyway.

"There's no chance the Madame'll show up?" Sandy flickered.

I choked on a mouthful of snow. "When I left the doctor was giving her a sedative. She won't wake up for hours, and then the performance'll be over."

Sandy opened the door. Nero was standing in the wings, biting his nails.

"Forget Madame," I said, girding my loins. "Look at Nero. He's out for raw meat."

Sandy looked and winced. And turned tail. "You've got more meat on your bones than I have. Let him take the edge off his appetite on you. See you in the dressing room."

And so I was left alone.

During the ensuing fifteen minutes I found out how Daniel felt surrounded by lions. At that, though, Daniel had more of a chance than I did. I'd prefer four or five of the beasts to Nero any day.

But I weathered it. After all, it wasn't my fault. I was only the bearer of bad news. After the first shock had worn off, he quieted down and resigned himself to the Strentoni strumpet.

"But will I have a job explaining this to Gaul!" he groaned. "Go ahead and get into your things, Tony. I'll wait till the last minute to make the announcement. It'll be up to you, boy, to put this performance across."

I went downstairs to my dressing room. Grazie should have been moving into the one across the hall from me. Well, what the hell, I thought. But I would have given a night's fee to see that note. And another one to know who had left it.

Sandy had everything in readiness. It was two o'clock, he informed me. I stripped to the waist and dived into the cosmetics, Sandy standing by to offer suggestions. A moment later we heard a babble of Italian from across the hall and knew that Perelli and Strentoni had taken possession.

Then all at once there was a modern-dress eruption of Krakatoa. Vocables peppered the air. The wall shook as something struck it. There was a crash of glass. A woman screamed. Perelli's voice rose to high-C and stayed there, agonizing. A second woman's voice cursed fluently and with all the vigor and color of a Neapolitan fish-wife. A chair smashed.

"God almighty, go out and see what that racket is," I shouted to Sandy. "Tell them if they don't can it, I'll refuse to sing. Tell them I'll have peace and quiet for the next half hour or they can get another tenor."

Sandy leaned against a trunk and croaked wisely: "Offhand, I'd say that Grazie's arrived and is throwing Strentoni out on her beautiful rear-end. Strentoni, she don't like going. *Voila! C'est la guerre.*"

"Grazie!" I pulled on a dressing gown, aware that the earthquake had died into ominous calm.

I dashed out into the hallway. At the far end of the alley, barely visible in the glow of dim bulbs, a drooping, hefty blonde was being led along, weeping, by a little dark man. Perelli and his wanton. By all that was holy, Grazie *had* arrived and taken the fort.

I burst open the door.

Marina's ample figure was settled before the dressing table. Wrapped in a dressing gown, with a towel pinned around her hair, she was plastering on the grease paint in vehement gobs. Elena was scooping up broken glass in a newspaper. The sundered chair was piled in forlorn fragments at the foot of the couch.

"Madame Grazie!" I said. "I'm delighted to see you. Are you sure you've quite recovered?"

She turned. The broken wreck I had left at the Olympia had vanished. Marina Grazie was here in person, eyes gleaming. The hand she extended was steady. I bent over it.

"Nonsense, Signor Graine—er, Anthony. I never felt better."

"But the doctor—"

"The doctor is a fool. He would have put me to sleep. Me! Grazie! When I am to sing my Gilda! I simply put my foot down and walked out. Medicine!" She snorted.

"Brava!" I smiled. "And La Strentoni?"

"Was that the creature's name?" she said vaguely. "A trifle difficult perhaps, but me, I am accustomed to dealing with difficulties. That horrible little man with the falsetto voice was?"

"Only Perelli," I told her gravely.

She was not fazed. "Indeed. Well, he is in his place for the moment. I shall watch his tempi particularly. One inaccuracy—and your Mr. Gaul will hear from me. Now go, young man." She waved a casual hand. "I must collect myself. There is nothing like relaxation to clear the voice."

Elena opened the door for me, and I had my first close-up of her. She was lovely. Beautifully lovely. But infinitely sad, distraite. I smiled at her. Her answering smile was a bare curving of the lips.

As the door closed Madame's voice rang out: "The steak, Elena. Is it fresh? I insisted that it be—"

I could hear the orchestra already tuning up. And I was not yet in my costume. I tore into the dressing room.

"Sandy, my pants."

He held them out. "How is she?"

"You can't kill an old war-horse," I said, slipping into the satin breeches and hip boots of the Duke of Mantua. "Advised me to relax."

He smiled sardonically. "She'll need plenty of nerve to get through this performance. The audience will probably toss her enough vegetables to stock a store."

But they didn't.

They were friendly, more than encouraging. I had a little talk with Barona, our baritone, who was the afternoon's Rigoletto. Together we cooked up a plot for assisting Madame whenever she found herself in a tight spot. As most of Gilda's scenes are with him, he bore the brunt of the scheme, and he deserves a medal for the shouting and bellowing he did that afternoon. It was not good singing but it did succeed in drowning out Marina's most flagrant deviations from pitch.

The audience was child-like. They had come to be entertained and they were quite prepared to like everything about the performance. My *Questa o quella*, I say modestly, put them in an enthusiastic mood at the start. My ovation stopped the show. Rigoletto's *Pari siamo* monolog at the opening of the second scene was another smash. By the time Barona had taken ten bows and repeated the aria, they were ready to applaud anything.

And so we got along. Even the *Caro nome* aria was passable, although Madame's cadenzas and attacks left a trifle to be desired.

But what she lacked in voice she more than made up for in assurance and manner. She took twelve bows and was happy.

The afternoon wore along. Now and then I saw Nero's face; it was pleased. The day was saved and Gaul, back in New York, would never know how close the Portland engagement had come to disaster.

The curtain finally fell and after the twelfth call I lost count. Barona, Grazie, and I were, naturally, the most favored. We beamed and shook each other's hands and Barona and I were kissed by Madame until we were dizzy. The audience loved it. In the wings I could see Elena, Thorndyke, and Julian Porter. They, too, looked pleased. Madame threw them a kiss, and then yanked me on stage for a final bow.

It was over.

The crush backstage was terrific. Supers and stagehands, officials of the Portland Opera Association, and visitors who had rushed back for autographs, clustered around us. Madame was gracious, "accepting with assurance." But under the grease paint her face was drawn. Now and then she closed her eyes wearily, but the smile remained fixed on her face.

At last, giving up, she pleaded fatigue and asked me to escort her to her dressing room. I forced a passage through the mob and dragged her through. I stationed a stray stagehand at the head of the stairs with instructions to allow no one except members of the company to pass. Madame, I told him, wanted no interruptions until she had rested a few moments.

In the dimly lighted passageway downstairs Marina withdrew her arm from mine and halted. Her eyes were like a cat's, gleaming with a strangely topaz glow. She said nothing for a moment. Then she patted my arm and for a moment I thought humanity would break through her reserve. But it didn't.

"You sang very well, Anthony," she said quietly. "I myself—thank you. You gave me splendid support."

With that she turned and moved slowly, almost painfully to her door. I stared. She had come as close to frankness as she would ever permit herself. I understood what lay behind those words—remarkable words for Marina Grazie to have uttered. And I could not find it in me to be annoyed even at her slightly patronizing air.

Sobered, I went into my room and closed the door. Sandy was gone. Probably caught in the crush upstairs, but never mind, he would be down soon.

I was tired myself. I sat down before my mirror and stared at myself. What would it be like to be old and weary? To feel one's voice going, going, going—and be able to do nothing about it? To see the Present slipping relentlessly into the Past—and be able to discern no Future? Better die, I thought, than hang on, clutching at Time while, moment by bitter moment, the process called disintegration went on. And then and there I made a vow. When the time came, I—

I jumped. What now? Surely that was a scream, half-stifled. I listened. From across the hall—from Marina's dressing room—came the sound of a thump. Like—like a heavy body falling down.

I ran from the room and into Marina's.

I stood in the doorway, stunned.

She lay in a heap on the floor. A trickle of crimson emerged from under her head and gathered into a small pool. And I knew it was blood.

Automatically I raised my eyes and looked around the room. There was no one there. There was only the still, white-robed figure on the floor. Everything was the same except for that.

Or was it? No, I was wrong. There was something else—something that had not been there when I had last seen the room.

On the mirror of the dressing table were two words. They were the title of Gilda's aria that afternoon. They were the words, *Caro nome*.

They were scrawled on the glass as with a blunt forefinger.

And they were written in blood.

8

IT WAS NEARLY MORNING before I could go to sleep. Sandy deserted me early. After an evening of arguing round and round the subject and arriving nowhere, he threw in the sponge, said he never wanted to hear Grazie's name again, and went to bed.

I couldn't. The exhilaration of the performance coupled with the subsequent excitement had jacked my nerves so high that I could not relax. I simply sat and thought. I could not get that scene in the dressing room out of my mind: over and over I heard Marina scream and fall; countless times I flung open her door and saw her crumpled figure and the puddle of blood. And every time I looked across the room at my windows I saw again that macabre writing on the mirror.

Practical jokers have always annoyed me. It isn't, it seems to me, that I have no sense of humor; rather I'm convinced that theirs is perverted. They say: a joke is a joke. I say: not always. This was one of the times when it was not.

Yet it was evidently intended to be. Only on that score could it be explained.

Where did the blood come from? Fantastic as it seems, you have already had the answer. I myself had heard Madame ask Elena for the steak. And Sandy had told me he had read somewhere that Grazie drank blood.

Elena had explained it when she finally arrived in the dressing room. Before each performance it was her duty to crush a fresh, dripping beefsteak and catch the blood in a glass. This Madame sipped from time to time during the performance. It was, Elena said, a secret her aunt had learned from the great Luisa Tetrazzini, who maintained that the drink imparted a limpid fluidity to her tones.

The jokester had simply dipped his finger into the glass, which Madame, because of her lateness in arriving, had been unable to finish; had written the words on the mirror, and then poured the remainder of the congealing mess in a puddle in the center of the floor.

At least that was the explanation Marina gave when she came to. She stared at Dr. Thorndyke for a moment. Her eyes turned to me. She seemed to be struggling to remember what had happened.

Then realization dawned. She closed her eyes and every muscle of her body went limp.

"I am so sorry," she whispered. "So foolish of me. A joke. It was a joke, of course."

And that was all. Except that, a moment later, when she thought she was not observed, her eyelids flickered and she darted a quick, stealthy glance at the mirror.

I think I was the only one who saw her—who noticed the sigh of relief that escaped her twitching lips.

For there was nothing on the mirror. As soon as I had grasped the situation, and knowing that it would be the first thing she would see upon regaining her senses, I had washed it clean.

But not, however, before I had carefully copied down the words in my notebook.

It was this copy that lay on the table beside me that night in my hotel room. I give a reproduction of the words, faithful to the smallest blur and dribble:

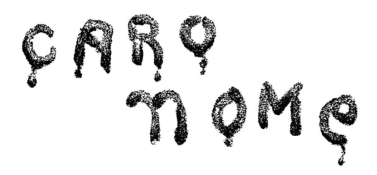

It haunted me. It was mad, insane. The only person I could think of who might have done it was Strentoni, out for revenge. I had suggested as much to Marina, and she had calmly informed me that she wished only to forget the whole incident. Someone else had suggested calling in the police, whereupon she had flown into a fury, blasting us all with maledictions in five languages. She was, she told us, quite capable of managing her own affairs; she would be grateful for being credited with enough intelligence to recognize a childish prank when she saw one; she would personally throttle anyone who dared mention the thing again.

And so I had left. But I could not forget that fear-stricken glance she had directed at the mirror, and I could hear, too, her sigh of relief when she had discovered that the writing was gone. I knew the writing had been no prank. Madame knew it too.

Even after I finally did go to bed I dreamed of it. When Sandy arose to dress for eight o'clock Mass, he told me later, I begged him to "wash it off." I wouldn't know about that, though. I didn't really awaken until nine.

It was the telephone. This time, though, it was not Nero, but a woman.

"Mr. Graine?" she said crisply. "This is Ambrosia Swisshome. Will you hold the wire for Madame Grazie?"

I held, wondering what now.

"Good morning, Anthony," came Madame's throaty accents. "You have slept well?"

The resilience of the woman bowled me over. She was indomitable. After three emotional upheavals, any one of which would have floored an ordinary woman, she was bouncing about like a rubber ball at nine in the morning, wondering if others had enjoyed their night's rest. I gave up. She was unique.

I told her I had slept fairly well and was glad to hear her quite herself again.

"Me!" She actually sounded amazed. "But I am never daunted. Naturally, I am well. Quite. And that you, too, are rested pleases me because I am wishing to invite you to make an excursion with me."

"An excursion?"

I glanced out the window. A blizzard was in progress. The snow was being forced from the leaden sky with such velocity that it beat against the panes with an almost audible impact. I am no orchid, but the idea of an excursion even to the bathroom on a day like that left me less than enthusiastic. Bed was the place.

"An excursion?" I repeated.

"But yes. A holiday. How do you say—a jaunt? How would you, Anthony, care to see Lucifer's Pride? With me and my party?"

I could not have been more surprised if Dante had called and asked me to join himself and Virgil on a week-end tour of *Purgatorio*.

"But," I stammered, "I thought—the reporters—"

"Ha!" Madame snorted. "They are why I go today. If I wait until later, others will crowd there, too. And I do not wish that. I wish to be alone. Without prying eyes."

"But—Madame—after all—"

"No, no, no. You are not like the others. You are *simpático*. I like you, Anthony. I wish to do something to repay—to please you. You say yesterday that you wish to see what you call 'the barn'. Well, I give you your opportunity. Eh? You will come?"

"But I should feel like an intruder."

"Nonsense. I wish you there. Say, please, that you will come."

I hesitated. After all, I had nothing on that day. I was not due for another performance until my Enzo in Wednesday night's *La Gioconda*.

"You are there, Anthony?" Madame asked anxiously. "Why do you not answer?"

And then I saw the sheet of paper with the two dribbled words. My mind was suddenly made up. I was curious to know more about the happenings of the past few days and this would be a splendid opportunity for field-work.

"I accept with pleasure," I said. "When do you start?"

"But we are getting into the bus now. I have chartered a bus to take us. Can you not be ready immediately?"

"But Sandy is out at the moment. I—"

Murder Ends the Song

"Sandy? What is a Sandy?"

I explained who Sandy was.

"Get him and bring him along," she commanded.

"Very well," I said. "But it would be better if you went on ahead. I shall have breakfast, pick up Sandy, and follow you in my car."

Madame was ecstatic. "But it is all so simple. The very thing," she cooed. "There is, you should know, a ferry to be crossed. I shall leave word with the man to bring you over after us. You will hurry?"

I promised all speed. With mutual felicitations, we hung up. I glanced at my watch. Nine fifteen. Sandy would be out of church at nine-thirty. If I were to catch him at the Cathedral steps I should have to hump myself.

Flinging off my pajamas, I rushed for the bath.

I did not know it then, but the curtain had already risen on the second act of the *Caro Nome* affair. Tragedy was in the offing; and I, like a fool, was rushing to meet it.

9

"Nuts!" Sandy exclaimed.

I reached around the wind-shield and brushed away a little of the caked snow.

"Us or Bollman?" I asked bitterly.

It might have been either, but I was inclined to the belief that he meant us. Portland had been unprepossessing enough with its dun-grey sky, its gusts of snow-laden wind, and its frozen pavements. But when we rounded Crown Point and started the descent into the Columbia Gorge, I thought, "*All hope abandon, ye who enter here.*" Dante had had, however, a more pleasant prospect: he could take his Inferno a little at a time. Ours was a combination of the first and seventh circles. (Wasn't the first a place of howling winds and the seventh, a refrigerator? I think I'm right.)

Down the canyon raced and tore a wind that shuttled our car like a bobbin from one side of the road to the other. The trees and shrubbery bowed earthward with a coating of ice and snow as impenetrable as armor. At one side of the highway the roiling torrent of the river was peaked with ominous caps of foam. Once, when the wind picked us up bodily and set us teetering on the very brink, Sandy gulped and croaked, "Oh, my God!" My nerves are not exactly fragile but three different times before we reached the ferry I almost turned back.

Sandy's exclamation had, however, been intended for old Lucifer Bollman. For, slewing down the embankment to the river, we were having our first glimpse of the old man's "abortion."

Or rather, Sandy was. I had my hands full negotiating the frozen, rutted grade. It was a nightmare, straight up and down and tilted at an angle crazy enough to have come from *The Cabinet of Dr. Caligari*. I discovered that for once I had enough temperament to satisfy even Madame; I was sweating like a Fourth of July orator. Not a single easy breath did I draw until, with much creaking and groaning of ancient timbers, we rolled onto the ferry and I braked the car to a halt.

I took off my hat and sopped my streaming forehead. I knew how Hannibal felt when the last of his elephants clumped out of the pass and stamped on the broad Italian plain. A chain rattled behind us and there was a wailing as the wooden runway was hoisted up. The boat teetered and jiggled, and we were off.

"Have you by any chance looked ahead?" Sandy's voice was strangled.

I shook my head. "I'm postponing it as long as possible." (Damn, I thought; there must be a limit to a man's ability to give off moisture. My handkerchief was soaked; my eyebrows were still dripping.)

The ferryman, a superannuation minus his plates, came up and peered at us. He was so bundled up in sweaters, coats, and mufflers that he could barely squeeze between the car and the railing.

"You opera singers, too?" he wheezed.

Sandy, green from the wallowing of the boat, muttered profanely. I said I was and asked him if he wanted to make anything of it.

He eyed me bitterly, spat into the water, and walked forward without a word.

"He doesn't exactly love us," I said to Sandy.

"Can you blame him? Madame probably tried to throw him overboard and run this contraption herself."

Contraption was the word for it. More ancient, if possible, than its owner, the boat was long and wide enough to accommodate four cars parked in pairs. Fore and aft, frail wire ropes ran up to a three-inch steel cable stretched from bank to bank. These ropes could be taken in or let out by means of winches, so that, with the aft rope always longer, the craft was held at an angle; the current thus carried the contrivance across. The wires were rusty and frayed. The river came suggestively near the rotten planks of the floor. All in all, it looked like an earlier Ark discarded by Noah because of its unseaworthiness. Its name was the *Minerva*.

After taking that in, I looked ahead for the first time and I understood why Sandy's voice had sounded so queer.

Lucifer's Pride was a new-world Elsinore, gaunt and stark. Even through the blinding snow it was nightmarish and forbidding. Perched on a bluff some three hundred feet above the river, the entrance looked straight down into the water. At the west end a canyon gashed through the sheer rock of the cliff so that a second side of the building was a sheer drop into blackness. From the ferry-slip an almost perpendicular road climbed through the jagged lava rocks. Behind—to the north—stretched miles of snow-covered, treeless hills gulleyed and pitted with ravines and declivities. A thin stream of smoke issued from one of the chimneys atop the three-story box—the only indication of life within sight. The palisades of the river stretched bleakly for miles up and down.

And the wind howled. And the sky lowered.

I couldn't speak. Sandy glanced at me, lifted an eyebrow, and nodded. A home for a bride! It was the gauntest, ugliest thing I had ever laid eyes on, so grim and cold that I felt hollow inside. It was a horrible place, created for horrible happenings.

How we docked I don't know. With the wind beating at us I couldn't see how the rusty little cables held. Once the wires buckled, then snapped taut; the singing vibration was like a scream. I fully expected the strands to part and the boat to go careening into the saw-toothed rocks ahead.

But it didn't. It docked.

The old boatman snaffled off the chain barricade and lowered the runway with much creaking of the rusty winch. Then he approached.

"You tell that ole porpoise to be here at four-thirty," he said.

"Porpoise?"

"That there Madame What's-'er-name. Tell her I ain't waitin' fer man er beast longer'n five minutes. Now git. I'm froze."

There was no answer to that. I started the engine, shifted gears. "Four-thirty?" I shouted as we started to move off.

He spat. "Ef I kin git the Minervy acrosst. Wind's got to die down a heap er you kin stay till she does." He jerked his thumb impatiently.

"Agreeable old cuss," Sandy said. He looked at the Alpine trail ahead. "Jesus Christ, are four wheels supposed to climb that?"

I gritted my teeth. "If Madame's bus did it, we can."

But we couldn't. Halfway up the grade the car coughed à la Mimi and expired. Sandy jerked the hand-brake; it was the only thing that saved us from rolling back over the precipice. It was insanely cold and the wind cut like a razor but we had to pile out. I looked at the gas tank; it was half full. There was nothing else I could do. I can run cars but I've always maintained that garages and mechanics were created to nurse them. Sandy growled about my incompetence and raised the hood.

"I'll help," I said, getting my head in his way.

"You'll get the hell out of here! You don't know a gadget from a widget. Go on up to Frankenstein's castle. I'll fix this thing and drive it up later."

So that is how I arrived at Lucifer's Pride alone. My hands were numb and my thighs ached. I saw as through a glass, whitely; my eyelashes were frozen together.

But I could see enough to recognize Julian Porter, his sleek hair coated with snow, his coat collar turned up around his throat. He was standing just outside the door, his languid manner dropped for once as he laid hold of me and dragged me towards the door.

"I thought you'd never come," he said breathlessly.

"What's the matter?" I managed to get out.

"It's Marina. She's having hysterics and she's practically beaten Tait to a pulp. Hurry."

10

THERE WAS NO LIGHT in the entrance hall. Like a blind-man I stumbled along, clutching at Porter's sleeve. It was like Poe's pit or Dracula's cellar. And, like Mélisande, I was not happy.

Porter opened the door into the hall proper; the darkness dispersed somewhat, and I saw a broad rectangle of greyish light. We walked towards it and I looked up curiously. The ceiling was cut away through the two upper floors and one stared up through the heart of the building to the sky-light. Cobwebs dripped from the panes, hung in festoons over the waist-high railing of the stairway that wound up and up. Dust motes rose and fell in shafts. It was like looking up into the burial vault of a very large and mouldering family.

As I stared up I became conscious of a strange beating on my eardrums, a beating that gradually revealed itself as a voice, shrill and furious. It was Madame. And it was nerve-wracking. Clamor was the word for it. I looked at Porter.

"It's been going on like that for an hour," he said moodily. "The Taits are locked in the kitchen."

"Locked in the kitchen?"

He nodded. "They didn't bring along any implements."

It sounded like Greek to me. I opened my mouth to explain that there must have been some mistake because I hadn't brought any either. But I didn't get it out.

For Porter opened a door and shoved me into a room. There was a burst of caterwauling and I seemed to be drowning in a pool of noise. Then there was silence, and all of a sudden I heard a scream, saw a blur rushing towards me; it swept down on me like whirlwind and two arms went around my neck.

"Signor Graine! Anthony!" the whirlwind cried, sobbed into my ear. "You have come. You have come at last. Now I shall have some sympathy, some understanding. These pigs . . . they insult me. Me! La Grazie! Oh, but I have suffered. I freeze. I starve. And do they do anything to help me? No, they do not. I am helpless. Thank God, you have come."

It was Marina in one of her better moments. As she flung herself on me I staggered but managed to keep my balance. After all, I was totally unprepared. I stood there, the human Rock of Ages. I felt like a fool. And looked it, too, I have no doubt.

Conscious of that, at last, I tried to disentangle myself.

"Madame—" I began.

"Madame is a fool." A hoarse voice broke in.

The room rocked and reeled with the silence. I glanced around blankly, wondering who had dared that heresy. I saw only lowered heads, vague ellipses spotting the gloom.

Marina drew in a hissing breath. Her dumpy body quivering with rage, she pulled her arms from around my neck and turned.

"Who . . . who said that?" she pronounced.

No one spoke.

"I repeat," Madame thundered, "who said that? Who dared to insult me?"

The silence deepened. A clicking came from the far end of the room. I strained my eyes through the dusk and made out the figure of Ambrosia Swisshome. She was sitting on a davenport, knitting away for dear life.

Someone sighed.

"Who, I ask you . . ." Marina began for the third time.

"Oh, please, Auntie. No one meant to insult you. It's just that you've worn our nerves thin during the past half hour. No one knows what he is saying. Can't you be human and have a little mercy on us?"

It was Elena who spoke. She was standing beside the fireplace, her head flung back. Her little clenched fists were rammed against a table. Every line of her body told of nerves tensed to the breaking point.

Madame choked. Then with asthmatic intensity she said, "You . . . Elena! You dare . . ."

The girl should have been shattered by the fury of those syllables. But she wasn't. Some demon had taken possession of her. She stood her ground.

"This is not pleasant for any of us, Auntie. You dragged us here; none of us wanted to come. If there were anything we could do, we would. We are just as cold and hungry as you are. Why make it more difficult for us?"

She was superb. Lohengrin's Elsa facing Ortrud. Outwardly she appeared calm and poised enough, but I could see the little yarn boutonniere on her breast fluttering with the inner agitation.

Marina was momentarily paralyzed. This was treason. Heresy. She never had met it before, I'd swear. Then her fat face clouded. Her pudgy hands contracted into fists. She took a step forward. From the far end of the room came a tinkle of steel on the hardwood floor. Ambrosia was standing, her knitting in a heap at her feet. Two shadows moved threateningly: Julian Porter and Dr. Thorndyke stepped protectingly towards the girl. Only two figures remained motionless: a man across the room whom I could see only indistinctly. And Elena.

Madame wavered, halted. Her painted lips parted, surprisingly, in a wry smile.

"So! That is how it is, eh? Very amusing. You agree, Ambrosia?"

The spinster simply stood. She said nothing.

Madame turned her head a fraction. "Beale?"

Thorndyke cleared his throat. "I think we are all more than a little unstrung," he said carefully.

Madame snorted. "And you, Julian?"

"I, Marina?" He turned away with a shrug.

"Very amusing," she repeated. "Will you all please leave the room . . . except you, Anthony."

There was no movement.

"I said, will you all please go? I do not wish to see you."

"But where shall we go, Auntie?" Elena asked.

Marina gestured widely. "Any place. Into the hall . . . outside . . . any place. Will you obey me? Paris, get out of that chair and get out of this room. Instantly."

The man across the room unjointed himself. It was the chauffeur-pilot. With a strange smile he looked at the others, strode towards Madame, hesitated as though to speak, then walked on. A blast of icy air struck through the room as he opened the door.

"Coming, you others?" he asked with a chuckle.

In slow procession Ambrosia, Thorndyke, and Porter moved after him. Elena was the last to go. The door closed.

Marina sagged. With a great sigh she crossed to the fireplace and dropped into the chair behind which Elena had stood. Raising her hands she began gently to massage her temples.

I stood where I was. I hadn't stirred since I had entered the place. Since Marina seemed to be wrapped up in her brooding, I glanced around at the room.

It is difficult now to recall just what I noticed particularly on my first visit to that room. We saw so much of it, later on, though, that I came to know every corner and crevice almost by name.

Recollections? Well, it was enormous. It was called the library, even though there were no books in it. My feet were half-buried in a great Chinese rug which swirled with dragons and urns vomiting wistaria. I remember the huge chandelier above my head, its pendants and prisms and faceted crystal strings swaying and tinkling. I remember the concert grand piano hulked in one corner. (God, do I remember that piano!) There were quantities of chairs and davenports and divans and sofas and tables littering the place.

Most of all, though, I was attracted by the tiny fire burning timidly in the massive carved fireplace. The sight of it made me realize the numbness of my hands and feet, my aching, tired legs. More than anything else in the world I wanted to stretch out before that fire and bake myself to a crisp.

I moved over to it and warmed my hands.

Marina sighed. "You are ashamed of knowing me, yes?" she said presently.

I could think of nothing to say.

"Yes, I see you are," she went on. "But there is my side, too, Anthony. My great day!" She laughed a little bitterly. "The day I have looked forward to for so long. I wanted this day, you see. I planned it beautifully. There was a time, long ago, when I was very fond of that strange old man who built this place for me. And I thought, perhaps, to relive one of those moments again . . . today."

She shaded her eyes with her hand.

"Will one ever learn not to plan, Anthony? I thought I had learned that lesson, but I . . . I tell you this from my experience: hope, if you will, but let it be with indifference. The fates conspire against you. Never put your soul into a dream, Anthony. There is always . . . only disappointment."

She raised her head and turned in her chair to face me.

"I have so little left . . . and I have given up so much. And I thought: Here . . . away from the world . . . I might be able to see again . . ." She broke off. "What was that?"

From outside came the sound of a motor. Sandy had got the car to running at last and—wonder of wonders—had negotiated that climb.

I explained to Madame about the accident. She listened abstractedly, without interest. She seemed sunk in lassitude. When I had finished she said:

"Go and welcome him, then, this friend of yours. But I do not wish to see him. I do not wish to see anyone. Keep the others outside."

"But surely you can't mean—isn't it inhuman to leave them out there in the cold?"

She shook her head. "I feel nothing for them. They may go wherever they wish, so long as they keep out of my sight. Let them go into the kitchen with that crooked caretaker and his grotesque wife. There is a fire there, I suppose. Only keep them away from me." She waved me away. "Go and admit your friend. You may come back later. Now I wish to be alone."

At that moment I felt an overwhelming pity for this weary old ruin of a woman. Arrogant, overbearing, self-pitying as she was, I still felt sorry for her. She looked infinitely worn and tired, pitiably crushed and battered. I did not as yet know what had upset her but I wished with all my heart that I could have forestalled it.

I left the room quietly. She did not raise her head.

Mutiny was brewing in the hall. The exiles were huddled at the foot of the stairs, their faces bluish-grey, their teeth chattering. They looked up hopefully as I approached them.

Paris, the chauffeur, stood up. "Has the old fool come to her senses yet?"

Elena said crisply, "You are not to speak of Madame Grazie like that, Paris. I shall not tolerate it." Then to me, "Has Auntie forgiven us?"

"She doesn't want to see any of you," I said. "You'd better all steer clear of her for a little while anyway. I'll try to smooth things over later."

"I am sorry." Elena looked troubled and contrite. "We behaved very badly. And she had planned on this day for so long."

"I regret nothing. Marina is a pig-headed, spoiled, childish old woman. I shall freeze to death before I utter one word of apology."

That, you might know, was Miss Swisshome. I noticed that her hands, purple with cold, still moved in queer jerks. Then I remembered the knitting she had dropped in the library. She was lost without it.

I shrugged. "My secretary has just arrived with my car. Madame suggests that you go into the kitchen with the caretaker and his wife."

"Horrible old things!" Julian shuddered delicately. "I don't suppose they'll let us in."

Elena stood up. "I'll explain to them. Come with me."

They trooped down the hall and I went on to the front door. As I opened it Sandy rounded the corner, leaning forward against the howling wind. I got him in and slammed the door shut.

"I'm frozen, Tony," he said and I could barely understand him. His face was grey.

Without a word I took his arm and hustled him down the hall, past the door behind which Marina was brooding, to another door beyond which I could hear voices raised in tempestuous conversation. I opened it and pushed Sandy through.

"Time for introductions later," I said brusquely. "My friend is almost dead with the cold. Let him get near the fire."

We shucked him out of his overcoat, pulled the gloves off his stiff fingers and got his shoes off. Dr. Thorndyke took command. Someone got some snow outside the back door and we commenced rubbing Sandy's hands and feet.

While we worked over him I found out a little of what had gone on before I arrived.

The bus with the party had arrived promptly at ten-thirty. Mr. and Mrs. Tait, the caretakers, had fires going in the library and the kitchen; they had been all eagerness to be helpful. Marina had been in fine form, gracious and good-humored. She had liked the room and seemed pleased with everything.

Then the misfortunes began to heap up.

Stretching her hands towards the fire Marina commanded the Taits to set a luncheon table before the fireplace. The caretaker was amazed.

"There ain't any food here," he said.

Marina smiled as at a child. "But of course not, Mr. Tait. I have brought the food. It is in the auto-bus outside. You and Mrs. Tait are only to set the table."

"But we ain't got anything to set the table with," he protested. "We didn't know you was going to eat here."

The truth was out: except for the ancient kitchen stove, Lucifer's Pride possessed no facilities for cooking or serving food. Most of what Marina had brought along was in cans and as there was not even a can-opener, much less a knife or fork, the problem became acute.

Marina controlled herself with difficulty. Was there not, then, an axe or hatchet of some kind?

Tait shook his head. There was nothing. No one lived at Lucifer's Pride. He and his wife merely came over to see that the

Murder Ends the Song

place was warm. He lived across the river and he had supposed the party of visitors would merely walk through the building and then leave.

Marina tapped her foot. Well, then, she indicated, if they could not eat, at least they could be warm. Would Mr. Tait be good enough to pile some wood on the fire?

Even that, though, was not to be. Marina's cup was not yet full. Tait proceeded to pour in the drop that caused the overflow.

"Ain't no wood neither," he said. "Nobody never comes here in t'winter time. Had jest a little bit left over frum last Fall. Whyn't you let me know you uz goin' to make an all-day party out'n it? I'da fixed things up proper."

That had been more than Marina could bear. In her rage and disappointment she had snatched Tait's walking stick and struck him across the shoulder, the forehead. He had tottered. She had struck him again.

Mrs. Tait had rushed to her husband's assistance. "You ought t'be ashamed," she cried. "Hittin' a old man like that. 'Tain't his fault, nor it ain't mine, neither. I'll have the law on you, you see if I—"

Marina was beside herself by that time.

"Be quiet, you blind old hag," she had screamed. "Take your husband and get out of here. And stay out. Don't let me catch you within my sight again."

And she had flung the walking stick full in their faces.

Mrs. Tait, weeping with chagrin and anger, had led her husband out of the room. They had barricaded themselves in the kitchen and had seen no one until Elena had persuaded them to allow the fugitives to join them around the kitchen stove.

That was the story as it came to me. Everyone chimed in from time to time, interrupting, interjecting a detail, coloring up a point. But that was the story. And it was a mess.

I regarded the Taits with interest. He was a gnarled old man with kindly, bewildered eyes; his forehead was bandaged. As for Mrs. Tait, Marina had used the word "grotesque" in describing her. It was well-chosen. She had also called her a hag. And she was.

But she was not blind; she merely had a cataract on one eye. The grey film, the exact color of her skin, made her look as though she were winking. The effect, I could see, might become a little annoying after a time.

But that did not justify Marina's cruelty. I felt sorry for both of them.

Sandy was coming to life. He had listened with interest to the story. Now he grinned. "Wonder if she'll come out here to pay her respects to me?"

Instantly Mrs. Tait made for the door and locked it. "She'll not set a foot in this kitchen while I'm alive," she said furiously. I wondered idly whether her ire had been aroused by the blows given her husband or by the epithet which Marina had hurled at her. It has been my experience that no woman, no matter how old or hideous, relishes being called a hag.

I remarked that I thought such a visit very unlikely since Madame had expressly ordered me to keep them all out of sight.

"No trouble about that," Miss Swisshome muttered. "I've had enough of her for one day."

Assured that Sandy was recovering satisfactorily, I decided to return to the library. Perhaps I could persuade Marina to relent. After all, the kitchen was rather cramped.

Mrs. Tait let me out, locking the door again after me. I knocked at the library door and identified myself.

"Oh, come in, Anthony. I was hoping you would come."

By this time I should have been inured to Marina's mercurial changes. But I wasn't. She still had the power to take my breath away with her lightning changes of mood. She slipped them on and off like gloves.

She was standing beside the piano. The leather case I had first seen on her arm at the Swan Island airport was open before her on the broad back of the piano. She had just slipped a platinum chain over her head. There was a sparkle and glitter upon her bosom.

She crooked an arch finger at me. "Come, *mon ami*. You shall be the only one to see my glory."

When I reached her she took my hand and dropped something into it. Something hard that felt like a small egg.

"Glory" was the word for it. It was the most awe-inspiring thing of its kind I had ever seen. The Lucifer diamond was cut in the shape of a prism; purple, topaz and cerise flashed from its core. How large it was I do not know; when I held it I was conscious only of the fact that it seemed to burn into the palm of my hand. And I jerked back from it automatically. It fell, swayed slightly on its thin, silverish chain, came to placid rest in the valley between Madame's breasts.

"It frightens you," she laughed. "But that is droll." She looked down at it over a cascade of double chins. "But then sometimes it frightens even me." She caressed it with her fingers. "But it is my love . . . my one treasure."

I said, "Old Bollman must have been very fond of you."

She carolled with laughter. "Fond? Yes . . . for a time. This was his ransom, you understand."

I didn't. "Ransom?" I repeated.

She gave me a level look, as though wondering if she had said too much. Then she dropped the gem and turning away, seated herself at the piano. "Never mind, my friend. You could not understand. I am a strange woman. Very strange. The others—where are they?"

I told her they were in the kitchen.

"Let them stay there. Your friend arrived?" I nodded.

"*Bon.*" She ran her fingers over the keys. "Now please to find some fuel. It is nonsense that there is no wood in this great place. Replenish the fires. Tear down a wall if necessary, but I must be warm."

She was in one of her grand lady moods. I forebore to remind her that even if there had been a suitable wall to demolish, we had no axe. I said, "I'll do what I can."

In the kitchen I called a meeting of the ways and means committee. Nobody had any suggestions. We sat and gloomed at each other. Finally Julian raised a sullen head.

"There were some mammoth packing cases in the garage. Someone could break them up."

Tait came to life. "If it's packin' cases you want, there's plenty upstairs. Thousands of 'em."

"Empty?"

He scratched his stubbly chin. "Don't rightly know. Even if they ain't, we could empty some of 'em, couldn't we?"

There was applause. It was amazing how the group came to life. Even Mrs. Tait smiled, like a cock-eyed crow, out of one corner of her twisted mouth. But she said acidly enough, "It's for us, though. I wouldn't turn a hand for *her* . . . not if she was froze stiffer'n a board."

I got up. "You wait here. I'll talk to Madame Grazie."

As I entered the library Marina was playing the piano. The fire had burned low. I could barely distinguish her, all alone at the keyboard. She was playing the opening measures of the *Caro Nome* aria. "Madame?" I said.

She swung around abruptly. The Lucifer diamond trembled in a pear-shaped blaze on her bosom, and I thought again that never in my life had I seen anything so breathtaking. She smiled graciously at me and seemed delighted when I told her the news.

"*Bene*," she approved. "Perhaps now I shall restore circulation to my body."

I smiled. "I could use a little circulation, too."

"You are cold?" she said with concern. "How stupid of me. You must have some amontillado to stir your blood."

"But I wouldn't dream of putting you to—"

"Nonsense. We have all had some." She smiled wryly. "It was the only thing we could open." She pointed back over the piano. "There . . . in the angel."

I stared. "The angel?"

"The angel-bottle. Beside my treasure chest."

I saw it then. It was perhaps a foot high, of purple glass. And it was a lovely thing: the angel of the Annunciation with great wings joined at the top above the head to form the bottle-neck. While I got a glass from the mantel Marina explained that she had picked up the bottle in a little Neapolitan shop—"for a song . . . but literally a song. I sang *Caro Nome*. The shopkeeper was in ecstasy."

When I tasted the sherry, I remarked that the shop-keeper had nothing on me. It was grand stuff, nutty and smooth. I finished it off and did feel warmer. I put the glass back on the mantel and rubbed my hands.

"And now to work," I said. "We'll bring in the wood very quietly—"

"You will do nothing of the kind," she exclaimed. "I have said I do not wish to be disturbed."

"But—"

"Place it in the corridor outside . . . anything . . . only I will not see anyone. Now go."

I shrugged. Madame had spoken.

They were the last words I was ever to hear her say.

11

THE PACKING CASES WERE EMPTY.

We climbed to the third floor and finally found them after breaking into three rooms that appeared to be bedrooms. The Taits did not accompany us, insisting that they would not consider leaving their impromptu fortress. Sandy, who was not yet quite thawed out, elected to remain with them.

As I say, though, we found the place without the caretaker's help. It was piled almost to the ceiling with furniture crates stamped with the name of a Portland store. I appointed myself chief wrecker. As I had no axe or hatchet, I used my feet. The others cheered as the boards shattered. We all had visions of roaring bonfires and even Ambrosia, at sea without her knitting which was still in the library, joined what she referred to with a sniff as "the bucket brigade."

Thorndyke was the first to gather his load and depart. I heard the barrage of bright remarks that showered over him as he started down the three flights of stairs.

But he is the only one I was sure of. After he left I became so engrossed in my jumping and smashing that I paid little attention to the others. They picked up loads and left, returned empty-armed for another trip. There was little conversation as the long flights of stairs took all one's breath. My back was to the door and I was beginning to work up a good sweat.

Marina came in for a goodish bit of unflattering comment. I learned from stray remarks that she was still ignoring them, remaining behind her closed door, playing and singing *Caro Nome*.

Later on I heard a grumbling behind me. It was Julian Porter. I gathered that he was starving and freezing at the same time and couldn't decide which was the more unpleasant. I remembered some sandwiches I had put into the car before going to meet Sandy at the Cathedral. Neither of us had been hungry on the way out; they should still be there. So I told Porter about them and suggested he get them and bring them up on his next return trip. He cheered up immensely and said he would be right back.

Minutes later I straightened up to get the kinks out of my back and the sweat out of my eyes. Elena came in. I looked at her in surprise. She was white and shaking.

"Sometimes I could cheerfully commit murder," she said and fell rather than sat on a box.

"Think of the fire we can have," I said, hoping to cheer her up.

"Oh, I don't mean this. It's rather fun. I meant Auntie."

"She want the steam heat turned on?" I remarked flippantly.

She was not amused. "My arms were so tired I couldn't hold my load any longer . . . and I dropped it in the hall. Out she came and gave me a tongue-lashing. Sometimes I think—"

I patted her shoulder. "She'll wear herself out soon. And when we get the fire going she'll be more human. Forget about it. We're all with you."

With a wan smile she got up, sighed, and took another load.

The work went on. I broke boxes until the soles of my feet ached. The others came and went until finally it dawned on me that we should have had enough wood piled downstairs to last us till doomsday. I decided to call a halt.

The others were only too eager to stop. One by one they came in, draped themselves around on boxes, and talked about food. I told them about the sandwiches and said that Porter should have been back hours ago. They brightened up and actually mustered the spirit to make a few wisecracks.

We began concocting an imaginary dinner from the materials on hand. Thorndyke, with an amazing display of ingenuity, was just describing a fricassee of building-lathe with shingle-nail sauce and garnish of excelsior when Porter walked in. He looked half-frozen. There were beads of ice on his eyebrows; streaks of powdery snow traced every seam in his clothes. Beating his arms around his body, he glared at me.

"If that's your idea of a joke," he said through chattering teeth, "I don't think you're very funny."

"What're you talking about?" I said. "Where's the food?"

"Don't make me laugh. There isn't a crumb of food in that car of yours and I think you knew it. You haven't liked me from the first and this is just your way of showing it."

Well, I've already admitted I didn't like him, but I had not consciously done anything to demonstrate it to him. At some other time I should have been angry, but now I was only puzzled about the sandwiches. I'd put them in the car; we hadn't eaten them. Then where the hell were they?

Wondering about that, I ignored Porter. But Elena didn't.

"You're being very silly, Julian," she said. "If Mr. Graine said there were sandwiches there, he thought there were. There is no need to behave like a child. Please apologize."

Porter looked at her sullenly.

"Apologize, please," the girl repeated.

By that time everyone was thoroughly uncomfortable. Trying to smooth things over, I said it really didn't matter in the least. But Elena waved me into silence and stood waiting.

Finally Porter gave up. "Sorry, Graine," he said ill-naturedly. "Nerves, I guess."

Ambrosia Swisshome stood up.

"There are," she announced, "few people in this world more tolerant of artistic temperament than I, but I have had enough of this. I am going down and demand that Marina come to her senses."

Paris, the chauffeur, shifted his bulky legs. "I bet she chews your head off."

Miss Swisshome gave him a withering glance. "I prefer decapitation to slow congealing. Are you all worms or must I go alone?"

I realized that I was beginning to cool off. The comparative warmth of the library had a sudden infinite attraction. So, feeling that if anyone could get results with the tempestuous creature downstairs it would be I and not Ambrosia, I offered to go. They took me up on it with alacrity. I think Ambrosia had a difficult time concealing her relief. She said:

"Well, run along then and don't keep us waiting until we have to be carried down."

I "ran along."

As I was going down the stairs I reflected that Marina's devotion to *Caro Nome* was almost pathological. She was still singing it and she had been at it all afternoon. The tones shivered up through the well of the staircase. The voice grew stronger as I neared the ground floor and I realized with amazement that she was singing better than I had ever heard her. Even muffled by the closed door and the intervening space, her voice had a fluidity and brilliance that was almost incredible at her age.

I marveled at it, wondering if her explosion were responsible for the improvement. I know for a fact that there is nothing like a good tantrum to relax the vocal cords; I've utilized the procedure many times myself. And I thought that if Marina were going to continue her career she should adopt the motto: More and better blow-ups.

She finished the aria as I reached the downstairs hall. Knowing that she would still be under the spell of that afterglow that is the second of three rewards accruing to the singer of a song, I knocked very softly.

There was no answer. I waited. Then I knocked again.

There was still no answer. Instead, she began singing the aria again.

Once, at La Scala, I sang Des Grieux opposite a young Viennese Manon. She had paid out a good fat fee for her debut but it was money well spent: she had brains and a voice and she used them both. Everything was going along swimmingly until all at once, during the St. Sulpice scene, I became aware of an uneasy twitch in my brain. There was no reason for it that I could discover; it was one of the best performances I had ever taken part in. I tried to shrug the feeling away. But I could not. An inner consciousness kept whispering, "Careful . . . something is going to happen . . . watch out for trouble." Ten minutes later the debutante went completely to pieces. Crashed. Gave up the ship. Couldn't sing a note. She never appeared on a stage again.

It was that same inner warning that came to me as I stood before that door, listening to Marina begin her song anew. It was nothing tangible . . . just that same vague uneasiness . . . warning me that something grim was in the offing.

So, gathering all my courage, I opened the door instead of knocking for a third time.

I called softly.

There was no break in the flow of sound.

I opened the door wide and looked in.

The room was icy. A draft that turned one's very marrow to slush was pouring in from somewhere. And yet Marina went on carolling as though the temperature were that of a balmy spring day. Across the room I could see a wraith-like flapping: the window was wide open, the draperies pulled back.

Had Marina lost her senses utterly? I thought: Good God, she'll catch her death.

The voice sang:

"Caro nome che il mio cor
Festi primo palpitar . . ."

and, I realized, it came not from the vicinity of the piano but from one side of the room. I looked closer—and discovered why Marina had sounded so fresh and youthful.

It was the phonograph, a large, old battery set, playing a recording that must have been made ten years before.

Again the uneasiness assailed me. I called, "Madame Grazie!" and I could hardly believe my ears: my voice was quavering.

But there was no answer.

And then I saw her. She was sitting on the piano bench, her body bent forward over the keyboard, her head resting on her arms. And seeing her, I had an impulse to laugh at my fears. The poor

Murder Ends the Song

old thing, I could see, had put on the recording in order to relive her past glory—and had fallen asleep.

I would have left her to finish her nap—but there was the open window. No one knows better than I that, to a singer, a draft is the most fiendish visitation an unkind Providence can devise. And Madame had been dozing in the path of the open window for Lord knows how long.

I went over to awaken her. I called her name softly but she did not stir.

And so I put my hand on her shoulder and shook her.

If I live to be a thousand I shall never forget what followed. Under my hand the great body swayed for a split second, then like a sawdust doll, it rolled slowly to one side, further and further. Paralyzed, I watched it lean towards me, heard the dissonant crash as the head struck a cluster of keys. And then the velvet-clad bulk went sliding down between the piano and the bench, coming to rest in a dark mound on the floor.

I couldn't move. Inside my head was a rumbling like the ominous tympani in a Sibelius symphony.

"The woman will catch her death," I had thought a moment before.

I choked back an ungodly impulse to break into hysterical laughter. For she had. There was even a tiny tracery of blood threading around her neck from where a steel knitting needle protruded like a pin impaling a specimen.

Across the room Marina's voice began again:

"*Caro nome che il mio cor . . .*"

"Carved upon my inmost heart . . ."

12

I don't know what the conventional reaction to sudden death is supposed to be, and I don't care. I've never pretended to be a strong, silent man. All I know is, I wanted to be sick.

It wouldn't have been so bad if her eyes had been closed or if there had been some sort of decent repose in her face. But there wasn't. Her eyes stared up at me as though they were looking at the devil himself. As if that weren't enough, the lipstick had been smeared out and up one cheek so that she smiled with all the twisted inanity of a jack-o'-lantern. It was that smile under the terror-stricken eyes that got me.

I managed to fight off the waves of nausea that swept over me. But I wanted company. I didn't much care who it was as long as I wasn't alone with that quiet, inert mound on the floor.

I went to the kitchen to get Sandy.

At first, the Taits wouldn't unlock the door. The old man kept asking who it was and I could hear Mrs. Tait's Greek chorus commanding him not to let "that woman" in. I realized finally that I had been talking up in high falsetto, vaulted two octaves down to my normal register, and convinced them that I hadn't changed my sex since they had last seen me. Grudgingly, they opened up.

As I have remarked before, Sandy's cadaverous face is not exactly matinee-idolish and he appears to have all the vigor of a perambulating corpse, but when I walked into the room and saw him blithely toasting his stocking'd feet in the open oven, he looked so alive and vital compared to what I had just left that I swear I could have put my arm around his shoulder and kissed him.

Instead I told him gruffly to get into his shoes; I wanted to show him something.

"Important?" He eyed me resentfully.

"Rather."

"More than this stove?"

"God damn it, yes! Will you crawl out of that little hell and come on?"

Mrs. Tait clicked her plates at the profanity. Sandy got into his shoes with the resigned air of Mother going out to look at a grasshopper Junior has captured under a jelly glass.

I didn't warn him of what to expect. I simply opened the library door and shoved him in. The phonograph was still hitting the high spots of *Caro Nome*. (Don't be worried about how it kept on: I had already discovered that it had a metal contraption which lifted the pick-up and carried it back to the beginning. It could play until the record or the batteries wore out.) As I had, Sandy naturally thought it was Marina singing. He was, therefore, halfway across the room before he took a good look at the piano. He stiffened, turned, looked in bewilderment around the room. I pointed to the dark heap on the floor.

For a moment he stood as paralyzed as I had been, then went over, bent down—and poked it with a long forefinger. He drew in his breath.

"Dead," he muttered. "Dead, by God."

The phonograph took high-C with a gusto that demolished the ear-drums. Suddenly I could hear Marina saying, "My Gilda is *con brio* . . . a delicate young girl in the first ecstasy of passion." Again I had to fight down a desperate urge to be sea-sick.

"Will you, for Christ's sake, shut off that phonograph," I said. "It's getting me down."

Without a word he got up and shut off the machine. Then he came back and stood beside me. "What's the matter, Tony?" he said quietly. "Did you have anything to do with this?"

"Don't be an ass," I snapped. "Of course, I didn't. I didn't know anything about it until I walked in three minutes ago and practically fell over her."

"O.K. Skip it," he said. "It was just something to say. I guess what we both need is a drink." He went over to the piano and picked up the angel bottle. It gleamed with an amethyst glow in the dying firelight. He shrugged. "Well, I always say sherry's better than nothing." He filled two glasses and handed me one.

I could hardly get the first gulp down because all of a sudden it seemed rather ghoulish to be standing over Marina's body drinking her sherry. But I finished it. Then we had another.

Warmed a little, steadied a trifle, I crossed over to stoke up the fire. Sandy, glass in hand, was looking down at Marina. As I threw on some boards, he said:

"It couldn't be suicide, could it?"

(I wonder why the average human mind, confronted by violent death, always brings in a first verdict of suicide. Did Eve, looking down at Abel's limp body with its shattered skull, say to Adam, "Could it be suicide, do you suppose?")

"Don't be an ass," I said again.

"No, guess you're right," Sandy agreed.

Nevertheless the same thought had occurred to me. And yet, obviously, suicide was out of the question.

In the first place, she would have needed the power of a pile-driver and the ability of a contortionist to drive that knitting-needle into the back of her neck. There were other considerations as well. Marina could have exhibited herself in a sideshow as one of the world's prize egoists. As far as she was concerned, the world not only revolved around her but existed because she existed. No one who savored life as she had would deliberately cut off that life. She might dramatize her petty misfortunes, but even in her most *farouche* moods she was jealous of each passing moment, spurning contemptuously any suggestion that she was not as she had been twenty years before.

Finally, however, there was the fact that the weapon was a knitting-needle. If by any chance she could have brought herself to the point of self-destruction, it seemed to me that she would have been impelled to choose something highly exotic and picturesque: a Petronius-like severing of her veins in a petal-strewn bath; a delicate nibble at one of Agrippina's arsenic-dusted peaches; plunging into her breast a tiny jewelled dagger with which Cesare Borgia had despatched a too-promiscuous mistress. But impaling herself on anything as prosaic as a knitting-needle! No, no, it was out of the question.

I went on poking the fire. Sandy was quiet, but in his silence I sensed the same suspicions that were beginning to trouble me. And because sometimes you can fool yourself into believing an idea doesn't exist until you put it into words, I hoped that if I kept on prodding the fire Sandy would keep still.

You can, however, poke a fire only so long. At last, I had to give up. I turned and found Sandy's eyes on me. We looked at each other for a moment, and I was suddenly conscious of the cold pouring in from the open window. But it didn't feel like a draft; instead, it trickled along my spine like icy fingers counting my vertebrae.

Sandy must have felt it, too. He started over to close the window. And in a gruff voice he said what I had been trying not to hear:

"Which one, then?"

And there it was. Out at last. Yet, while I was afraid of it, perversely I was a little relieved that the thing had been dragged out into the open.

For we were face to face with a murder. And someone in Lucifer's Pride had committed it.

Which one? There were nine of us in the building. And I knew them all. It was not a pleasant thought. One reads about murderers, but somehow one doesn't actually *know* a murderer.

"I don't know," I said. "I wish I'd never—"

But I didn't finish that sentence. I had been watching Sandy in his slow progress towards the window, so abstracted that he was seeing nothing.

But I was. I let out a yell.

"Sandy! Don't move."

He froze, teetering there on one foot like a stork playing hopscotch. His head jerked around and he looked wildly at me. I made a dash towards him. He leaped sideways, tripped over a coffee table and crashed in a tangle to the floor. He sat there and gaped.

I said, "Sorry, old boy. You were just about to step on these."

"These" were what appeared at first glimpse to be the soles of two white shoes, detached from the uppers and planted there on the bare oak floor. One was directly beneath the window; the other a few inches nearer the piano.

I squatted down and examined them. They were two footprints moulded in snow. It was only luck that they had not long ago melted into puddles. As it was—because the fire had burned to embers and the open window had admitted a frigid blast—they had retained their shape perfectly. Even the peculiarities of the leather sole had remained imprinted in the packed snow.

Sandy had recovered his poise and what might be called his voice. He joined me beside the prints. "Looks like a ditch digger's boot," he said.

It did, too. It was broad and shortish. A line of elongated pockmarks outlined the rim. In the center of the heel was a large star, which I recognized as the trademark of a well-known brand of rubber heels. It—

"Don't do that!" I yelled and made a grab for Sandy's hand. But I was too late. He had tried to pick up the print and it lay now in mushy fragments.

I glared at him. "You dope," I exploded. "When the police come they'll want to see this thing. And now look at it!"

"It was melting anyway," he said defensively. "They won't last ten minutes with this fire going."

He was right, of course. The ferry wouldn't be back for us until four-thirty; we would have to make the slow trip across, drive to the nearest town, sound the alarm, and then make the return trip with the police. The prints would not only have melted; they would have dried completely.

I decided on action. "Got a pencil?"

While he fumbled through his pockets, I ripped a blank sheet from an opera score propped on the music rack of the piano. Then with suggestions from Sandy, I made a faithful copy of the remaining print—star on the heel, welt marks and stitching, every thing. I labeled it "Footprint found on floor beneath window sill," and tucked it away in my inside coat pocket.

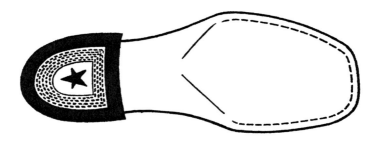

"Let 'er melt," I said with satisfaction. We stood up and brushed off our knees.

"Maybe there's something in the snow outside the window," Sandy said. "Looked?"

I went to the window, pushed back the velour draperies and leaned out. I was almost knocked over by the force of the gale. Obviously there was nothing below the window. If there ever had been, the marks had been obliterated by the fury of the storm. The ground was swept bare; it stretched to the palisades, brown and frozen.

I slammed the window shut, drew the drapes and returned eagerly to the grateful warmth of the fire. As I walked forward my foot caught in something soft. There was a tiny metallic tinkle. I stooped over and disentangled Ambrosia Swisshome's knitting from around my ankle. There were three needles enmeshed in the half-completed stuff.

I knew where the fourth one was.

With a feeling of repugnance I dropped the thing. As I did so I glanced automatically at Marina's body.

"Holy cow!" I yelped. I hurried over to the corpse.

I suppose seeing the body from a different angle brought the thing into view. For half hidden under Marina's hair was a fluffy wad of color. I picked it up. It was a knot of yarn flowers, purple, pink, yellow, and green.

Sandy came over and examined it with me. "What is it?" he said.

I saw again Elena Grazie beside the fireplace as she defied her aunt. I could see the agitated rise and fall of her breast. I could see something pinned to her coat.

"A boutonniere," I said dazedly.

"Whose?"

"Elena Grazie's."

He made an obscene noise. "You're nuts. That nice kid couldn't have—"

"No one said she did. I only said these flowers belong to her. I know, because I saw her wearing them."

We stood in silence, looking at the little blob of color. It was incredible. But there could be no mistake. And then I remembered the girl's face as she came into the room upstairs, pale and shaken; remembered her queer expression as she said, "Sometimes I could cheerfully commit murder."

I stooped over and replaced the flowers.

"What now?" Sandy said.

"I don't know. But I've read enough murder stories to know that everything in the room must be left as it was. And if Elena—" I broke off.

"Yeah? If Elena—?"

I shrugged. "Skip it. Put some more wood on the fire. We've got to get the others down. They're probably frozen."

While he piled on more wood, I took one last look at Marina. Dammit, I thought, she was a great person. She had added something very definite to the world; she had made a contribution and so had justified herself, no matter what else she had been or done. She had deserved something more from the world than this: a stab in the back . . . death in a lonely room.

I gave way to a sentimental impulse. After all, those staring, terror-stricken eyes were indecent; she would not have liked

Murder Ends the Song

being left so. I knelt down beside her and pressed the lids down. Then I got an Indian robe from a divan and started to spread it over her. It was little enough but somehow I felt she would have been grateful for it.

But with the robe in midair I halted. I had seen something else.

She had fallen from the piano bench so that her left arm and hand were beneath her but not completely hidden. I could just see the clenched knuckles of the hand—and the fingers were holding something white. I tried to disengage it and succeeded with some difficulty. I smoothed it out—and stared, dumbfounded.

It was a page of Gilda's aria from the first act of *Rigoletto*. It was the first page of *Caro Nome*.

Again, that confounded song! Were we haunted by it? First, the words smeared in blood on Marina's dressing-room mirror, then the phonograph singing it over her dead body . . . and now the song itself crumpled in her stiffening fingers.

The right margin was torn and jagged, as though the page had been ripped from its moorings. The score was propped on the music rack of the piano. I had, without realizing what it was, torn from it the blank sheet on which I had made the copy of the footprint.

I remembered that Marina's head had been resting against the rack when I entered the room. I could picture what had happened.

Wrapped in her memories, she had been sitting at the piano, playing and singing the aria. As she had reached up to turn the page, the murderer had appeared, in one hand the needle withdrawn from Ambrosia Swisshome's knitting. Seeing that and understanding in a flash what was to happen, she had opened her mouth to scream . . . a hand had been clasped over her mouth, smearing the lipstick. The blow was struck; Marina's fingers had contracted spasmodically, jerked back, pulling the page away with them.

In the silence that followed, the murderer had, with macabre humor, started the phonograph. And Marina had sung on . . . in death.

It was a horrible thought. But it all held together. Over at the fireplace Sandy muttered, "I'll be glad to get out of this damned morgue."

Alfred Meyers

Well, for that matter, I heartily agreed with him. I bent over Marina to replace the page from the score. But I did not accomplish it.

Footsteps sounded in the hall outside and there came an imperative knock.

"Mr. Graine, are you there?"

I recognized the acid syllables of Miss Swisshome, and called that I was.

"Well, I think you had better come upstairs. Julian and Dr. Thorndyke are killing each other and I can't make up my mind which I should like to win. Could you help me decide?"

13

"It's all so delightfully feral," said Miss Swisshome.

To me it sounded less like wild beasts than house-wreckers at work. The din was terrific. The three of us stood outside the locked door—down the hall a little from the room containing the packing boxes—and wondered what to do. My knocking aroused no reaction on the other side; if anything, it seemed to spur the combatants on to more violent sound-effects.

"What happened?" I asked when it became apparent that I was only bruising my knuckles to no purpose.

Miss Swisshome leaned towards the door, drinking in the sounds of the scuffle. Her eyes glittered. They did not swerve from the door as she explained briefly.

"They were in one corner talking. I had not been paying attention to them but all at once I heard Beale say something about 'the box.' Then Julian hurled a rather improper epithet at the doctor. A 'son of a bitch,' I think he called him. I always think that is such a virile term, don't you?"

Her eyes swung to me momentarily and her lips twitched with suppressed amusement. Then she again became absorbed in her eavesdropping.

"Before we knew what was happening, the two of them dashed out of the room and locked themselves in here. That is all I know."

"But didn't someone try to stop them?"

She smiled a little malicious smile. "I wouldn't have dreamed of it. There is little enough excitement in life."

"I didn't mean you. But Paris might—"

"Paris is really a sort of servant," she interrupted stiffly. "Such a thing would have been out of place. Elena came out here with me, but when we heard what was going on, she put her hands over her ears and ran back. She has always disliked violence."

"Most unusual girl," I commented gravely.

Miss Swisshome ignored my sarcasm. "Listen to that crash," she said with relish. "I think someone was knocked down."

Sandy made a face at me over the woman's shoulder. I said, "Do you have any idea what is behind this row?"

"A fair one," she admitted, looking like an aged Mona Lisa.

"What box were they talking about?"

Her face was expressionless. "Box?"

"Yes. The box you said Dr. Thorndyke mentioned?"

She gave me a look in which were shrewdness, caution, and the vaguest touch of annoyance. "Oh, that one," she said, and went on with her listening.

I waited. Nothing was forthcoming. Finally I said, "Well, what about it?"

"About it? Oh, you mean the box. I see no reason why I should tell you, Mr. Graine. After all, who are you?" All that said very sweetly.

I bowed. "As you say, after all, who am I?" Sandy made another face at me. I grinned back. "Would you like us to break the door down?"

She stepped back, delighted. "Please do. I dote on brute strength."

Fate, however, robbed us of the dubious pleasure of being doted on by the sadistic spinster. At that moment the key turned in the lock, the door opened, and Beale Thorndyke appeared.

Blood oozed from a cut on the doctor's forehead. His hair, usually so neat, was rumpled and tossed. His coat hung over his arm and he sucked at a knuckle of his right hand. He eyed us with clinical dislike and lowered the hand from his mouth.

"Sorry, but do you mind letting me pass?" he said coldly.

Miss Swisshome's jaw dropped and Sandy emitted an admiring whistle. I was so awed by his poise that I stepped back.

"Thanks," he said. "Come along, Julian. We've had an audience."

The accompanist had obviously got the worst of the fracas. His left eye was one grand and beautiful mouse, and his nose dripped blood like a leaky faucet. He glared at us sullenly but said nothing.

Thorndyke put on his own coat and helped Porter into his. Then the two of them strolled casually back to the store-room.

"Of all the effrontery!" Miss Swisshome gasped. "You'd think they might at least offer a word of explanation."

"Perhaps they feel it's none of our business," I suggested wryly. "After all, who are we?"

She would have liked, I know, to scalp me but she restrained herself. "Shall we follow them," she said instead.

The store-room was quiet when we got there. Elena was standing with her back to the wall facing the two gladiators, who were calmly ignoring her tense and questioning gaze. Porter was tightening the knot of his tie. (I was glad to see that the cold air had had a salutary effect on his nasal trickle.) Thorndyke was seated on a packing box, still abstractedly sucking his knuckle.

Miss Swisshome took it all in and then exploded. "Well, all I have to say is—"

Porter turned smouldering eyes on her. He said slowly and distinctly:

"You keep quiet."

Miss Swisshome's mouth shut with a snap. She tossed her head and sniffed. She kept quiet.

In the silence that followed I suddenly remembered that I had come up to tell them of what had happened downstairs. I cleared my throat. As at a signal, everyone turned and looked at me. Then it was that I received a shock. For in their eyes I saw an expression of resentment and—yes, defiance. It was as though they knew what I was going to say—knew, in fact, more about it than I did. And they resented me as an intruder. They tied my tongue as efficiently as though they had gagged me.

I wasn't imagining it, either. I know, because Sandy put a hand on my shoulder and whispered, "Don't let them get you down." He felt it, too.

That was all I needed. Forcing myself to remember that huddled body beside the piano and fixing them with what I hoped was an impressive eye, I told them. I didn't go into any of the details of what Sandy and I had discovered. I simply said that Madame Grazie was—dead.

I don't know what reactions I expected. Tears and hysterics from the women, I suppose; shock and controlled sorrow from the men. Whatever it was, though, I was disappointed. What I got was something like this:

Elena said, "Auntie . . . dead?" Her hands went to her breast, fumbled, became motionless. (Was she, I wondered, searching for something that was no longer there?) Then she simply sighed, and I'll swear it was a sigh of relief.

Beale Thorndyke raised professional eyebrows and said, "Oh, I'm sorry." It was the purely conventional regret of a physician who has jabbed a thermometer into a patient's mouth a bit too roughly and feels he must say something.

Ambrosia Swisshome patted Elena's shoulder. "I knew this would happen and I'm—" She didn't finish, but even a fool could have told that she was going to add, "I'm glad."

The accompanist went on arranging his disordered clothes. He said nothing, but the way his lips twisted into a wry smile could have meant any number of things.

It was Paris, though, who turned in the star performance of the afternoon. While I was talking he straddled his packing-box and eyed me as though I were "Uncle Wilbur" spouting a bedtime story on the Krunchy Krispy Kiddy Hour. As I finished, a change came over him. His blunt fingers clenched into fists; beneath the tight whipcord of his breeches the muscles of his thighs twitched convulsively; he leaped to his feet and charged past me out the door. His booted feet clattered as he took the stairs three at a time.

I looked at Sandy. Sandy looked at me.

"Is that man utterly mad?" Miss Swisshome asked. She stood up.

I don't know what happened then. There must have been some sort of tacit signal exchanged between them, because all at once everyone made a rush for the door. How they got through so quickly, again I don't know. But they did. They were gone before I could blink.

Sandy was still looking at me. And I was looking at Sandy. The room was very still.

14

PARIS WAS WAITING for the two of us as we came downstairs a few minutes later. He had a very large, ugly-looking revolver in his hand. It was pointed at us.

"Been waiting for you," he said, punctuating the words with little jerks of the gun. "Just walk right in and join the others."

With the muzzle of that gat ooh-ing in our faces, it was a little difficult to refuse his invitation. We walked in.

"And stick your hands up," Paris went on. "I don't want to play favorites."

I saw what he meant. The others were standing along the wall, hands above heads, for all the world like the receiving end of a blood-purge. I hadn't the vaguest idea what it was all about but the chauffeur's grim manner discouraged the questions I might have asked.

So we upped with our hands and joined the lineup. I was amazed to see Mr. and Mrs. Tait along with the rest. They, too, had their hands above their heads and were looking very unhappy about the whole thing. Paris must have seen the look of surprise that came over my face.

"Found the old man sweeping up some snow. At least that's what he said. The old woman was helping him," he explained.

My eyes sought the spots on the floor where the footprints had been. Now there were only two darkish splotches. I thanked heaven I'd had sense enough to copy the outline. Unconsciously I lowered my hand to my pocket to reassure myself that the paper was still there.

"Keep your hands up, Graine," Paris barked, "or I might get a twitch in my finger."

I obeyed hastily. I'm always oppressed by the thought of possible twitches in trigger fingers.

If this were fiction I suppose I should have to say that Paris leered at us. But it isn't. And he didn't. He grinned. Although his eyes remained cold and determined, his rugged face crinkled into a strangely likeable grin.

"Now that we're all together," he said, "suppose you just hand it over."

No one moved.

The revolver swept the ranks. "I said hand it over. I'm getting tired of talking. In a minute I'll show you a little action." The grin broadened. "And I don't think you'll like it."

The indomitable Miss Swisshome cleared her throat. "I think this is all very silly. Perhaps the rest of you may have some idea of what the man's talking about but I for one think it is gibberish."

Well, I for one agreed with her, but I knew better than to say so.

The gun swung to her. "You know goddamn well what I mean. Hand it over."

In answer, Miss Swisshome lowered her arms.

Paris's grin faded. "Put 'em up!" he cracked.

"I shall do nothing of the kind," she said firmly. "I have had quite enough of standing here like a department store dummy. My shoulders are aching. You may shoot me if you wish but I intend to be comfortable while you're doing it."

And she walked calmly to a chair and sat herself down. She folded her arms, arranged her thin lips precisely.

"Now," she said.

I couldn't take any more. I'm afraid I disgraced myself. I collapsed . . . literally . . . fell on the floor and rolled with laughter. At the moment of writing this the scene doesn't seem particularly funny. But when it happened it struck me as the most hilarious thing I'd ever seen. Nervous tension, I suppose.

Elena was the next to succumb. She started to laugh with me, caught sight of Marina's body and began to cry, then laughed and cried at the same time. One by one the others joined in; even Mrs. Tait added a shrill cachinnation to the uproar.

And all the while Marina lay there before us, the blanket pulled off her body. It was a shocking scene but no one could stop it.

Paris fumed and threatened. No one paid any attention to him. In fact, far from quelling us, he only added to the merriment for whenever one of the howling hysterics showed signs of tapering off, one look at his red and scowling face started the bedlam all over again. At last he tossed the gun down in disgust and, flinging himself into a chair, pouted like a sulky little boy.

The sight of the discarded gun had an astringent effect on my nerves. I picked it up and pocketed it. Then I went over to the seething man.

"Now suppose you tell us what is gone and what we were to hand over."

The words brought a quick return of sanity to the room. Only Elena could not control a few last exhausted moans. Otherwise the room was quiet.

He glowered. "Maybe you don't know," he conceded, "but the others do. Why don't you ask them?"

"Because I'm asking you. Come on. Out with it."

He glared at me, then lowered his eyes. "It's the Lucifer diamond. That's what's gone."

Across the room Sandy gaped at me. We had been so engrossed in footprints and knots of flowers that we had completely forgotten the diamond. Now that I thought of it, though, I couldn't remember seeing it when I stooped over to examine the wound in Marina's neck. But to make sure I went over to the body.

The chauffeur was right. The thin line of congealed blood was the only thing encircling Madame's neck. Earlier that afternoon I had seen the platinum chain there.

I looked up and started to speak. But there was no need for words; my face evidently spoke for me.

Instantly there was pandemonium. Within twenty seconds the room looked like something in the wake of a Kansas tornado. Pillows flew through the air like upholstered snowflakes. Beale

Thorndyke attacked the sparsely populated bookshelves, pulling the volumes out and dropping them with thuds to the floor. Elena was running her hands deep down into chairs and divans. Ambrosia skulked around Marina's body.

I sought refuge beside Sandy, whose thin lips twisted with contempt.

"Undoubtedly motivated by love for the deceased," he muttered.

It was a repulsive exhibition. I could think of nothing but swine rooting through a straw-heap for a forgotten carrot. Sandy and I didn't exist; the search went on around us as though we were not in the room. The Taits, looking wild-eyed and fearful, joined us in our corner. We waited.

It went on until the place was a shambles. I swear every nook and crevice was explored. Finally, however, there was no place else to search. They stood where they were and looked at each other. The looks were not kindly. I saw suspicion in more than one pair of eyes.

I said brightly, "I don't suppose every prospector in Kimberley makes a strike every time."

Thorndyke threw himself down on the cushionless davenport. "It isn't the diamond," he said wearily.

I swallowed. Good God, if that were true, then the egg-hunt became all the more inexplicable.

"You weren't looking for the diamond?" I repeated stupidly.

Ambrosia snatched up her knitting, made as though to start to work, fumbled for the fourth needle, looked involuntarily at its resting-place, and turned pale. She fell down into a chair.

"No," she said, weakly. "It's the chain."

"Chain?"

Elena came to my rescue. "You see, Mr. Graine, Auntie had something else on that chain besides the diamond. It—it was a key. We—we were hunting for it."

"A key?" Then it dawned on me. I remembered Ambrosia's remark about the argument upstairs over "the box."

"You mean . . . it was the key to the jewel-case?" I said.

She nodded.

Murder Ends the Song

I looked around. "But where is the case?"

After all, they had turned the room upside down and I had caught no glimpse of it.

The same thought occurred to the others. They had been so intent on the tree they had forgotten the forest. Beale Thorndyke started to spring up, but Ambrosia stopped him.

"Why do you bother?" she said. "We've been all over the room and it isn't here."

"But it must be somewhere," Elena insisted. "It can't have just flown away."

Again I noted the suspicious dart of eyes. I couldn't resist saying, "Perhaps it didn't need to fly. Perhaps someone took it away."

"Don't be ridiculous," Miss Swisshome snapped. The others seemed to agree with her.

Just the same, my remark hit the bull's-eye. That was what they were afraid of; that was why there was an atmosphere of distrust and suspicion which could have been cut with a knife.

"Of course, no one took it," Thorndyke said. "We're not thieves."

So I had to take their word for it . . . until I found the jewel-case, that is.

I found it all right. Only a few moments later, too. It was in the piano bench. For want of something else to do, I had gone over to spread the Indian robe over Marina again. And then I lifted the lid of the bench. Why? I don't know. I just did. And there it was—the one place in the whole room that hadn't been ransacked.

I picked the box up but before I could examine it there was a stampede. It was Elena who snatched the thing out of my hands. It was Ambrosia whose sharp eyes made the discovery before the others.

"The key," she shrieked. "It's in the box."

Elena jerked the lid open. Her eyes widened. Then she dropped the box and burst into tears.

I expected to see a cascade of jewelry go spilling over the floor. I was disappointed. The box was empty.

Everyone stood and looked down at it. No one spoke.

Finally I said, "So the diamond is really missing, after all?"

Thorndyke turned away. "To hell with the diamond," he growled. "I told you we weren't looking for it."

I was bewildered. The first search had been for the key. Then they had hunted for the case. They had found both. What in hell, I thought, did that crew want for a nickel?

"But the diamond—" I began.

Miss Swisshome stiffened. "If you mention that diamond once more, Mr. Graine, I—I warn you I shan't be responsible for what happens."

I was not deterred. I still wanted to know what the fuss was all about, and, by God, I was going to find out. "But I still don't see—"

Miss Swisshome's teeth came together with a crack. She looked as if she were embarking on an epileptic fit.

Elena dried her eyes hastily. "Of course, you don't, Mr. Graine," she said, motioning to Ambrosia to control herself. "But you may take my word for it that the diamond is comparatively unimportant to us. At the moment we're all much more interested in the other—"

"Elena!" Thorndyke erupted.

The girl straightened defiantly. "Mr. Graine is in this as deeply as the rest of us. I think he ought to know that—"

Julian Porter strode to her, grasped her wrists. "Will you for God's sake shut up?" he blurted.

They glared at each other. Then she wrenched her arms from his grasp and massaged her wrists gingerly. "Oh, very well," she said, beaten. "I'm sorry, Mr. Graine, but I'm afraid you'll have to keep on just being curious."

Sandy shot me a look that said plainly: "Nuts—all of them!"

And I agreed.

But whatever I might think of them and the mysterious "other," whatever-it-was that they were much more interested in at the moment, this was getting us no closer to the main point. Marina Grazie was lying dead in the room. So far her dying had had about as much effect on us as the squashing of a bluebottle fly.

"All right, let's forget about it," I said. "But don't you think we ought to do something about—about Madame Grazie?"

Miss Swisshome plaited her bony fingers. "Have you any suggestions, Mr. Graine?"

"Yes, I have. I think we might at least try to find out who—who—"

"Who assisted Madame in her departure from this world?" Julian finished for me.

"Exactly," I said, struggling to conceal my irritation at the smirk on his face.

"I don't know what we can do about it, Mr. Graine," he went on. "I don't think any of us were involved. You see, we were all dependent on her; we would hardly kill our golden goose, you understand?"

The smirk broadened.

"And," he added, "you were the last person to see her alive."

Now what do you think of that? I didn't get it for a moment. When I did, I saw red.

"If that means what I think it does," I said, advancing on him, "it'll give me more pleasure than I can say to push in that pretty puss of yours."

He retreated. "That would not disprove anything," he said truthfully. "We still know that Marina called you back when we left the room. You also were the first one of us to come down here. You will find us ready to swear, too, that you took a very long time at it."

At first I couldn't find words. Sandy nodded his head at me and moved his hands with a strange suggestiveness. I stared, then caught on.

"I'll join you in that little swearing-bout," I said. "But I won't swear that I was the last one to see Madame Grazie. She happened to be alive when I went upstairs. She was dead when I came down. Obviously someone had been in the room in the meantime. I know of at least two of you who were."

He eyed me calmly. "Prove it."

"In the first place, when I came in and found Madame dead, the window was wide open, the wind was pouring in—and there were two footprints of snow on the floor, one under the windowsill and another a little nearer the piano. That should prove something."

They all glanced toward the window. All except Porter. His smirk was rapidly becoming maddening.

"It proves that you should, perhaps, be writing fiction," he said. "The windows are closed and there are no footprints on the floor."

I felt like kicking myself. As soon as the words were out I remembered the efficient Mr. Tait and his activities. Even the damp spots on the floor were dry now. And I myself had closed the window and drawn the curtains.

But at least Tait would bear me out on the footprints. I put the question to him.

"Didn't see no prints," he said positively.

"But you did see snow? You did clean up some snow?"

The rheumy old eyes bleared. He shook his head. "I uz jest cleanin' up. Jest saw somethin'. Don't remember."

"But you told Paris you were cleaning up snow."

"Don't remember. Maybe 'twas. Maybe 'twasn't." I turned away in disgust. After all, I had the paper tracing of the print in my pocket. I started to pull it out, but didn't. The thought occurred to me that it would prove nothing to that bunch of dead-pans; they could say I had just drawn the thing out of my imagination. Sandy would back me up, of course. Then they would say, naturally, that we were sticking together. That line was hopeless.

So I turned to my second point. I hated to use it—but there was Marina's body before my eyes.

I pointed to it. "If you won't believe that, look on the floor beside Madame. You'll find a little bunch of knitted flowers. I think they'll prove that at least you, Miss Grazie, were here in the room with your aunt."

"You find them yourself. I shall believe you then."

In a fury I went over to the body, lifted Marina's arm.

There was no boutonniere. The yarn flowers were gone.

I looked up, bewildered.

"You don't mean these, do you, Mr. Graine?"

Elena was fingering the flowers. They were pinned to her dress, exactly where they had been earlier in the day. I stared, speechless.

"Well, are those the flowers you thought you saw?" Thorndyke demanded.

"Thought, hell!" I jumped up. "Those flowers were on the floor when. I left this room. I saw them, handled them myself. Who picked them up? Who gave them back to you, Miss Grazie?"

Her cheeks flushed a little but she looked me straight in the eye. "You must be mistaken, Mr. Graine. You can see they're pinned securely to my jacket. They've been here all the time."

This was too much. I whirled on Sandy. "You saw them there, Sandy. Tell them you did."

And then I did begin to believe I was losing my mind.

Sandy shrugged. "I thought we did. But I guess we were mistaken, weren't we, Tony?" And he frowned at me to keep still.

But I was beside myself. I shouted, "This is a conspiracy. You're all trying to make me look like a fool—"

"Trying!" Miss Swisshome sniffed.

"But you won't get away with it. After I've told my little tale to the police we'll see just what's what."

If nothing I had said heretofore had made any impression, that one word, police, created plenty. You could fairly feel them tightening up.

"Police?" Elena quavered. "But surely—surely—"

"Quiet, Elena," Thorndyke broke in. "Graine is just bluffing."

"Bluffing, my foot," I said. "You didn't think this was a little game of spin-the-bottle, did you? This is murder. Madame Grazie was a celebrity. When the newspapers get wind of this story we'll see how long you'll be able to keep up this cute little game of yours."

At that even Julian Porter paled. Miss Swisshome, fumbling at her knitting, said, "But there's no need for this to be in the papers. Couldn't we—couldn't we—"

"Not by a damn sight, we couldn't," I said. "You've all had a lot of fun pulling my leg. Now I'm going to have a little sport myself."

Elena looked up at Thorndyke. "Beale, is that right? Will the newspapers—the police have to know?"

The doctor's face clouded. "I'm afraid so. We aren't out of this by a long shot."

"Long shot is right," Paris put in. "Somebody's got that diamond and I want to know who it is."

For all his bravado, the man looked frightened. For the first time it occurred to me that perhaps Mr. James Paris might have reasons of his own for disliking the idea of policemen.

"So do I, Paris," I said. "Even though the others seem more interested in something else, I resent the implication that I might have the diamond or that I had anything to do with this. I suggest we have a general search of each other."

No one moved.

"Well, how about it?" I said. "I'd like to volunteer to be the first one searched. Shall we do it?"

Porter's eyes smouldered with dislike. "I can't think of anything more boring, Graine. Search yourself if you want to. I certainly don't intend to have this mob pawing me over."

I looked at the others. Their silence seemed to indicate that they agreed with him.

"But what are we going to do?" I demanded. "We surely don't intend just to sit here?"

"I'm quite comfortable," Ambrosia said acidly.

"But it's over an hour until the ferry arrives. Are you seriously proposing that we just sit here around Madame's body and wait?"

"It boils down to that," said Thorndyke. "Have a cigarette?"

I refused curtly. "I think—" I began.

"No one cares what you think, Graine," Porter interrupted. "You've caused enough trouble already. I for one am tired of hearing you sound off."

"Julian, there's no need to be rude," Elena said before I could make a comeback. "Mr. Graine is only doing what he thinks is right, aren't you, Mr. Graine."

"What I'm doing—" I began hotly.

Miss Swisshome pressed a bony hand to her forehead.

"Please, Mr. Graine! Won't you please relax?"

I gaped. "Relax?"

She waved a hand. "Yes, relax . . . sit down . . . retire . . . anything. Let us take thought."

I looked at Sandy, who winked at me.

And so I sat down.

For an hour we "took thought."

15

SOME TIME AGO I SAW PHOTOGRAPHS of an ascent of Nanda Devi. They were mildly interesting but on the whole, no more than amusing. You see, I went to meet the ferry at four-thirty.

As a matter of fact, we all went. Even Tait and his grotesque wife. Ambrosia bundled them up with as much cooing and care as though they were the Dionnes going for their first outing. "I wouldn't be able to swallow a mouthful for worrying about you poor dears," she said, tucking the old man's muffler securely around his neck.

The "swallowing a mouthful" referred to our polite little fiction that we were crossing over for a steak and a change of atmosphere in the inn at the ferry landing; we knew we should have to return when the police took charge. The truth was that I insisted on going over to call the police and the others were afraid to let me out of their sight.

It wasn't only I, for Julian offered to remain and keep a sort of death-watch over Marina while we were gone. The idea was voted down *viva voce*. So much so, in fact, that I understood that what I suspected was true: until the contents of Marina's jewel-case turned up, we would have as much individual freedom as a member of a Georgia chain-gang.

I knew it was the jewel-case that was behind all this, because it was the only way of explaining their sudden devotion to each other. It was the only way, too, to explain the furtive suspicion that blanketed us like a pall. I didn't understand what it was all about but as it turned out, my intuition was correct.

And so at four-ten we started out.

I was the last to leave the room. The drapes were drawn tightly across the window. The fire was burning low; mahogany shadows flickered over the Indian robe under which Marina lay. It was a strange way for the great Grazie to lie in state.

Tait locked the door behind us. Ambrosia tried the knob, clicked her teeth with satisfaction, held out her hand to the old man.

"The key, please," she said peremptorily.

Tait hesitated, then resolutely shoved it deep into his trouser pocket. "Always kept it," he grunted. "Always will."

"And quite right, too," Dr. Thorndyke spoke up. "I fail to see, Ambrosia, why you should have charge of it."

The spinster looked flustered. "I merely wished to be certain that nothing intrudes upon poor dear Marina's last repose."

I'll admit that that sounds like something out of Jane Austen but I also insist that it didn't quite deserve the juicy Bronx cheer that came from Paris. Ambrosia's face darkened thunderously, but she only tossed her head and marched ahead of us down the hall.

I found myself walking beside Elena. I hadn't realized she was so small; her blonde head came only to my shoulder. We took a few steps in silence, then she said:

"It seems so strange that she is gone. I feel a little queer about leaving her like that."

I tried to be reassuring. "What could happen?"

"I know," she said wistfully. "But it just doesn't seem right."

"Many things aren't."

"You mean—death?"

"In a way. As it happens, I meant murder."

I suppose I shouldn't have said that. It hurt her. And yet I didn't care. The indifference of this gang—yes, and that included Elena—was getting under my skin.

"Do you enjoy being cruel, Mr. Graine?" she asked quietly.

"Not particularly. Certainly no more than I enjoy seeing a defenseless woman done to death."

She busied herself with the fastenings of her gloves as she said, "You think us all very callous, I suppose."

"I hadn't realized that anyone was interested in what I think."

She laid a small hand on my arm. "We have been dreadfully rude, and I'm sorry. As for the other, perhaps sometime you'll understand that we aren't quite as heartless as we seem. You should remember that you knew Aunt Marina only casually. We who have lived with her know that she was—"

She broke off with a suddenness that startled me. I had felt, listening to her, that for the first time I was to learn something definite. No more words came.

"You were saying?" I prompted, trying not to appear too eager.

The hand was withdrawn. "I was about to be indiscreet. Forgive me for changing my mind."

I wondered if they would ever get over their habit of leaving sentences and ideas half completed, dangling in midair. It seemed to me they never finished anything; if they didn't catch themselves, someone else shut them off. I was getting a little fed up with it.

But I could say nothing more. We had joined the others at the end of the hall by that time. And someone opened the door.

There were, I can only suppose, two reasons why we hadn't noticed what was going on outside. One was that our own private affairs had been dramatic enough to hold the attention of a blind deaf-mute. The other was that old Lucifer Bollman must have built the strength of the Pyramids into his old rookery.

For all hell had broken loose. Combine all of Joseph Conrad's hurricanes and typhoons into one gigantic, whipping cataclysm and you have a vague idea of what assailed us. The snow and sleet did not fall; it peppered along horizontally like a barrage of darts from a mammoth blow-gun. Ambrosia's hat sailed off her head and went kiting into the river, lost forever. Tait's muffler unwound and the end went flying into his wife's one good eye. The scream she let out was a banshee wail, choked off by the wind almost before it could be heard.

I don't know yet why we plunged out into that boiling maelstrom. But we did. Gasping, gulping, bent double against the fury of the gale, we struggled towards the garage.

And we reached it. That is why I say you can talk all you wish about ascents of Nanda Devi! I'm content to rest on my laurels for having crossed that forty feet of level space. Make no mistake about it; it was a feat, especially when all the while you could see that sucking, inky river at the foot of the cliff, lashing and foaming with eagerness for anything blown in its direction.

But we reached the garage, almost crawling, our clothes half torn off, our eyes blinded, the exposed portions of our anatomies numb and frozen. (I discovered later that there had been a worse storm on the Columbia River in 1867. God help the pioneers!)

And so, exhausted and battered, we straggled into the garage—only to discover a final outrage.

The cement floor of the place was a lake. I was puzzled, at first glimpse, as to why it was not frozen stiff. My nose gave me the answer. It wasn't frozen because it wasn't water. It was gasoline. A nail had been driven into the gas tanks of Marina's bus and my car. Now and then a discouraged drop of fuel fell from the neat little holes. It was a very thorough job. If we were going to get to the ferry, it would be only under our own power.

Elena began to cry and said she wished she were dead. Miss Swisshome looked grim and began fumbling for smelling salts. The others were either too cold or too paralyzed to say or do anything.

Sandy came over to me. I was still irritated with him for deserting me over the matter of the boutonniere. So when he suggested that the women could never navigate the steep road to the ferry-slip, that they go back to the house and that he would be willing to go over alone and get the police, I didn't bother to tell him of my discovery that, sink or swim, our little band would stick together.

I simply said, "It's o.k. by me. Go ahead and tell them," and stood back to watch the fun.

And so he did.

And so we all started for the ferry on foot.

When we reached the road, Thorndyke and Porter took Elena between them; Tait and Paris helped Mrs. Tait; and despite her protests, Sandy and I grasped Miss Swisshome firmly by her elbows and propelled her along.

We had just begun the descent of the nearly perpendicular road when Thorndyke pointed out across the river. The snow stung my face like needles but by releasing my hold on Miss Swisshome's arm and peering through my fingers I managed to catch a glimpse of the *Minerva*. She was well out from shore by that time. I remembered the old boatman's remark about not waiting longer than five minutes "fer man er beast," and quickened my pace. We would have to make ungodly speed to come within the deadline.

Halfway down the slope I happened to glance out again. The yell I gave was potent enough to be heard above the wailing of the storm. The others stopped in their tracks and stared out to where I was pointing.

The *Minerva* was standing on end, whirling round and round. In that split second, she wallowed up on the crest of a wave and smashed into one of those rocks which, I discovered later, gave the Oregon town of The Dalles its French name. The old craft seemed to fold itself around the rock in an ardent embrace. Then, as though a bomb had exploded in its vitals, it flew to pieces. Fragments of board and planking shot high above the water, seemed to hang static for an instant, then sped along like arrows on the breast of the wind.

And then there was nothing to be seen.

They found the body of the old boatman two weeks afterwards, rammed into a five-inch crack in the rocks below the water line.

As I say, we stood and stared. Numbly I saw three men rush out of the inn beside the ferry-landing, drag out a row-boat that looked like a pea-pod, and strike out for the scene of the disaster. I suppose they actually thought they could make it. Perhaps they were surprised when, before they had taken a dozen strokes, the oars were snapped out of their hands; perhaps they were surprised when their boat, like the *Minerva*, whirled dizzily, turned up on end, and capsized. I wasn't. Nothing could have weathered that storm.

We saw it all as in a dream. I suppose we were so numb with cold and shock that we weren't rationalizing. Like automatons, we watched it, absorbed it, and then turned around and trudged back to Lucifer's Pride. Without a word of consultation, I mean. It was simply the natural, the only thing to do.

I honestly believe that nothing more could have penetrated to our consciousness; we were immune to shock. I know it barely registered when Tait unlocked the library door and I saw that Marina's body was no longer covered with the Indian robe. I noticed it, and that was all.

And yet the last thing I had seen before I left the room, had been the reflections from the fire playing over the robe, which then was covering the huddle that had once been Marina Grazie.

But as I say, the change did not startle me. The only thing that made any impression on me was hearing Elena cry, "I wish I'd never come to this horrible place. I'm afraid, Beale . . . I'm afraid . . ."

16

"IN THE FIRST PLACE," SANDY CROAKED, "this is a job for the police. In the second place, you couldn't crack these dead-pans if you were Charlie Chan himself. In the third place, it isn't any of your business in the first place."

"Nuts!"

"As far as I know," he said severely, "nuts has never been recognized as logical rebuttal of one argument, much less three of them."

A gust of wind roared down the chimney, splattering us both with sparks and smoke. Despite the barrage I edged closer to the fire.

"If it's rebuttal you want I can do it in three easy lessons," I said. "In the first place, the police can't possibly get here before morning—if then. Secondly, as for cracking these dead-pans as you so elegantly put it, I happen to think I can. Anyway, the only way to find out is to try. In the third place, anything's my business that I choose to make my business."

I lighted my pipe, and went on, "I suppose you've forgotten that our little piano-playing hothouse flower practically accused me of doing a knit-one-purl-two with poor Marina."

The argument was being staged in our bedroom on the second floor. Yes, I said bedroom. Lucifer's Pride had risen to still another occasion.

At our cozy little luncheon at the hotel Marina had told me that old Lucifer Bollman had left his love-nest uncompleted. I naturally expected to find a gaunt, naked shell with perhaps one room chinked up and hastily furnished with a buffalo rug to keep the dirt from between our toes. But only the third floor was unfinished. On the second floor there were eight bedrooms, all with fireplaces in working order, all with beds—huge, canopied monstrosities— and chairs of a sort. Stored in the unplastered third-floor rooms were packing cases of blankets, sheets, etc. Enough for a small army. Tait had known about it all the time, but the blasted old curmudgeon had let us stew in our juices for half an hour before he had seen fit to give out.

Spirits rose instantly. It dawned on us that at least we wouldn't have to choose between huddling together in the cramped kitchen or sitting rigid around Marina's corpse in the library.

The stairway, as I have indicated, pierced the center of the building. The bedrooms opened directly off the hall, four on each side of the rotunda. They were all alike: dank and clammy, cold as zero, and smelling like old trunks in an attic. But you know how human beings are: we had to poke our noses into every one and argue about who should occupy which.

It was finally decided that Elena, Ambrosia Swisshome, Dr. Thorndyke and Julian Porter would occupy the four rooms in the east end; Sandy and I, the Taits, and Paris found quarters in the west end, leaving one vacant room in the corner. Immediately adjoining the wall of the staircase were two bathrooms—without water— and two rooms evidently intended as storerooms for luggage.

But to make the whole thing clear I'll give you a rough sketch of the lay-out as it was finally settled:

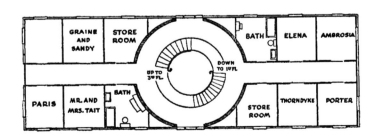

It was, as you can see, all very shipshape: the two women side by side for protection; the jealous swains, Porter and Thorndyke, side by side for mutual observation; the Taits together as befits the holy state of wedlock; Paris by himself because, as Ambrosia had pointed out, he was not exactly a member of the party; and Sandy and I together chiefly because I wanted to talk.

There had been plenty to do, though, before we could get around to words. A raid on the third floor netted a crate of candles; we stuck them on small boards and distributed them around the first and second floors. Another sortie to the source of supplies, a forty-five minute assault on the inexhaustible array of packing cases, another bucket-brigade of wood-carriers—and each bedroom had enough fuel to warm and dry it out. We went from room to room and spread blankets and sheets over bedposts and chairs to air until the effect was that of a Chinese laundry overtaken by Hallowe'en.

Little was said. We went about in silence, oppressed by the never-ceasing gale that howled and catcalled down the chimneys as we laid the fires and coaxed them into burning. I don't know about the others, but I myself was not exactly cheered by the thought of Marina lying downstairs under the Indian robe (which I had unobtrusively replaced) and the memory of the old boatman as the *Minerva* whipped over and burst into fragments.

Either of those recollections would have been enough to tie one's tongue in knots. But there was more. For one of us, going quietly and intently about his business—one of us was a murderer. It was not a comfortable feeling.

When Ambrosia reminded us of the fact that we never had gotten around to the matter of food, I persuaded Beale Thorndyke to relinquish a scalpel from his bag and sent Tait and his wife downstairs to open the cans in Marina's lunchbasket. The old man grumbled about how in tarnation he was expected to pry open tin cans with a knife. Mrs. Tait indicated that she couldn't feel "gasslier" if she were catering in a morgue. But they were finally persuaded. They would bang a pan or something when the food was ready.

Finally the home-making process was, in a manner of speaking, done, and Sandy and I were alone in our room. We had hauled

Murder Ends the Song

the huge bed up to the hearth. Sandy was sprawled on it, cocking dubious ears. I was sitting by the fire on something by a footstool out of an ottoman.

"But, good God, you're not paying any attention to what Pantywaist said are you?" he said in response to my comment on Porter's accusation. "He was just shooting off his face. No one took him seriously."

"Maybe not then," I conceded. "But after they've had time to think things over, I wouldn't be too sure. Pinning the thing on me would make a swell out for all of them. If they ganged up, concocted some story they could all stick to, and maintained a united front when the police take over, they could make things hot and heavy. It would be their quintet against my solo."

He nodded solemnly. "Like the boutonniere."

"Like the boutonniere," I said, wrath rising. "And why the hell did you desert the ship then? You saw that damned yarn as plainly as I did."

"Why didn't you show them the drawing of the footprint when they called you a liar?" he countered. "We couldn't have proved anything. If I'd backed you up they'd only have called us both liars."

I saw the point, and seeing, couldn't blame him.

"Which brings us back to the main issue. If they get together and decide to make me the goat, it'll be the devil's own job to break 'em down. After all, they can show I had plenty of opportunity."

"Yeah," he jeered, "but how about motive? Could they say Marina had been singing *Caro Nome* until you got sick of it and finished her off to give your ears a rest?"

"Nothing that funny, McGee. But they'll dig one up. Swisshome is capable of anything. And offhand I'd say our friend Panty-waist could do a pretty fair job of mud-slinging if he set his little mind to it. And that's why I intend to get to work."

I tossed another stick on the fire. Sandy heaved himself over on his other side and regarded the fire for a while. The room was warming up nicely. Nothing lavish, you understand; but at least you could no longer chin yourself on your congealed breath. As I sat there relaxing I decided to try out on Sandy an idea that had occurred to me a few minutes earlier.

"Sandy?"

He grunted.

"Has it ever occurred to you that we might not be alone here?"

"There isn't one of this gang I'd want to be alone with," he said, adding dreamily, "Except the little Grazie. I could do with her."

"Control your ruttish instincts," I said. "I didn't mean that. I meant, what about some stranger, some uninvited guest having joined us on the sly?"

He flopped over again, eyes bulging. "Have you gone nuts? Who? Where? How?"

"Remember your epilepsy," I said mildly. "It's just that several things around here look suspiciously like an outside job."

"Such as?"

I told him about the sandwiches and Julian Porter's excursion. "I know I put them there," I concluded; "just as I know we didn't eat a crumb of them."

He snorted. "That's easy. Of course, Panty-waist ate them himself and pulled that story to justify it."

That was, I thought, a simple way of getting around the point. But somehow, remembering Porter's face on his return, I was inclined to think he had been telling the truth.

"Then Porter also punctured the gas tanks?" I said.

"Who else? He was the only one out there. According to your story he was gone long enough to have inched the whole damn garage into the gorge."

"But why did he do it?"

"Don't ask me." He gestured. "I was only trying to show you that he could have done it."

"And the footprints inside the window?"

"Naturally. You can check up on that easily enough. Make him let you see his shoes."

I played my trump card, to coin a phrase. "And I suppose he pulled the blanket off Marina, too?"

He groaned. "So it really did happen? I noticed it when we got back but I thought I must be mistaken. You're sure you spread it over her?"

"Of course, I'm sure. And so are you. You saw me do it."

"Yeah." He sighed. "But I was beginning to wonder if I ought to trust my eyesight any more."

"I spread that blanket over her," I said doggedly, "and someone pulled it off. We were all together on the way down the hill, so it couldn't have been any of us. And don't forget your friend Porter was with Thorndyke and Elena Grazie all the time. He wasn't out of sight for a minute. The other things might have been done by him, but not this."

"So what?"

"So any one of three things." I ticked my fingers. "One: we're haunted and a ghost did it. Two: We weren't all together on that trip and one of us did it. And three: Someone we don't know about is here at Lucifer's Pride and—"

He propped himself up in his excitement. "The murderer?"

From downstairs came a sound like a junk-wagon being overturned. It was, I presumed, Tait's idea of beating on a pan. I got up.

"I don't know," I said. "But I'm going to start the ball rolling to find out."

17

I DIDN'T BRING UP THE SUBJECT for an hour or so. No one would have paid the slightest attention to me if I had; we were all much too occupied with food. Marina had brought two large hampers of cans and bottles. Since there were no dishes of any kind in the place, the Taits had simply set the array of containers on the kitchen table. Each one dived into whatever suited his fancy at the moment—or was not being monopolized by someone else. There was no rime or reason to it: I began with cheese straws and guava jelly and wound up with a hunk of canned baked ham in one hand and a gooseberry tart in the other.

It was not until the two thermos-bottle caps of coffee were being handed around the circle that I fired the first shot. I turned to Elena who was sitting between Thorndyke and Porter.

"Miss Grazie, when we returned to the library after starting to the ferry you said something about being afraid. Is that right?"

The room became miraculously hushed. The howling of the storm seemed to sweep in on us and the coziness we had managed to create over the food vanished.

Elena's delicate face went pale. "Why—why, yes, I believe I did," she faltered. "Why?"

"Would you mind telling me why you felt afraid? Was it something specific or just the atmosphere in general?"

Thorndyke's arm moved slightly and I knew that under the table his hand had closed warningly over the girl's. Porter scowled. No one else moved.

At last the girl shook her golden head. "It was nothing in particular. This horrible old place . . . that poor old boatman . . . Auntie lying there . . . everything . . ." She shivered. "I don't know. I just didn't like it. I still don't."

"You're sure that's all? You're sure you don't know something about your Aunt's death? Something that might—"

"That's enough, Graine," Thorndyke cut in. His handsome face registered cloudy-with-storms-ahead. "Madame Grazie is dead. It's too bad, but it's happened. Let's just leave it at that."

Sandy winked at me. It was the old stone wall again. I was getting no place fast.

I said, "This afternoon I might have been inclined to. But the suggestion's been made that I had something to do with it. I didn't like that. Not one bit."

"And so you're going to try prodding a stick in the ant-hill, Mr. Graine." Ambrosia Swisshome dunked a garlic olive in mayonnaise and nibbled. Like a horse with a lump of sugar. Except that her teeth were shorter.

"Put it that way if you like," I said. "The fact remains that Porter as much as accused me of killing Madame."

"Well, did you not?" Porter's olive-skinned face was bland.

There it was for the second time. But I knew better than to lose my temper. My only chance for success, I felt, lay in making them lose theirs.

I tried to be equally bland. "You could have done it, Porter. You were gone long enough after those sandwiches. The window was open and I still say I found footprints on the floor. I suggest that you came in through the window, quarreled with Madame for some reason, and then killed her, leaving through the window when the job was done. I'm also inclined to think you drove those nails into the gas-tanks. After all, you're the only one we're positive was in the garage. Now how about it?"

His face had gone livid. His long, spatulate musician's fingers gripped the edge of the table.

"You're a filthy liar." If it is possible to hiss that sentence he did it. "I went straight to the garage and looked where you told me. When I could not find anything I came straight back. Anyone who says I did not is lying."

Ambrosia clunked another olive-pit into a tin can. "Be quiet, Julian," she said, completely unruffled. "Can't you see Mr. Graine is merely trying to egg you on to say something you'll regret?"

"But he accuses me of murder!" Porter was close to tears.

"Bosh! I don't believe he thinks you committed murder any more than I did."

"Fair enough, Miss Swisshome." I turned on her. "We'll consider you now. Let's say you carried a load of wood down, thinking all the while of Marina's high-handed treatment of us. You were cold and furious. When you left the wood in the hall, you yielded to an impulse and went into the library. There was a scene. You became more and more angry until, beside yourself with rage, you picked up the nearest thing at hand—a needle from your knitting, remember—and killed her. Then you waited until you heard a load of wood dumped in the hall and the footsteps going back up the stairs. Whereupon you calmly opened the door and walked up yourself. No one was checking up on the order of carrying the wood. It was all perfectly safe."

The spinster smiled slightly, but her hands shook a little. "Fantasy, Mr. Graine. Pure Gothic romancing. As it happens, I had no occasion to quarrel with Marina. I was devoted to her."

I made a jeeringly triumphant noise. I had her there.

"No? How about yesterday afternoon at the hotel? It seems to me she slapped you rather hard after you threatened to—what was it you said?—'remember a few things.' And I seem to recall something about wishing you could strangle her. I think your exit line was a neat little bit about God-damning her and her performance. Strange devotion, don't you think, Miss Swisshome?"

The horsey jaw dropped. Her leathery face was grey. "You heard that?" she gasped. "Oh, my God!" Then she pulled herself together and the glint returned to her eyes. "Well, what of it?" she demanded.

"Nothing," I observed mildly. "Except that I suspect the police will be interested in your somewhat violent devotion."

Murder Ends the Song

Miss Swisshome stared, swallowed, and lapsed into stricken silence.

Mrs. Tait set up a clamor. She said she'd never heard anything like it in her life and that she for one didn't approve of pulling skeletons out of family closets. Tait said he didn't know what in tarnation it was all about but that he felt an attack of indigestion coming on. "Stummick ache," he called it. Mrs. Tait rushed to get him a glass of hot water from the kettle boiling on the stove.

"You keep out of this, you two," I warned them. "If I wanted to, I could include you."

"Us?" Mrs. Tait almost dropped the glass. "Tait an' me, we didn't do nothin'."

"Nothing but call down the wrath of Heaven on Madame Grazie," I reminded her. "You yourselves told me she beat you, Tait, with your own walking-stick and called you—unpleasant names, Mrs. Tait. You might have done the thing yourself out of revenge."

That shut them up for the time being. Mrs. Tait retired, weeping, to a corner. Tait went to console her, glaring at me and muttering through his plates.

Sandy rose to their defense. "Don't be hard on them, Tony. They were out here with me all the time."

"Shut up," I said. I had the center of the stage and I was enjoying it no end. Once in Paris Greta Kornulm, the Wagnerian soprano, told me about a performance of *Götterdämmerung* in which the Waltraute collapsed and Greta, as Brünnhilde, had the intoxicating experience of singing the whole Waltraute scene, both parts, by herself. "I was *Gott*," she described it to me with simple dignity.

Well, I was "*Gott*" here and I meant to have no interference.

"If this crew pins Madame's murder on me," I went on to Sandy, "you'll probably be rung in as my accomplice. However if it's bothering you any, I'll admit I think the Taits are out. After all, if they did it you'd know about it. And vice-versa."

Beale Thorndyke cleared his throat. "You're not overlooking me, I presume?"

"Quite right, Dr. Livingstone," I slammed back at him. "The mechanics in your case would be the same as in Miss Swisshome's.

Of course, instead of a knitting needle you might have used one of your scalpels. Why didn't you?"

Julian Porter had been sullenly spreading pate on crackers with a scalpel. He let it fall with a clatter.

The doctor gave me a bedside-manner smile. "My bag was out in the hall. I couldn't reach it in my hurry. Anything else?"

"You're damned right." His sarcasm stung a little. "It's rather odd, I've thought, that Madame Grazie's neck should have been pierced at precisely the one point that was certain to bring about death . . . the juncture of the occiput and the first cervical vertebra, isn't it?" (That was just about all the anatomy I remembered from college and did I make it count!)

He lighted a cigarette, his eyes never leaving my face. "Quite correct," he snapped, adding, "The fact is not widely known among laymen, Mr. Graine." There was innuendo in the crack.

I could afford to ignore it, however, now that I had gotten under his skin. "I'm a pretty unusual layman, Thorndyke. It's one of my boasts. You do admit, though, that any reputable medico knows it?"

I merely tossed that off for what it was worth. The reaction to it bowled me over. Thorndyke went white to the lips. Fists clenched, he half rose, his eyes shooting sparks.

"What do you mean by that insinuation?" he demanded. "For two cents I'd bash in your offensive face, Graine. We've stood just—"

"Beale! Please!" That was Elena's voice, strained and tense. Julian Porter's too handsome face was twisted in a vague sneer. Miss Swisshome emerged from her trance long enough to roar "Quiet, doctor." Mrs. Tait's wailing rose to high-C. The table was in an uproar. A raucous horse-laugh rang out over the tumult.

Then it was over. Thorndyke subsided into his chair, mopped his face with his handkerchief. Elena clasped her trembling hands before her and closed her eyes. I turned to Paris, who had uttered the laugh. He sobered instantly.

"You're in it too, my fine revolvered friend," I said. "The motive's obvious, too. You tried to take the diamond away from Madame Grazie. When she resisted, you killed her. Let's hear you laugh that off."

His eyes darted around the room. He wet his thick lips. "But I ain't got the diamond. One of you's got it. I was tryin' to get it away from you. You know that."

"Pure bluff. You could have staged that scene to throw us off the scent. The police won't overlook that possibility."

"Police!" His voice shot upwards, broke. His eyes looked haunted now. "But I didn't do it. Honest to God, Mr. Graine, I didn't do it. I didn't even know she'd checked out till you told us upstairs. An' that's more than the others can say. Honest to God, Mr. Graine, I'm tellin' the truth."

His voice had the ring of sincerity, but I refused to be convinced that easily. "I still say you may be a good actor, Paris."

"I ain't actin'," he protested wildly. "I swear I'm tellin' the truth, Mr. Graine. It's just a frame-up. You're tryin' to frame me."

"Which, if I'm not mistaken, was what you all were trying to do to me," I reminded the room at large. "I'll come back to you later, Paris. All I say now is that you didn't look any too much like a guardian of law and order when you had us lined up in the other room."

That shut him up. He sat there, moving his lips from time to time. I had no doubt he was still swearing, honest to God, that he was innocent.

I turned to Elena. Realizing what was coming, she shrank back in her chair with a little gasp. Porter and Thorndyke both bristled, leaned toward her reassuringly. It should have been a touching little picture, but it didn't touch me.

"We're back where we started, Miss Grazie," I said. "Don't be frightened. I merely don't want to hurt your feelings by leaving you out of the party."

Her voice was pleading. "I can't bear any more, Mr. Graine. This is torture . . . inquisition . . ."

"Maybe," I said, unimpressed. "But I just want to make it clear that I know you were in the library at least once with your Aunt because I did see that boutonniere of yours on the floor by her body. I remember, too, something you said to me upstairs. Your words were, 'Sometimes I could cheerfully commit murder.' Oh, yes, I have a good memory. It comes from learning my roles. Anything to say?"

She looked down at her hands. "Nothing," she choked.

"You're probably wise. Never talk without a lawyer. That's customary procedure in murder cases, I believe."

"Murder? You're not accusing me of murdering—" She broke off.

I said cheerfully, "The police might. You know how rude they are. They might insinuate that you didn't just talk to your Aunt in the hall, as you told me. I imagine they might even say you went into the room and killed her. After all, I'd have to tell them how upset you seemed when you were talking to me in the storeroom."

The violet eyes, which had been regarding me with horror, filled with tears. Thorndyke and Porter glared at me but did nothing about Elena, being helpless as men always are when confronted by women's weeping. Miss Swisshome got up quickly and put a consoling arm around the girl's shoulders.

"You, Mr. Graine," she said bluntly, "are a brute."

"Because I point out a few facts?"

"Because you distort facts," she corrected me. "You know very well Elena did not kill Marina."

It was my turn to correct. "I know nothing of the kind. She could have done it as well as any of the rest of you. It didn't require a great deal of strength to drive that needle in."

I selected a stalk of celery and chewed on it thoughtfully.

"However," I went on, between munches, "I've just been indicating some of the things the police might be interested in. I wanted you to see that we're all in this thing up to our necks."

Thorndyke picked up a scalpel, stabbed it down into the table. It stuck upright. The room was silent except for the sound of Elena's gentle sobbing. I watched the yarn flowers move on her breast. The silence wore on.

Finally I said, "Well, do you want to co-operate?"

"Co-operate?" Miss Swisshome snapped. "Why should we?"

I was ready for that one. "Because for one reason or another you've all made it perfectly plain by your behavior that you're afraid of the police." I glanced around. They were all staring. "Now wouldn't it help matters if when the police arrive we could simply turn the murderer over to them. The rest could save themselves some embarrassment, I fancy."

Porter did not look at me. "We have nothing to hide. We will not talk."

Then I sprang the surprise.

"Not even," I asked, "if I can show that someone else is here at Lucifer's Pride? Someone who doesn't belong to our party?"

18

TEN MINUTES LATER, swaddled in every spare bit of clothing we could lay our hands on, Julian Porter, Dr. Thorndyke, and I set out for the garage to try to prove my point.

During my silent period at dinner, before I began what Elena chose to call my Inquisition, I had remembered a bus trip I once made from Washington, D. C. to Mount Vernon, less to see the shrine than to sample the highly touted fried chicken at the Mount Vernon Inn. And remembering, I thought I knew how a stranger might have gotten to Lucifer's Pride.

It had to be the way. Tait, backed up by his cataractical frau, closed all the other avenues. "Couldn't no one be here afore we come," he insisted in answer to my question. "Front door uz locked an' anyways no fires. Man'd a-froze stiffer'n a board."

"He couldn't have come over on the ferry with you and Mrs. Tait?"

They shook their heads vehemently. "We'd a seen im. Nobody else uz on that boat."

"Couldn't he have been hiding in your car or anything?"

He cackled. "Haven't got no car. Maggie an' me, we walked. Feet uz invented afore engines. What uz good enough fer my grampaw uz good enough fer me, I alluz say."

"The ferry-boatman hadn't brought anyone over before you?"

"Could-a but didn't. Happens he said he hadn't made no crossin' fer more'n a month."

All of which left only the possibility I had thought of.

The idea had been greeted with an enthusiasm just short of cheers. Their eagerness to grasp at an exit for themselves was almost pathetic. Tension relaxed. Elena dried her tears. Mrs. Tait unveiled her monumental head and came back to the table. Even Miss Swisshome unbent so far as to pat my arm with bony fingers and say, "So you were just having a little game with us, Anthony."

I've always disliked coyness in women. Lola Pratt in *Seventeen* is the only arch female I've ever come across who was bearable. And she was funny. Miss Swisshome was not. Besides, it didn't ring true.

"Perhaps, Miss Swisshome," I began a little coldly.

"You are to call me Ambrosia," she interrupted. "We have had enough formality, don't you think?"

Porter broke into the one-sided love-fest, thereby earning my grudging gratitude. Of all of them he had seemed least impressed by my brainstorm.

"What makes you think anyone else is here?" he glowered. "Any one of us might have done everything you have said."

"Everything—but one." I reminded him—and them—of the disturbed blanket. "We were all together from the time I spread it over Madame. And besides—" I broke off.

Everyone looked at me. Thorndyke asked eagerly, "You have some proof?"

"What *I* call proof," I said. "You might not, though, since you ask me not to believe my eyes."

"Oh, go on and show it to 'em, Tony," Sandy put in. "They're going to be good boys and girls now, aren't you, children?"

Ambrosia sniffed.

Elena said, "If you have anything, Mr. Graine, please tell us. We have been stupid, a little unfair to you, perhaps, but it is different now."

Somewhat mollified, I brought out the drawing of the footprint and passed it around.

"That," I said, "is what I saw inside the library window after Marina's death. Sandy will bear me out. He saw it, too."

"I did," he asserted. "And I watched Tony make that drawing."

They studied it intently. Not one of them showed any sign of confusion or recognition. Finally Ambrosia looked up. "I think you must admit, Mr. Graine, that neither Elena nor I could have left this. Only a Bulgarian peasant-woman could have worn shoes large enough to have made it."

I agreed. After all, only Tait's brogans were broad and heavy enough anywhere near to match the print. He seemed to read the speculation in my eyes for he promptly thrust out his feet. There was not a sign of a star on his solid leather heels. Prompted by his example, the others did likewise. Result: nil.

And so Porter, Thorndyke, and I went out into that hellish night.

It was shortly after nine and black as a coal pit. If anything, the wind had increased in ferocity, whipping down the gorge with the force of a horizontal piledriver. The sleet cut into my face, burning like acid. We had to link arms, bend forward and batter our way. Beyond the palisade the river roiled and roared like an ocean gone berserk. I thought of the *Minerva*, shattered on the rocks, and of the old boatman swirling in that inky welter. And I shivered.

The garage was as we had left it at four twenty-five. It still smelled to high heaven of gasoline. In the beam from Tait's flashlight which I had borrowed, the blue and grey bus with my roadster beside it looked like a wretched, forlorn animal stranded in the dark with its equally miserable offspring.

"We'll look for the sandwiches first." I had to yell to make myself heard above the howls of the wind.

We searched every inch of the roadster, even pulling out the accumulation of junk from the dashboard catch-all. There was nothing. Not even a crumb.

Julian's lips moved, and I knew he was saying, "I told you so." As far as I was concerned, though, the fact that the sandwiches were not there proved nothing. He could still have eaten them.

I turned to the bus, scarcely able to contain my excitement. Would my brainstorm prove correct? Teeth chattering, Thorndyke and Porter rallied round, watching me skeptically.

It was an ordinary small passenger bus of the Whippet Line. You've seen thousands of them: blue and cream-colored two-storied monstrosities, roaring along the highways with a vibration that can be felt half a mile away. Riding in one of them on that trip from Washington, we had passed a freight train barnacled with hoboes and tramps. The sight of them had set me to wondering if there were any way of hitching a ride on one of these contraptions. Then I had remembered watching the luggage being loaded at the bus station and noting the huge luggage compartment under the raised floor of the bus. A man could easily have secreted himself far back in a dark corner. It would have been a difficult feat to accomplish on a regular commercial trip. But in a privately chartered bus? With no luggage?

While my two cohorts goggled, I opened the door to the compartment and turned the flashlight into the interior.

I still think I may be forgiven the triumphant glance I gave Thorndyke and Porter, the smugness with which I motioned them up to look inside.

For there on the floor was the waxed pasteboard box in which the sandwiches had been packed. Scattered about were half a dozen wads of waxed paper. There had been six sandwiches. Also there were four mashed cigarette butts, the cellophane wrapper from a package of cigarettes, and seven burned matches.

Thorndyke shook his head in puzzled amazement. Julian Porter brightened. "Bravo, Mr. Graine," he shouted. "You cannot believe that I did it now."

I wondered, but said nothing then.

19

I WISH SOMEONE WOULD TELL ME what good taste is. The average person simply takes it for granted until Slap! the need for explanation hits him in the face. Of course, when pressed for reasons why a given action is in poor taste, he can always say, "Because one doesn't do that sort of thing." But that is, at best, a lame and snobbish reasoning.

More than that, it doesn't, of necessity, hold. There come times when one *does* do it. For whatever reason, justifiable or otherwise, one *does* do it.

All of which is by way of excusing or justifying or rationalizing the situation Porter, Thorndyke, and I found on our return to Lucifer's Pride. When we stamped in, half blinded by wind and sleet, and numb with cold we found the group gathered in the library. The fire was roaring in the fireplace, casting a warm crimson and gold glow over the room. The piano gleamed richly; the wistaria-splashed carpet was lush under foot; candle-flames pricked the corner gloom. After that agonizing trek to the garage and back it was like heaven.

Except for a few details.

Marina's body had been removed from the floor. It lay on a chesterfield in a far corner, the Indian robe tucked around it like a shroud. A branched candlestick flared seven flames at her head. One single fat taper sputtered at her feet. And at the piano Sandy was beating out *Shall We Gather At The River*. Grouped around him, the rest of them bellowed (Paris), carolled (Elena), twittered

(Ambrosia), wheezed (Sandy), or chanted lustily in true camp-meeting style (the Taits). It sounded like bedlam.

Dumbfounded, we three newcomers could only stand staring while the song rolled on and on to its conclusion. Then Sandy swung himself around on the bench. "Think it would have pleased the old girl?" he grinned.

I can attempt to excuse them now. I couldn't then. My reactions were purely conventional. "What the hell's going on here?" I spluttered. "It's—it's outrageous."

Mrs. Tait squared her thin shoulders. If she'd had a rubber plant in her hands she'd have looked exactly like the woman in Grant Wood's "American Gothic."

"We're only holdin' a kinda prayermeetin'." She nodded toward the improvised catafalque: "She was an ornery woman. But she's dead. Seems like it's our Christian duty."

Sandy cheered. "There you are, Tony. It's our Christian duty."

"Christian duty, hell!" I exploded. "I'm surprised at all of you."

"You should be in a pulpit, Anthony," Ambrosia retorted. "Do you expect us to sit around here from now on with our hands folded in an attitude of prayer? Frankly, I am bored. I thought Mr. Sands' suggestion an admirable one. At least, it relieved the monotony."

So Sandy had been responsible for that outburst. I might have known. His Puckish sense of humor had a way of popping out at the most amazingly inappropriate times.

I said, "But it seems to me . . . with Madame Grazie's body lying here in the room . . ."

She snorted. "You are less observant than I thought, Anthony. It should have penetrated even your consciousness by this time that there isn't one of us in this room who regrets Marina's death."

She paused, sweeping the group with her cold eyes, challenging contradiction. There was none.

She went on: "We may deplore the violence of her passing, but I for one refuse to play the part of a hypocrite. I don't care who hears me. I'm glad Marina is dead. If the rest of you were equally frank you'd say the same thing."

Mrs. Tait drew in a shocked breath. It was the only sound.

Then Thorndyke sighed. *"De mortuis nil nisi bonum,"* he remarked to no one in particular.

Ambrosia shot out a forefinger at him. "That's what I mean," she cried in ringing tones. "Platitudes! Cant! We all know Marina was a grasping, egotistical, demanding slave-driver. Just because she is dead now doesn't alter the fact. And you should be the last one to preach to me, Beale Thorndyke. You don't have to marry her now."

I gaped. Of all the surprises that had been shoved at me lately, that one took the cake. Thorndyke and Marina Grazie? It was incredible. Marina was almost old enough to have been his mother. Into my mind flashed the picture of Marina's collapse over the note in her hotel room. Her first reaction had been to call for "Beale." Naturally I had thought it was because Thorndyke was a doctor. Now I wondered if I had been wrong. Had it been, instead, the instinctive turning of a woman in love to her lover?

Stunned, I glanced at Sandy. With a lighted cigarette between his lips and his head propped on his arm, he was frankly enjoying the show. I knew then that with his mordant sense of humor he had hoped the thing would work out this way. He, like Ambrosia, had probably been bored.

My reflections were brought to an end by Thorndyke. Lips a thin tight line, his lean face etched with fury, he advanced on the spinster, who stood her ground like a defiant clothes-pole. His long surgeon's fingers closed like vises on her thin arms. He said:

"Another remark like that, Ambrosia, and you'll join Marina in hell."

I'll say this for Miss Swisshome: she had the courage of her convictions. She didn't waver. Looking him straight in the eyes, returning glare for glare, she said, "You mean I can expect the same thing you gave her?"

If anyone was ever on the verge of murder, Beale Thorndyke stood there at that moment. Frankly worried for the woman's safety, I took a step forward. That movement of mine was, I swear, the only thing that stopped him. He saw me out of the corner of his eye and hesitated. Then his hands dropped from her arms. He stepped back.

"I gave Marina nothing," he said tightly. "But I'm warning you, Ambrosia. One more word about me and—and I'll wring that scrawny neck of yours. I'm telling you."

He meant it. I could tell from his voice. So, I was not too surprised to observe, could Ambrosia. She tried to brazen it out, but she wasn't equal to it. Her eyes fell. She darted a pink tongue over her dry lips and turned away.

Everyone began to breathe again. Elena's voice gushed out in a breathless burble of sound. "Please, let's not quarrel any more. Let's not make it any more difficult than it is."

"Prayer meeting's over, folks." Sandy got up from the piano and came over to the fire beside me to warm his hands. "Any report about the garage from the ways and means committee?"

The garage! I'd forgotten it completely. So much was happening that I was finding it impossible to keep all the threads in my hands at the same time. Everyone looked at me. Paris, who had been leaning on the mantel watching the brawl in noncommittal silence, said:

"Yeah, what about it?"

So I told them about the sandwich box and the crumpled papers, the crushed-out butts, and the wrapper from the cigarette package. They listened silently. As I talked, though, I became aware of an atmosphere that was strangely familiar. Those little signs—the quickly darted glances from one to the other; the almost visible drawing together; that tight, grim look of foreboding in their eyes. It was the same phalanxed fear I had seen when they realized that Marina's jewel-case was empty.

I finished my recital of the facts. After a moment's silence Elena faltered, "Then you think this—whoever he was—came in through the window and—and murdered Auntie?"

"It's possible," I said. "That's as far as I go."

"But who—why—?"

"I haven't the vaguest idea. You know as much as I do: the kind of print his shoes made, the fact that he ate the sandwiches, that he smokes, that he certainly was in the library. My guess is that he came here to rob your aunt, knowing from the newspaper stories that she always carried her jewels with her. Lord knows, there was plenty in the papers about them. Especially the Lucifer diamond."

"But no one," Ambrosia put in, "knew Marina was coming here today?"

I smiled. "I rather imagine, if you checked up, that you'd find plenty of persons who did. The hotel, the place where she ordered the food, the bus company where she hired the bus, all of us. I fancy that the things Marina did had a way of getting around."

Julian had been looking from one to the other with anticipation. He could contain himself no longer. Waving his hands with an almost Latin excitement, he burst out, "But all this is not the thing. Do you not see the fact? Must it be said to you that—"

Ambrosia gasped, "Oh, my God!"

Elena was the next to see. Her hand went to her mouth. "He's here," she whispered. "Whoever it was—is here in the house with us!"

Mrs. Tait went of the deep end. Flinging her arms around her husband's neck, she began mewling, "You git me outa here, Leander." (Leander! That wattled crow! Shades of the Hellespont!) "A murderer's loose. Git me outa here."

The old man firmly disentwined himself. "Don't go faunchin' around, Maggie," he said. "Far's I kin see, if he's here he's been here all t'time. We're still breathin'. Tain't likely he'd set out after you, anyways."

I applauded. That was exactly what I had been thinking.

"But what shall we *do?*" That was Julian, his voice cracking again as it rose.

"My suggestion," I said calmly, "is that we go hunting."

He shrank back, so obviously afraid that I wondered how he had ever mustered the courage to do battle with Thorndyke upstairs. "You mean—search for—him?"

"Exactly. Anybody any objections?"

Thorndyke began, "Do you really think—"

"Because," I added hurriedly, "whoever murdered Marina undoubtedly emptied her jewel-case."

"We'll search," he said brusquely.

20

WELL, WE SEARCHED.

At someone's suggestion—probably Julian's—we paired off. Like nuns on a shopping excursion, we went in twos: Maggie Tait with her Leander for protection; Sandy and I; Paris, the lone wolf, by himself; Elena and Julian, and Ambrosia Swisshome with Beale Thorndyke.

The latter two couplings were not arranged without a scene. Everything had been going along comparatively smoothly until Beale, taking Elena's arm, said, "We'll go together. Julian, you take Ambrosia."

Miss Swisshome, still smouldering from her encounter with him, sniffed, "I hope you didn't think I'd trust myself with you, Dr. Thorndyke."

I turned away, thinking everything was settled. Just then, though, Julian's voice broke in: "You are entirely wrong, Thorndyke, if you do not mind. You will take Ambrosia."

Something in his voice arrested me. I turned, to find we had another brawl on our hands.

"I do mind," Thorndyke said. "I am taking Elena."

To my surprise Julian stood firm. "And I say you are not, since I myself am taking her. No! Do not dare to strike me." He had cowered back a little. Then he straightened. "But you would not. For you know what I shall do if you touch me, Thorndyke. You know, eh?"

For an instant Elena's puzzled eyes played between them. Then she walked quietly over to the accompanist and thrust her arm through his. "You take Ambrosia, Beale," she said, not looking at him. "I—I'd rather go with Julian."

Thorndyke winced as if she had lashed him across the eyes with a bull-whip. His shoulders sagged. He turned to the spinster. "Come on, Ambrosia," he said roughly. "And for God's sake, don't pretend you're afraid."

"Who said I was afraid?" she asked, her eyes snapping. "But if I go with you, you must promise to tell me what Julian—"

"And keep your mouth shut," he snapped. "It's none of your business."

Oh, yes, we were just a group of happy, fun-loving children.

We searched that rookery from its foundations to the attic beams. I shan't linger too long over the expedition. We did the rat-haunted basement in a body, thrusting our candles into spider-webbed corners and crannies, climbing about over rubbish heaps and piles of iron pipe. We found nothing.

We did the first floor together too, since we arrived from the basement that way.

The upper floors were something else again. By the time we reached the second floor we had begun to go numb with the cold, the natural result of which was division of labor. The corridor echoed with cries of "I'll take this room and you take that one" . . . "I've already been in there. No need to repeat," etc. Couples became separated. Partners strayed. Lone candle flames zigzagged through and across the hall in mad flares of light. It was as weird as a Polish cemetery on Hallowe'en.

Strange combinations turned up, too. As I was about to enter one of the storerooms I saw Sandy and Ambrosia Swisshome climbing up to the third floor. Nearer at hand, Julian started into a room, bumped into Paris coming out.

"Are Miss Grazie and Dr. Thorndyke in there?" he demanded. His candle-flame illuminated a face like a tortured mask.

The chauffeur shut the door. "No one's in there. I've just searched it." Footsteps sounded over our heads. "Have you tried upstairs? Sounds like the whole mob's up there."

Julian turned and sprinted for the stairs, followed in a more leisurely manner by Paris, who winked as he passed me. "Little Boy Blue's sure got ants in his pants," he jeered. "Ain't love wonderful?" He went on up.

If I had answered him, made some remark of any sort, things might have turned out differently. But I didn't. I just stood there watching him out of sight. Then recollecting my intention of searching the storeroom, I opened the door and started in.

I didn't go in, though. What I did was to blurt, "I beg your pardon," back out hurriedly, and close the door behind me.

I've always thought it a pity that the second act *Liebesnacht of Tristan* must end as it does, so shatteringly, with the surprise entrance of Melot and King Mark. The lovers, laved in the sensuousness of the music and the sultriness of the night with its swooning perfume of roses, are so ecstatically happy, so blissfully unaware of imminent intrusion that it all seems too bad. Melot, I grant you, has the instincts of a Peeping Tom, but King Mark should have had the decency to withdraw quietly, without fuss.

As I did.

What had I seen? Two candles were set on a packing-case. Near them stood Elena and Beale Thorndyke, locked in an embrace so yearningly passionate that even now I feel ashamed of myself for having to mention it.

That wasn't all. As I opened the door I heard Thorndyke's voice, husky with emotion, just before his lips closed over hers. He said, "But there's nothing we can do, darling. Only death . . ." The words trailed off.

I climbed the stairs thoughtfully. This was getting to be too much for me. My so-called brain was whirling. For here was Thorndyke, engaged to marry Marina Grazie, making love to Marina's niece not twelve hours after Marina's death. It was obvious, too, that Elena was far from disapproving. Yet not half an hour before she had deliberately turned away from him and chosen Julian as her escort. And what was this about "nothing we can do . . . only death . . . ?" Do about what? Death of whom?

As I rounded the bend of the staircase, still pondering, I heard a door below me open and close. The two lovers, talking with ostentatious casualness, were behind me.

It was a good thing, too. As I reached the hall on the third floor a dark figure hurled itself at me, clutched me by the lapels. I turned the flashlight into its face. It was Julian, green with fury.

"*Madre de Dios*," he screamed. "Where are they, those two? If I find that they—"

"Control your blood pressure, Porter." I disengaged his fingers. "If you mean the doctor and Miss Grazie, they've been with me down below. They're right behind me."

He pushed past me, flew down the stairs. "Elena, where have you been? I have hunted all over for you. I have been beside myself with worry." He took her hand, flung his arm around her waist.

Her voice was gently chiding. "You shouldn't have worried. Beale and I were with Mr. Graine. We were just putting more wood on the fires in the bedrooms."

Well, I gave up. I don't understand women. I guess I never will. Men either, for that matter. For Beale Thorndyke slipped past the touching little reunion without so much as a sidewise glance and came on upstairs. The whole thing bowled me over. For the hundredth time that day I wondered if I should ever trust my eyes again.

I was certain I wouldn't when, later on, after we had reassembled in the library downstairs and Thorndyke remarked on the absence of Julian and Elena, I opened the door into the hall and stuck my head out to call them.

But I didn't call. I didn't even say, "Pardon me" this time.

There, in a pool of light from their two candles set on the newel-post, were the two of them. And from where I stood I should say that Elena was entering into the spirit of Julian's embrace with as much enthusiasm as she had into Beale's.

I closed the door. "They'll be here in a minute," I said weakly.

21

"THEN WE'RE AGREED ON THAT?" I asked.

It was five minutes later. Just short of midnight. Julian and Elena had slipped in a moment after I had closed the door. Nothing was said as they joined us. Thorndyke, who must have suspected something, was elaborately uninterested. Over by the piano he was studiously engrossed in unraveling Ambrosia's knitting.

By this time you have gathered that we unearthed nobody during our prowl. Every crack and cranny of the place had been peered into. We had found nothing. Nobody.

"You're all quite reassured?" I repeated. "There is no one but ourselves in the place?"

Heads nodded with such a wave of concerted affirmation that the candles flickered in the stirred air. Only Miss Swisshome looked a trifle dubious. Her angular face was set as she regarded the leaping fire.

"Ambrosia?" I queried. The name came with surprising ease. "What's on your mind?"

The iron-grey head turned to me. She said precisely, "I should like to ask a few questions before I am, as you put it, quite reassured."

"Anything, Miss Swisshome."

She looked around the room, drawing to herself the concentrated attention of the group. For a moment she peered toward the piano, then with a cluck of annoyance crossed over and yanked the knitting out of the doctor's hands. "Haven't you any regard for other people's property?" she snapped, and tossed the wooly stuff on the mantel.

"In the first place," she began after she had composed herself, "do you really and sincerely believe there was someone else here at sometime today, Anthony?"

I nodded. "I've given you my reasons, and they seem logical. I'm satisfied in my mind that there was someone."

Her grim eyes sought out Leander Tait. "Earlier, when Anthony asked you, Mr. Tait, you said you didn't remember whether there were footprints or not. Just some snow, I think you said. Have you changed your mind now?"

His rheumy eyes shifted to his wife, who ignored him. "Seems to me they was kinda prints, now you put it like that," he said slowly, studying his knotted hands. "More I think of it, t'more it seems like they was footprints."

"Well, why didn't you say so in the first place?" Again the eyes sought his scraggy wife. Maggie Tait gave no sign of being aware of it. "Guess I uz afraid," he said at last.

"Afraid?" The spinster bore in. "Afraid of what?"

His voice lowered to a mumble. What he said was all very involved but I finally grasped what he seemed to be driving at. He had seen the prints and had recognized them for what they were. Feeling, quite rightly, that they might be clues to the identity of the murderer, he had been worried for fear his having seen them might embroil him with the murderer. So he had destroyed them as quickly as possible, thinking that he was thus freeing himself from the power of the assassin. It was all childlike and confused. But what, as Sandy said later, could you expect from an old goat like Tait?

Ambrosia seemed to grasp what the old man was saying. Dismissing him with a snort of irritation, she returned to me. "And you honestly believe that the man who made those prints was the man who murdered Marina?"

Well, did I? After all, I had shown that there was plenty of opportunity for any of Marina's party to have committed the crime, but at the same time there seemed no motive sufficiently potent to point to any one of them. Beale Thorndyke might have done it to avoid marrying Marina. But that seemed improbable. Paris might have killed her in an attempt to rob her of the diamond. Yet there was no proof. And so—wishful thinking, I suppose—I fell back on the mysterious stranger.

"Yes," I said, not too firmly.

"Very well," Ambrosia went on. "And you are quite convinced that that person, whoever it might be, is not in Lucifer's Pride now?"

That was even more difficult to answer. "We've searched the place high and low. If everyone here will solemnly swear that he saw no one other than ourselves during the course of the search—" I broke off, looked around at the intent faces.

After a moment's silence, each one nodded. Watching their faces as they did so, I believed them. At that moment I was honestly convinced that there was no living person but the nine of us in Lucifer's Pride. I said so.

"Very well," the spinster said again. "Now I should like to know where that person is if he is not in this building or in the garage. Have you any explanation of that?"

"Frankly, I haven't. But if he isn't here, he must have got away some way. It's only logical."

"But how? In this storm?"

I threw up my hands. "Good God, woman, I don't know. All I can say is that if he planned so carefully how to get here he must have been equally careful to arrange for getting away. How he did it, I don't know. The fact remains that he evidently succeeded."

"And the nails in the gas-tanks?"

"Again you have me. It must have been part of the plan. Why ask me to explain it?"

She managed a wry smile. "Because you started all this, if you will remember."

"That was when I thought one of you was the murderer."

"And you don't now?"

"Frankly, I don't." Was it my imagination or did someone heave a sigh of—was it relief? I looked around quickly. Not a wisp of expression other than absorbed interest was visible on any face. I gave up. After all, it might have been the hissing of a board in the fire.

Then Ambrosia asked her last question. "You feel that you could go to bed without a worry on your mind? Without any fears whatever?"

I could answer that with certainty. I stood up. "I could. And furthermore that's exactly what I intend doing."

Maggie Tait screeched like a chicken whose head has been placed on the chopping block. "I ain't a-goin' to shet my eyes. Like as not we'll be murdered in our beds."

Miss Swisshome seared her with a glance. "I doubt that, Mrs. Tait. I am inclined to agree with Anthony. There is no murderer in Lucifer's Pride. I feel it in my bones."

"She's got plenty to feel with," Sandy remarked irrelevantly.

"And you, Miss Grazie?" I asked.

Elena looked at me with dull eyes. Her face was drawn, almost haggard. She looked half asleep. "I—I am awfully tired. Do you suppose it—it's all right?"

"I think we'd be fools to stay up," I said heartily. A gust of howling wind tore down the chimney. "God knows how long this storm will keep up or when a boat will be able to get across the river for us."

Everyone stirred. Leander Tait looked across the room. "What about her?"

Paris made a noise. "She'll keep. I'm goin' to hit the hay."

And so, with much palaver and bickering, it was decided. Eventually everyone had a board with a candle on it and the procession upstairs began. I lingered by the fire, listening wearily to the echoing voices on the stairs and the floor above.

Sandy was the last to go. He paused at the door. "Coming, Tony?"

"I'll be with you in a minute. You go ahead."

He hesitated, then asked gruffly, "Do you want to talk? If you do I—I'm not sleepy."

"You're a liar." I mustered a smile. "Thanks, fellow, but I think there's been enough talk in this place for one day."

He went out slowly, then poked his head back. "Don't catch cold. Remember you're singing *La Gioconda* Wednesday night."

The candle-flames at Marina's head winked maliciously.

22

I SAT THERE FOR TWO HOURS, listening to the creaks and groans of the building as the winds manhandled it. Now and then the heavy draperies at the windows bellied inwards and the crystal strings and prisms of the great chandelier over my head tinkled and whispered in agitation. Once I got up and replaced the guttering candles at Marina's head and feet. Otherwise I simply sat, feeding the fire with an occasional board, and thinking hard.

I had plenty to think about. For shortly after the footsteps and the stir on the second floor had died away an idea had come to me that simply knocked the props from under me. How I had overlooked it before I don't know. But I had. And it changed everything.

It all came about when I reached into my pocket for a match and my fingers encountered a crumpled wad of paper. I pulled it out, smoothed it flat on my knee, and sat looking at it. It was the ripped-out page of the *Rigoletto* score which I had pried from Marina's dead hand, and which I had stuffed into my pocket when Ambrosia had come beating on the door with the news of Thorndyke's and Porter's set-to upstairs.

The sight of the rumpled, creased page made me a little sad. How many times, I wondered, had Marina pored over those notes, reworking a phrase here, changing an inflection there, striving constantly for the ideal? No singer, however perfect, ever does an aria in exactly the same manner twice in succession. A mood, an inspiration, differences in audiences, a thousand and two complicating factors combine to make each performance a new experience. It may differ in only a minor respect from the preceding rendition, but something is always to be learned. Schumann-Heink must have sung the Brahms *Lullaby* or *Silent Night* thousands of times in her career, yet I'll wager she worked at them until the very day of her death.

Had Marina, on the evening of her death, been reworking *Caro Nome?* Or had she simply been amusing herself, as women will, by making herself sad? Attempting, as she put it, "to recapture a fleeting glimpse of what has been?" Had she been thinking not of the notes and the words she was singing but of old Lucifer Bollman who had built this crazy castle for a bride who had not materialized, of the man who had "ransomed" himself with a diamond as big as an egg? I wondered about that word "ransomed." It was a strange word for Marina to have used. I thought about that ill-assorted pair: Bollman, the crude and ruthless giant of commerce, and Marina Grazie, the opera star, spoiled, pampered, and as ruthless in her way as he in his. How had their paths crossed. What had brought them together?

Then it seemed I could see Marina sitting there at the piano, her plump fingers plodding away at the keys as she sang her song. She had been, I remembered, in one of her *farouche* moods. Undoubtedly her eyes had been closed as she concentrated on her thoughts and her song. "I know his name—Walter Maldè, I love thee!—*Gualtier Maldè! Nome di lui si amato,*" the words had come in her flawless Italian. "*Ti scolpisci nel core innamorata . . .* Ev'ry fond, tender thought for thee I cherish."

Suddenly she had broken off with a start. A sound had come to her ears. Opening her eyes, she had seen a window—that window in the corner—being raised stealthily. A man's foot had appeared over the sill. Wide-eyed, she had watched as Death, wearing stars in his heels, had climbed into the room, stood before her. Had she known, recognized the man, his intent, his purpose? Surely she must have read in his eyes what was coming. And she must have—

I sat up, excitement slashing through me. I twisted around to see the position of the piano. Yes, it was angled so that Marina must have been looking directly across at the window. She could not have helped seeing the intruder. And seeing—my hands began to shake—seeing, she would have cried out. Even if she had known the man, his clandestine entrance must have warned her. She would have made some sort of outcry even before he could cross the room to gag her with the flat of his hand.

Yet Sandy and the Taits had heard nothing. Only a wall between the library and the kitchen and they had not mentioned having heard a sound.

I sat there, stunned. It was impossible.

I looked down at the score on my lap, trying to collect my whirling thoughts. If Marina had not cried out at the entrance of someone through the window, then—then she had not seen the man come in. Yet, the piano placed as it was, she could not have helped seeing him.

Then what? If she had neither seen nor heard him, I was forced logically to the conclusion that she had been unable to. In other words, she was already dead when the man with the stars on his heels came in. He had not killed Marina Grazie because—because someone else had already done the deed.

Above me the chandelier swayed, its crystals rattling like ice in a highball glass. I threw my head back against the chair and stared up at it, feeling as dizzy as though I had had several drinks on an empty stomach. For now I saw that my assurances to Ambrosia and the others had been false. The murderer had not crept into the library through a window. He had walked in through the door. I was right back where I had started. The murderer was one of us.

It took me some time, not to grasp it but to admit it. After all, the solution I had worked out had absolved everyone in our party. I had been glad of it. I can't say I was exactly bursting with affection for them, but in a mild, indifferent sort of way I did like them. Yes, even Julian Porter, who was so obviously a snake that you could accept him on that basis. Ambrosia, in her blunt, craggy way, was likeable. Thorndyke, despite our differences, impressed me; I felt that under other, more favorable circumstances we might be friends. Elena's timid loveliness could easily have gotten under my skin if I had allowed it. Paris, the Taits—well, what of them?

Suddenly I wanted to talk things over with Sandy. I wanted to thresh things out, to put the ideas that whirled in my mind into good, solid, audible words. I looked at my watch. It was two in the morning. Monday morning.

I piled more wood on the fire, picked up Tait's flashlight, and started across the room. I glanced at Marina and then went on. The draft from the hall was frigid as I opened the door. Behind me the chandelier tinkled its glassy protest.

And then the chattering crystals were drowned out by other sounds.

It all happened so quickly that even now it seems to me everything occurred at once. Yet it couldn't have. It does take a moment for a body to fall two stories. My reason tells me that. But as I stood there in the doorway, looking out into the darkness, I could have sworn it was all one simultaneous sound: the rusty screech of nails pulling loose . . . the cracking of broken boards, the one moaning cry that seemed to tear at my vitals . . . and, quite close to me, that smacking thump that turned me sick at my stomach.

It was that last sound that did for me. For I had heard it once before. At the *Opéra* in Paris, the night of my second Faust, an electrician high up on a catwalk had tripped on a coil of rope and hurtled down to smash in a flopping heap on the stage. He had been dead when we reached him.

That was the sound I heard now.

It took me a moment to make my muscles obey. Then, aware that I was holding the flashlight, I lifted it and pressed the button. The beam shot across the rotunda, sprayed over a dark, motionless heap on the floor. I made my legs move forward, knowing, dreading what I should find.

It was a man. A man I had never seen before. He lay as he had fallen, the left arm twisted under his heavy body, his head—I gulped—almost buried under his chest. The skin over the back of the thick neck was stretched almost to the bursting point. He had fallen head-first.

Aimlessly I shot the flashlight up into the lightwell. High above, on the third floor, I could see a spindle dangling from the railing, a gap beside it. As I looked, the spindle came loose and fell with a crash beside the body.

Then it was that I saw, in the man's right hand, a little sheaf of papers. White and grey papers, the topmost one stained with blood which trickled from a deep scratch on the hand. Just as I had taken the sheet of the *Rigoletto* score from Marina, I reached down now, pulled the little packet out of his grip, and shoved it into my pocket. I couldn't tell you why I did it. It was purely an automatic gesture.

At that moment the second floor came to life. Doors squeaked open. Flickers of ruddy light danced in the darkness. Ambrosia's harsh voice rang out, "Elena, are you all right? It sounded as if the house were falling in."

Next I heard Sandy calling me. Then Beale Thorndyke's head appeared at the railing. He blinked into the glare of the flashlight. "Graine, is that you?" he called. "In God's name, what's happened?"

The sound of the voices, the sight of a living face snapped me back to normal. "Get down here as fast as you can, Thorndyke. There's been an accident. I think this man is dead."

Think, hell. I knew damned well he was. He had fallen on his head. His neck had snapped like a dried branch.

Other faces were peering down now: Porter, Ambrosia, the Taits, Sandy, all of them. I couldn't see Elena but I heard the sobbing cry she gave just before the stampede began. Sandy was still calling to know if I was all right.

When Thorndyke reached me I turned the flash down. By its light he examined the man quickly, his fingers searching over the neck. He turned the body over, and I thought I was going to pass out. For the head didn't follow. It just stayed there for a moment, and then with the sickening deliberation of a slow-motion camera, it rolled over, lolled down on the right shoulder at a grotesque, impossible angle.

Swallowing frantically, I made myself look down at the dead man. He was thick and heavy-set, with greying black hair. The face was coarse-featured with a large mouth; bushy black eyebrows met over a nose that was big and sensual. A heavy dark stubble covered his full cheeks and jutting chin.

Thorndyke stood up. His face was white. He brushed dazedly at his knees. "Dead instantly," he said in a voice so dry it sounded like Sandy's raw-hide rasp. "Who is he?"

Before I could say anything, the others erupted from the stairway. They rushed up, stopped dead, and stood, looking down at the body for all the world like a group of yokels viewing a sideshow exhibit at a carnival. Now that the stumbling clatter on the stairs had died away, it was all very still. Very quiet.

I was suddenly aware that I was shivering. Something had to be done. Evidently it was up to me to do it.

Sandy's hand was giving my arm a relieved squeeze. There was awe in his voice as he whispered, "Where did he come from, Tony?"

I made myself speak. "From the third floor," I said and shot the flashlight up to the splintered gap in the railing. Instantly Elena began to cry. Mrs. Tait gave a scream and ran for the library.

I shook myself. "We can't stand out here all night. Thorndyke, will you and Porter carry the fellow into the library."

Ambrosia led Elena away, assuring the girl through chattering teeth that everything was going to be all right. Julian and Thorndyke picked up the dead man and, with Sandy and me following as substitute mourners, carried him into the warm room. Tait had pulled another chesterfield over beside the one on which Marina lay. The pall-bearers deposited their burden on it.

Sandy whistled under his breath. "This is going to be a pretty sight for the police. It's looking more like a morgue every minute."

At the word morgue Maggie Tait set up a moaning wail that made the hair rise on the back of my neck. Everyone jumped. It was a little too much.

I turned on the old man. "Can you possibly keep that calliope of yours quiet for a minute? We'd like to keep what few nerves we have left in our bodies."

Murder Ends the Song

As Tait went over to console his wife I sensed rather than heard a movement behind me. I whirled around just in time to see Julian Porter reaching out toward the dead man's pocket. Seeing me, he straightened instantly, his face darkening.

I went over and pushed him away. "Hunting for something, my friend? You might at least wait till the man is cold before you take the gold out of his teeth."

He glared at me, breathing hard.

I wasn't impressed. "Go over and see if you can help Ambrosia quiet Elena," I told him.

He went. Without a word.

I turned to the others. "The poor chap isn't a very pretty sight, but I think we'd better try to find out, first of all, who he is. I'll hold the flashlight and—"

"No! No!" Elena cried. "I won't look at him. You can't ask me to do that." She buried her head in Ambrosia's none too ample bosom.

I went on inexorably, "I'll hold the flashlight and each one will look at him. Perhaps one of us will recognize him."

I focused the light on the dead face and waited. No one moved. I felt the antagonism rising like a tide. Something had to be done to halt it. I caught Sandy's eye and nodded slightly. He got my meaning. Ambling up, he peered down for a moment, then shook his head.

"No one I ever saw outside an Edward G. Robinson movie," he said casually, and strolled back to the fireplace.

His indifference impressed them. The trick was turned. One by one, timidly, diffidently, they approached, gazed, retreated. I watched each face closely. There was no sign of recognition. Ambrosia and Elena were the last. The girl kept her eyes averted until the very last moment; then she shot a hasty glance down, shuddered, shook her head, and moved away.

Ambrosia was a sight. She had not even taken time to drag a comb through her hair. It surged over her head in a tangled mass. As she stalked up to go through her ordeal, she looked half-asleep. She bent over the dead man. Her eyes opened a trifle wider. She looked again.

"You know him?" I asked eagerly.

"N-no," she said doubtfully. "It's just that—well, he seems to have a slight resemblance to someone I know. Not so much the features as a—oh, I don't know—the general expression."

The light in my hand wavered with my excitement. "Well, think, Miss Swisshome," I urged. "Who is it he makes you think of?"

She studied the face again and then gave a triumphant cluck. "I know what it is, Anthony, but I'm afraid you'll think me silly when I tell you. But—doesn't it strike you that he has the same—er—well, gangsterish look that Paris has."

Paris! Something had been nagging at me for some moments. Now I knew what it was. Paris was not in the room. Neither had I seen him in the group around the body outside.

I flung the flashlight to Sandy. "Run upstairs as fast as you can to Paris's room and see if he's—if everything's all right," I said.

He caught the worried look on my face and dashed off. We could hear him clattering up the stairs. The others huddled together. Fearfully.

Ambrosia cleared her throat nervously. "Is it—is that man the murderer?"

In my excitement I had forgotten to look. I took a candle, went around to the dead man's feet. Each heel was marked with a large star. I saw them without surprise.

"Well, is it?" Julian demanded.

I chose my words. "It's the man who made the footprints, yes."

Thorndyke caught the distinction. "Why do you say it like that?" he demanded. "Either he's the murderer or he isn't. Which is it?"

I opened my mouth to explain. But I didn't get the words out. Just then the door opened and Sandy burst in, followed by Paris. The chauffeur didn't waste an unnecessary glance on us. He crossed the room and pushed past me to the chesterfield.

Sandy said, "He *says* he was asleep and didn't hear anything. I got him out of bed."

Paris turned away from the couch. His face was thunderous. His accusing eyes burned over us all.

"So you got Caruso, too," he snarled. "Well, which one of you was it?"

23

No one stirred. I remember thinking, witlessly: But Caruso's been dead for years. Dead and embalmed and lying in that awful place in—is it Naples? I've seen him. I've watched the crowd of ghouls ogling his corpse. I've seen the fat wax taper beside his tomb. Caruso? What is the fellow talking about?

Ambrosia was the first to speak. "We're in no mood for jests, Paris," she said, for all the world like a governess reproving a little boy who has burst out laughing at his grandmother's funeral. "Perhaps if you would explain what you're talking about we might be able to appear a trifle more intelligent."

"Big words don't scare me," the chauffeur said with a sneer. "Which one of you killed my pal?"

I began to track again. I even found I had a voice. "You know this man, Paris? You mean this is Caruso?"

"What d'ya think I'm talkin' about? You're damn right I know him. And I know one of you did him in. All I want to know is which one of you was it?"

"Curiouser and curiouser," I reflected à la Alice. I turned to the newly laid-out corpse. He looked as much like Caruso as I did. He was heavy-set—and there the resemblance ended. I shouldn't have cared to meet him in a North Beach alley at midnight if he were put out with me.

Beale Thorndyke raised a calm voice.

"You're quite mistaken, Paris. Your friend fell through the third floor railing and broke his neck. I'm prepared to swear to it. You can see the broken rail yourself if you care to look."

"I don't need to look." The chauffeur spat the words out of the side of his mouth. "Sure, the railing's broke—if you say so. Sure, his neck is busted. I can see that. But fall! Don't make me laugh. Caruso could see in the dark. Like a cat. If he fell, then somebody pushed him. An' *I'll* swear to that."

"But it's too absurd," said Ambrosia. "Why, this is the man who murdered Madame Grazie. Anthony just said so before you came in."

I felt no especial affection for the dead man but at least justice demanded that I clear him of that charge.

"You're quite wrong, Miss Swisshome—Ambrosia, I mean. I didn't say that. I said this was the man who made the footprints."

"Why quibble?" She brushed my statement aside in exasperation. "Isn't it the same thing?"

"You're goddam right it's not the same thing," Paris rose to the defense. "Sure, Caruso made the footprints. Sure, he came in the window. But he never killed Madame Grazie. An' I'll tell you why. He never killed her because she was already dead when he got inside the room. Now what d'ya think of that?"

During the ensuing silence I concealed my elation as best I could. I didn't know how Paris knew all this, but I realized with pardonable pride that I had reasoned it out for myself. I haven't been so set up since the *régisseur* at La Scala complimented me on a bit of business I had worked out on my own for the second act of *Manon*.

I said, "How do you know all this? You weren't by any chance there yourself, were you?"

He snorted. "I wasn't in this room after she kicked us all out. You can't pin that thing on me, brother. How do I know? Because Caruso told me." He jabbed a forefinger against my chest. "An' even if he was a yegg like me, he wouldn't lie. Not to me. If he said she was cold, she was cold."

I shoved his finger away. "O.K., bud. I believe you. You don't have to ram that thing through my ribs." He backed away, muttering.

"That's better. Now suppose you tell me when you saw—er, Caruso. When did he tell you all this?"

For the first time since he had come in the room Paris's face brightened. He almost chuckled. "While all you dopes were hoppin'

Murder Ends the Song

around huntin' for him." He turned to Julian. "'Member when you bumped into me up on the second floor an' ast me was your girl friend an' the doctor in that room I was just comin' out of? Well, they wasn't. But Caruso was. Under the bed. I just finished talkin' to him. Then's when he told me."

Julian went a little pale, thinking, no doubt, of the closeness of his call.

"I see," I said. "And you simply forgot to mention that you saw him?"

"Sure," he said easily. "I couldn't go back on a pal, could I?"

"No, I suppose not." I looked at him thoughtfully. "And now that he is dead, you still don't want to go back on him, is that it?"

"What d'ya mean?"

"I mean simply that you'd like to find out how he came to die."

The face darkened again. "You're damn right. An' I'm goin' to."

Very casually I said, "Then suppose you tell me the whole story. Who he is, how he came to be here, everything. Maybe I can help you. You see, I'd like to get the straight of this whole thing myself."

I watched him in fear and trembling. Would he take the bait? For a moment he looked doubtful enough. You could almost hear the ponderous cogs of his brain meshing and slowly, reluctantly beginning to function. His eyes shifted from face to adamant face, returning always to mine.

Finally he said, "You're on, Mr. Graine. I'll tell you the truth, so help me God. But you're the only one around here I'd trust. Where do you want me to start?"

The others bristled. There was a general murmuring and much business of being outraged at the imputation on their honor.

"Just ignore them, Paris," I said reassuringly. "Start at the beginning. Who is he? Where did you meet him?"

He licked his lips once and then began. I had no way of knowing at the time that I was hearing only the first of an amazing series of stories that would occupy most of the night and the next morning. Talk about Haroun al-Raschid! Scheherezade's tales couldn't hold a feather to the ones that poured into my fascinated ears. I crammed a thousand and one nights into twelve hours.

"We was cell-mates in San Quentin," Paris said simply. "What got us there is nobody's business but ours. Anyways, his name wasn't Caruso. Not his real one, I mean. He just used it fer a sort of handle. His real name was Horston. Cobbett Horston. He told me that one night when we was talkin'. Funny name to give a kid, ain't it? But nobody ever called him that. He was always just Caruso.

"Funny guy he was, too. Couldn't talk about nothin' but opera an' opera stars. Just like some fellows go for—oh, baseball an' the Di Maggios an' all. Caruso went fer opera. That's where he got his name, I guess. Every time he seen a picture of someone in opera he'd cut it out an' paste it on the wall of our cell. Place was damn near papered with mugs of people like Lawrence Tibbett an' Martinelli an' Lily Pons. An' say, she ain't bad!" He paused a moment, reflecting with relish on Miss Pons's undoubted charms. "You was there, too, Mr. Graine. In sorta tights an' a piece about how you'd took fourteen bows at some place in Paree."

I took another slight bow then. It wasn't everyone, I felt, who rated a place on a cell-wall in San Quentin. I was genuinely flattered.

The chauffeur continued: "I ast 'im one night how he come to go fer opera that way. Most fellows don't, ya know. Think it's kind of sissy. Well, sir, would you believe it, he said one time he was goin' to be an opera singer. I mean, he planned on it till somethin' happened to his voice. I never found out what it was. Somehow I kinda couldn't ask 'im. Ya see, he always got a kinda funny look in his eyes an' closed up tight whenever he mentioned it. So that's all I know about it.

"He was a swell guy, though, after ya got used to him. Even if he was a little screwy. We was together until he got sprung. I kinda hated to see 'im go. Even if I didn't know much about his damn opera, we got along fine together." He paused, scratched his head. "Ya know, it's a funny thing. But I useta think that guy kinda pitied me. I dunno."

I waited while he attempted to puzzle out the riddle. The room was quiet except for the roaring of the fire, sucked up the chimney by the wind outside. And I had thought it would be unpleasant to meet Caruso Horston! Well, if he was screwy, so, I supposed, was I. Things equal to the same thing are equal to each other. Or words to that effect.

Maggie Tait's hacking cough roused Paris from his reverie. He lighted a cigarette and inhaled deeply.

"I didn't get out until six months after him," he went on. "I joined some pals in L.A. an'—uh, worked with them for a while. I never saw Caruso again until tonight.

"Then one day I read in the papers about Madame Grazie joinin' this opera company. There was a long spiel, too, about the diamond and all the other rocks she owned. An' so I thought—" He broke off, looking uncomfortable.

"You thought you'd like a look at them," I supplied for him. "Just skip that part, Paris. I think we understand."

"Well, a fellow's got to live," he said, giving me a grateful look. "Anyways, it was a cinch. I got a pal of mine to fix me up a swell bunch of references an' I barged in on the Madame an' ast her fer a job drivin' her around. I'm a good chauffeur an' before the police got me I worked fer an airplane company. So she took me on. That's all there was to it."

"But your friend Caruso . . ." I prompted.

"Oh, yeah, I was forgettin'. Well, I didn't know he was even around till he stuck his head out from under that bed upstairs. Was I knocked over!"

"How did he know it was you?"

"He seen my picture in the paper with all the rest of you down at the airport an' reconnized me. He said he'd been workin' fer this bus company in Portland since he got out but there wasn't no future to it. So when he read about Madame Grazie's rocks he—well, just like me, he thought he'd make a grab fer 'em. Said he was just tryin' to think of some way to get holt of me when the Madame calls up the company Saturday. He was in the office an' heard her order the bus. Right away quick he thinks where he can hide in it. That's how he got here. I told 'im how you figured it out, Mr. Graine, an' he thought you was awfully smart. He told me so."

I bowed again. I was beginning actually to wish I might have known Caruso. There was one man who appreciated me.

"And he punctured the gas-tanks?" I asked.

"Yeah. Just in case he couldn't grab the diamond up here. He thought if you was walkin' down to the ferry he'd stand a better chance of coppin' it."

"What!" I jerked to attention. "You mean to say he didn't get the diamond?"

"Not when I talked to 'im, he hadn't," he grunted. "He said he was meetin' someone later tonight who did have it an' he'd get it then."

I thought that one over. Light was beginning to glimmer. Someone who did have the diamond. But that meant . . .

"Did he say how he intended getting it away from this person?" I asked excitedly.

In the infinitesimal silence before Paris answered I could feel the room tightening up. Every eye was riveted on the chauffeur.

He spoke. "Sure. He'd promise to keep 'is mouth shut about the Madame's death."

Someone gasped.

"You mean—you mean Caruso Horston knew who killed Madame Grazie?" My voice was shaking so I could hardly get the words out.

He flicked his cigarette into the fire. "Yeah, he knew."

"But how?" I blurted. "How could he?"

"Easy. He seen it."

"He—"

"Sure. He was lookin' in the window when it happened."

24

ONCE I WAS AT A METROPOLITAN PERFORMANCE of *Götterdämmerung* when, toward the conclusion of the Immolation Scene, the hefty soprano who was singing Brünnhilde leaped on her white horse preparatory to plunging into Siegfried's funeral pyre. The horse had other ideas. Rearing up, it deposited Brünnhilde in a neat heap on the stage and then sat down on her leg. For long moments after the curtain fell hurriedly, the audience sat in utter, stunned silence, too petrified even to make a move.

That audience had nothing on us. I hadn't known eight people were capable of such concentrated stupefaction. Beale Thorndyke was standing behind me, but I could see Elena, her violet eyes wide with horror, sagging against Julian, who looked as if he needed a prop himself. Ambrosia Swisshome seemed so close to keeling over that I hurriedly located Marina's angel-bottle on the piano and held myself in readiness to administer alcohol. The Taits goggled like hypnotized rabbits.

This time it was Sandy who broke the spell. You couldn't keep him down long. "Did your Peeping Tom friend tell you whether it was a man or a woman he saw, Paris? You can't just leave us like this."

The chauffeur flushed, realizing in a dim way that his friend was being maligned but not quite sure just how.

"I ast him," he answered, "but he said he'd handle it. Less I knew about it, he said, the better off I'd be." He added bitterly, "He was right, too. I'm glad he didn't tell me now."

Seeing that quiet figure on the chesterfield, the horrible lolling head, I was inclined to agree with him.

"May I say a word?"

Heads swung as one to Beale Thorndyke. He appeared a little confused at the barrage of eyes turned on him, but stood his ground.

"You're asking us"—he directed his words at Paris—"to believe that your friend made an appointment to meet the hypothetical murderer on the third floor, offering to exchange silence for the Lucifer diamond. Is that right?"

Paris hesitated, warily. Then he nodded.

"Furthermore, you suggest that he met the murderer, who seized the opportunity to rid himself of a witness to his crime and pushed Horston through the railing, your implication being that one of us was that person. Am I right?"

I don't think Paris quite grasped the whole thing but at least he understood the last phrase. "You're damn right you're right," he said. "One of you did it."

A glitter came into Thorndyke's eyes. "That's your version, my friend. Mine is that you were the one he saw through the window. You met him upstairs—and you pushed him through that railing."

Paris blinked before the directness of the attack. "Me?" he brought out.

"Yes, you. Either that or you worked together and then quarreled over the spoils. Either way it would account for this cock-and-bull story you've manufactured to save your own skin."

Rage flamed up in the chauffeur's eyes. "Why, you dirty bastard," he snarled and took a step forward, fists clenched into small hams. "That's a goddam lie! Caruso and I never had any trouble. Why, he even give me—" He clamped his lips together, suddenly aware that he had said more than he had intended.

I picked him up. "Yes, Paris? You were saying that he gave you—what? You're sure it wasn't the Lucifer diamond?"

"I tell you he didn't have it to give me," the badgered man flung out. "That's what he was killed over. I know it. He was tryin' to get it. He didn't have it. I haven't got it either."

"But you said he did give you something. Come on, Paris. What was it? What did Horston give you?"

His eyes flickered around the hostile group. Defiantly, he began, "I ain't goin' to—" Then, strangely, he wilted. All the fight went out of him. He looked exactly as he had the afternoon before when he threw his gun away.

"Oh, what the hell," he said. "You can't pin anything on me. An' I don't want 'em. Not any part of 'em."

Saying which, he proceeded to uncork another surprise. Plunging his hand into his coat pocket, he pulled out a fistful of glitter and hurled it to the floor. Sapphires, pearls, diamonds went skittering over the rug. A diamond and crystal ear-clip rolled over and over, ticked out onto the polished hearth, teetered and came to rest, shooting out orange and purple rays from the fire-glow. Marina's jewels! I stood staring at the gleaming blobs that had peppered around my feet.

"That's what he give me, if you wanta know," he said bitterly. "That was my share for keepin' mum about seein' him. But I don't want it now. If the police found it on me they'd think right away I done the whole thing. An' I didn't. I swear I didn't. Mr. Graine, you believe me, don't you?"

I didn't know what to believe. I said, "If Horston didn't murder Madame Grazie, how did he come to have these things?"

He was only too eager in his efforts to make me understand.

"I ast him that. He said whoever killed the Madame yanked the diamond off her neck so hard the chain broke an' a little key flew across the room. Caruso saw where it fell, but this other guy didn't. Hunted around fer awhile an' then beat it.

"When the coast was clear, Caruso hopped in the window an' got the key an' finally found the Madame's box where she'd hid it under her." He looked distressed. "He said it wasn't no picnic gettin' it but he did. He took out everything in it an' put the box back an' then—"

"Everything?" I would never have known it for Elena's voice if I had not seen her lips move. She was leaning forward, her slight body rigid, a feverish light in her eyes.

"What d'ya mean, everything?" Paris asked, nonplussed.

Ambrosia drew a hissing breath. "Did your friend take everything out of the box?" she asked in spaced syllables.

Again I observed that queer drawing-together of all of them, that intangible phalanx that I had been aware of before. Julian's long fingers were opening and closing. The doctor's face was a lean, sculptured mask, tight and unrevealing. Even the Taits had drawn nearer the circle, hovering on the outskirts like two filmy-eyed vultures.

Paris took a step backward, as if an atmospheric battering-ram had come up against him. "That's what he said," he told them doggedly. "Said the box was empty when he put it back."

For an instant the line-up held. It was like that split second after the kick-off when the pigskin goes sailing down the field and you think the players will never start moving. It is only a flash of an instant, but it is there. Then the storm breaks, and the field becomes a blur of surging, uniformed bodies.

What happened in the library was just like that. The group broke. Once in a movie short I saw a dead dog attacked by white ants in Africa. The dog lay there. You could see the thick column of ants approaching nearer and nearer. Closer. Closer. Then all at once you couldn't see the dog any more.

So it was with poor Caruso Horston. As at a signal, everyone rushed forward, swarming around him until he was lost to sight. Paris, who had been shoved out of the way in the confusion, stood gaping. Sandy and I, by the fireplace, were only a little less obvious in our astonishment. All you could see were hands and arms moving over the body, in and out of pockets. A button, wrenched loose from the man's coat, kited high, fell to the floor.

The sight of it made me think of Horston falling through the air, landing in that grotesque heap. Then I remembered. I took out of my pocket the little sheaf of papers he had been holding, his blood still damp on the uppermost one. Was this what they were looking for? Were these scraps of white and grey the "other things" Elena had mentioned the afternoon before?

Sandy looked over and saw them. "What have you got there?" he whispered.

I was thinking furiously. Then all at once I made up my mind. I handed him the flashlight and got a grip on Paris's revolver which I had kept ever since I had picked it up when he threw it away.

"Get over by the door and be ready to make tracks," I said quietly. "We're going to have fireworks. And how!"

When he had taken his position I turned to the milling mob of ghouls around Horston's corpse. I said loudly, "I don't think you'll find what you're looking for."

They didn't pause. Julian flung over his shoulder, "You keep out of this, Graine." The words were thick. "This is not any business of yours."

I clutched the papers tightly. "I may be wrong, but I think these make it my business."

The words penetrated. As one, they turned. Ambrosia took one look at what I was holding and went white to the lips. "Julian! Beale!" she cried. "He's got them."

The two men did not need her words. Porter's face was a sickly green. He looked close to fainting. Thorndyke, however, was far from it. He held out his hand.

"Those don't belong to you, Graine." His voice was like steel darts. "Give them to me."

Shoving them into my pocket, I edged back toward the door. "If I recall correctly, they belonged to Madame Grazie. Which gives me as much right to them as you have." I took another step. "I think I'll just keep them for reference."

"You'll give them to me, Graine." Thorndyke began to move toward me.

It was, I felt, time for action. Julian had got control of himself and was standing shoulder to shoulder with the doctor. Ambrosia Swisshome's face was living fury. I whipped out the revolver, trained it on them.

"I'm keeping them, Thorndyke," I said stoutly. "Furthermore, I'm going up to my room. If any of you come to your senses and want to talk this thing out like intelligent human beings, I'll be glad to oblige. Otherwise, I'm sure the police will be as interested in these papers as you are."

I backed out of the room, kicked the door shut.

25

IN OUR ROOM I handed Sandy the revolver.

"Sit on the bed facing the door," I said. "If anyone tries to rush us, use the gun. I'm going to see what's so damned important about these papers or I'm going to die in the attempt."

He sat down a little sheepishly. "I can't see what's so dangerous about that bunch," he grumbled. "I feel like a fool, hiding from Panty-Waist."

"So?" I said no more.

I am no coward but if I ever saw stark naked menace in human eyes I had seen it downstairs as those people moved in on me. It wasn't a comforting sight. They meant to have Marina's papers, and if I could read signs rightly, they intended to stop at nothing to get them. Even murder. Or should I say, another murder? My experience with crimes of violence is not extensive, but it seemed logical that anyone who has successfully carried off two murders would not split hairs over engineering two more. I was taking no chances.

For I was firmly convinced now that Caruso Horston's death was no accident. I tried to be open-minded about it. After all, he might have misjudged distances in the dark and run into the railing. But I rather thought not. The railing was strong. It had been built into what had been planned—madly or not—as a home. A good round amount of momentum would have been required to go through it. Even if Horston could, as Paris had said, see in the dark, he would not have been running fast enough to smash through it.

The only other way it could have happened was through a quick, powerful shove.

Paris's story lent weight to the idea. I can't say I swallowed his whole recital, but at least part of it held together. I had demonstrated, to my own satisfaction, that Horston was not the murderer. Paris maintained the same thing. I had no doubt, now, that Horston had seen the crime committed while peering through the window. Just as I had no doubt that, having come to Lucifer's Pride for the purpose of filching the diamond, he would not balk at a little polite blackmail of the murderer to obtain it. Marina Grazie meant nothing to him. That she was dead meant less than nothing. It was the diamond he wanted. If he had to shield the murderer to get it, I had no doubt he would.

I thought I could see what had occurred during that rendezvous on the silent, dark third floor.

Having made arrangements to meet the murderer there—after all, if he held his conversation with Paris during the search, he could likewise have communicated with the criminal—he had hidden himself in one of the deserted, half-finished rooms up there. Then after everyone had retired and the second floor was quiet, he had crept out and kept his appointment. There was no danger of interruption except for the very unlikely possibility that someone would run out of wood and come upstairs to lay in another supply.

Anyway, they met. Probably in total darkness, since neither would care to risk lighting a candle. Horston made his demand: the diamond in exchange for his silence. The murderer probably quibbled, demanded proof. To supply it, Horston would take out the papers.

"You see," I could almost hear him say. "You couldn't find the key. But I found it. I saw where it fell when you pulled the diamond off. Now do you believe me?"

I imagined the murderer's eyes lighting up with a sudden flash of inspiration. There were the precious papers. There was the sole witness to Marina's murder. Why not? It could be done in two lightning, simultaneous movements: a quick, purposeful push with one hand . . . a driving grab with the other . . . and the thing was done. Two birds with one stone.

It was a beautiful plan. It deserved to work. But didn't. The first part came off successfully, but in the darkness the murderer must have misjudged distances. Or perhaps a reflex movement caused Horston to jerk his arm up suddenly in a wild attempt to regain his balance. Whatever it was, the murderer had missed. His hand grazed Horston's causing the deep scratch I had seen, and instead of the papers he found himself holding thin air.

The thing had failed. Caruso had gone through the railing and down, the papers with him. The cry that echoed through the darkness had been his only sound before he crashed and his neck snapped.

There had been no opportunity to retrieve them immediately. My sudden appearance beside the body had killed that hope. There had been nothing to do but wait.

I looked down at them. They and the Lucifer diamond had brought death to Marina and Caruso Horston. Now that I had them, would I be the next?

Sandy's voice broke into my reflections. "Do you believe that mugg's story, Tony?"

"Parts of it," I said abstractedly, without taking my eyes from the packet. Somehow, now that I had it, I felt a curious reluctance to open it. What would it contain?

"Thorndyke made a good point," Sandy said. "It could have been Paris."

"Yes. As well as any of the rest of them."

He fidgeted, twiddling the revolver. Finally he burst out, "For God's sake, Tony, aren't you ever going to open the blasted things? If you haven't any curiosity, I've got enough for two."

Curiosity? I smiled at that. Sheer, unmitigated curiosity had gotten me into the thing in the first place. I recalled the first time I had felt a twinge of it. It had been at the airport when Elena Grazie had appeared in the door of the plane and Julian and Beale had almost come to blows. I had wondered then what it was all about.

Murder Ends the Song

The other things, too: Marina's Wagnerian rage at poor Nero over the publicity . . . the imprint of Marina's hand on Ambrosia's face . . . the note that had caused her collapse at the hotel . . . the blood on the floor of her dressing room and the scrawled words on the mirror: all those puzzling bits raced through my mind.

Curiosity? I wished suddenly I hadn't had quite so much. As Thorndyke had said, the papers did not concern me. What business was it of mine? Mightn't it be wiser just to take the unopened parcel downstairs and throw it, like a bone, to the desperate group down there to dispose of as they chose? Pandora, I seemed to recall, would have been much happier if she had left a certain box unopened.

Sandy nudged me. "Tony, I'm going to go bats if you don't open that pretty soon."

Well, Pandora lifted the lid. Bluebeard's wives opened the forbidden door. I pulled the rubber bands off the package and shuffled through the papers.

In *Lohengrin*, Elsa, a fool if there ever was one, spends two acts brooding over what her husband's name is. Instead of enjoying her honeymoon like a sensible girl, she dashes around in circles, pestering the poor man until it's a marvel he even knows it himself. By the time she breaks him down she has built up such a monomania about it that she probably expects to find out he is the reincarnation of Alexander the Great. Instead, she discovers (a) that he is a knight, which she must have known already, and (b) that his name is Lohengrin. So what? I ask you.

All of which is by way of pointing out that her let-down could not have been more complete than mine. After all the fuss and furor, I expected nothing less than the plans for a death-ray or a map of Cocos Island with explicit instructions for locating the buried treasure.

What did I find?

When I had arranged the collection, it resolved itself into three piles: legal documents and papers; newspaper clippings; and letters minus their envelopes. With Sandy peering avidly over my shoulder I went through them all, one by one, making a complete listing on the back of the footprint drawing.

Here is the list, without comment.

LEGAL DOCUMENTS

(1) An old contract with the Metropolitan Opera Company, signed by Marina and Gatti-Casazza. By its terms Marina was understood to be prepared to undertake the coloratura roles in *Mignon, Rigoletto, Lucia, Il Barbiere, Lakmé, Dinorah*, and *Zauberflöte*, for each performance of which she was to receive twelve hundred dollars.

(2) A thirteen-week contract with the Conch Oil Company for a weekly broadcast at three hundred dollars a week.

(3) A contract with Anatole Gaul, calling for appearances with the Monte Calvo Company in Portland, Oregon, and Seattle, Tacoma, and Spokane, Washington. Roles: Lucia, Rosina, and Gilda. Salary: eighty-five dollars a week.

(4) A birth certificate. Name of child: Elena Grazie Marsh. Date of birth: September 23, 1919. Place of birth: New York City. Mother: Rachel Marsh. Father: Blank.

(5) An inventory of jewelry totaling one hundred and seventy-five thousand dollars.

(6) A savings account pass-book from the Golden State Trust and Savings Bank of Los Angeles, showing a balance of two hundred and fifteen thousand dollars and some odd cents.

(7) A will, dated three months previously, leaving her estate to Elena Grazie "provided said Elena Grazie never marries." Otherwise the entire estate was to be devoted to the purchase of Lucifer's Pride from the heirs of Lucifer Bollman, the remodeling of the building into a museum and theatre, and the establishment therein of "The Marina Grazie Festival of Italian Opera."

NEWSPAPER CLIPPINGS

(1) Bundles of press notices in all languages concerning Marina's appearances in her various roles.

Murder Ends the Song 163

(2) A story about a Dr. Scott Newell who had been dismissed from his hospital in disgrace for performing an operation while drunk.

(3) An account of the killing in a Kansas City bordello of a cattleman named Rufus Gore. The establishment, called "Glory's" had been closed by the police but Glory herself and the man who had done the shooting in her room had escaped before the officers arrived.

(4) A clipping in Spanish concerning the smashing of a drug-ring in Mexico City. A peddler of the stuff, one Juan Portales, had betrayed the gang to the police and then disappeared, leaving no clues as to his whereabouts.

LETTERS

(1) A letter written in longhand without date or salutation. It read: "Your urgent communication received. Herewith bank draft for five thousand ($5,000) dollars." It was signed by Lucifer Bollman.

(2) Five other undated letters, all alike, all reading: "Herewith bank draft for twenty-five thousand ($25,000) dollars." All were signed by Lucifer Bollman.

(3) A much creased, jaggedly torn piece of wrapping paper on which were printed the words, "God help you, Marina Grazie". It bore the signature, in blocked letters, "Caro Nome".

(4) A crumpled sheet of note paper from the Hotel Olympia, Portland, Oregon. The message on it was printed. In pencil. "Caro Nome", it read.

That was all.

I looked at Sandy. He looked at me. And made the obvious comment.

"The old girl was crazy."

I picked up the papers one by one and straightened them into a rough bundle.

"She must have been," he went on. "The Marina Grazie Festival of Italian Opera! For Chrissake!"

I said nothing.

"What's the matter? What's eating you?"

I sighed. "I give up. I thought that once we'd laid hands on these things everything would be clear. After all, we know how both the murders were committed. All I want to know is why. And all I get is this mess of junk."

"It seems to me there're plenty of leads there," he said seriously. "Maybe it's just that we can't figure them out."

"Brilliantly put, Watson," I said sarcastically. "The trouble is, my brain's so tired I couldn't add two and two on my fingers."

The fire was burning low. Except for an occasional crackle to indicate that its spirit was willing, there was no sound except the moaning of the wind. I got up and threw a few more pieces of wood on the embers.

"Speaking of fingers," he complained, "mine are getting numb to the elbow. How long do I have to hold this piece of artillery?"

I sat down again. "Until they come."

"What the hell makes you so sure anyone's coming?"

"I just have a feeling that—what did I tell you?"

A knock, loud as the crack of doom, had sounded from the door.

Instantly Sandy perked up, aimed the revolver. "Shall I shoot first or—"

"Come in," I called.

The door opened.

By all that was holy, it was Ambrosia Swisshome.

26

My weariness left me at the sight of her. I had naturally supposed it would be one of the men: Thorndyke breathing fire, or Julian attempting to follow Lady Macbeth's advice by looking like the innocent flower but being the serpent underneath.

But Ambrosia! I couldn't have been more surprised if Elsa Maxwell had rolled in.

She closed the door carefully and walked over to the fire. Sandy put on a look of alert intelligence, like a watchdog determined to do his duty, and trained the revolver on her. I took a firmer grip on the papers.

She noted our movements and then turned, quite indifferently, to spread her bony hands out to the warmth. Over her shoulder she said, "There is nothing to worry about, Anthony. You may not believe me but our interest in the papers has ceased for the moment."

She paused.

"And you, Mr. Sands, won't you please put away that ridiculous weapon? You look like a homicidal Buddha."

Sandy flushed, uncrossed his legs hurriedly, and dropped the gun on the bed. He barely stifled the unchivalrous epithet that rose to his lips.

As for myself, I was frankly bewildered by this new twist to the affair. Obviously, she was quite sincere, for after her first quick glance at the papers, she had ignored them completely. Bewildered, did I say? I was flabbergasted. What had caused this sudden about-face? What devious scheme had that crew hatched out after Sandy and I had left them?

To test her I threw the papers carelessly to one side. They fell to the floor with a muffled slap. I waited.

Ambrosia toasted her hands. "That was a very melodramatic little scene you staged downstairs," she remarked presently.

I smiled. "Like a bit out of *Tosca*, wasn't it? But there come times, you understand."

"Yes, of course," she hastened to agree. "We did behave like badly brought up pigs."

Sandy couldn't take it any longer. "This," he pronounced with disgust, "sounds like third-rate Noel Coward. Will someone wake me when the final curtain falls?"

She turned then. The wry smile that seemed so much a part of her played about her thin lips. "You are quite right, Mr. Sands. It would be stupid to continue like this any longer. And do please leave that gun alone."

He jerked his hand back as if she had flicked a live coal on it.

"May I sit down, Anthony?" she said. "I'd like to talk to you."

I got up from my chair and sat on the bed beside Sandy. I should add that I kept my foot in readiness to drop it on the papers if she made an overt move.

But she didn't. She sat down, plaited her fingers under her bony chin and regarded the fire. I found myself admiring her no end. It was three in the morning. Except for a possible hour's nap before Caruso Horston was thrown to his death, she had had no rest since early the morning before. Violence and death, strain and excitement had loaded the intervening hours. She had even played the part of a packhorse in the bucket-brigade from the wood-room on the third floor. She might even—

And yet there she was, grim but perfect; she had found a comb since I had seen her last and not a hair of her cropped, waved head was out of place. Her hands were steady; her voice, clipped and precise, displayed no sign of fatigue. Erect and controlled, she sat there, and the eyes which turned to me were frank and candid. She was magnificent.

"You're wondering why I have come bursting into your bedroom at this ghastly hour, Anthony?" It was said almost casually.

"I supposed . . . the papers . . . but you say . . ."

"In a way, the papers are involved."

"There you see, Tony," Sandy broke in excitedly. "It's a trap. Thorndyke and Porter are probably out in the hall now, just waiting till we're off guard."

She shook her head.

"Sorry to disillusion you, Mr. Sands. Beale and Julian have both gone to bed. Everyone but me has retired. I tried to, but I couldn't sleep. Downstairs we decided we would not approach you, Anthony, until morning. But I—I had to come tonight. You see, there is a favor I want to ask of you. A very, very great favor."

Beneath the gravity of her voice there was a faint pleading note, pathetic yet dignified, that impressed me. Yet I steeled myself against it. I could not forget the tricks that had been played on me during the past day and night.

I said cautiously, "Yes, Miss Swisshome?"

She made a gesture of understanding. "You are right to be suspicious, Anthony. We have treated you very shabbily. But that is over now. You have read Marina's papers, and you know now, of course, what was behind our behavior. Or at least enough to indicate that we had good and sufficient reason for what we did. And you must see, too, that there was nothing personal in our efforts to keep the papers from you. You were simply an outsider. Any outsider. We were only attempting to protect what few shreds of pride we have left to us."

Now, of course, I know what she was talking about. Then I was as bewildered as Sandy, and he sat there with his mouth unashamedly open. I might have confessed my ignorance. I might have told her that I had barely finished reading the collection and had had no time to reason anything out. But something told me that if I did that, her flow of words would come to an abrupt halt.

So I avoided Sandy's reproachful eyes and said, "I understand."

"I am not," she went on, "familiar with everything that was in the box. I'm not even interested in anything that does not concern me. Unlike Julian, I have never made inquiries."

"Julian has?" I followed her lead.

Her lip curled. "Julian shared a great many secrets with Marina. More than any of the rest of us. They were two of a kind, if you know what I mean."

I didn't, but I said, "I see."

"You think you do, perhaps." Bitterness overflowed her voice. "But no one who has not lived with Marina as we have, who has not been under her domination day in and day out, could know what it really means. But I knew her. Right down to the ground. God knows, I had more opportunity than most." Her fingers contracted. "And I tell you, Anthony, that if anyone ever deserved to die horribly, violently—that one was Marina."

She paused, made an effort to control herself. "You see now why your efforts to discover who killed her left us all completely cold. It must have seemed heartless to you. But we knew her as she really was. And there wasn't one of us who couldn't have sung for joy over her death. There wasn't one of us who was not capable of killing her and feeling no more regret than if we had crushed the head of a snake."

The words hung, tumid with hatred, on the still air. In them was even a kind of fiendish triumph that chilled my blood, that compressed the lungs and made breathing a conscious effort. I had thought the scene I had overheard in the hotel was evil enough. But this surpassed it. I found myself looking down at my hands. They were shaking.

But she seemed unaware of having said anything extraordinary. Her attitude implied that it was the truth and that this truth was its own justification. When she spoke again she was quite calm.

"I have never been able to understand why Lucifer Bollman didn't murder her himself. Sometimes I used to think he was on the point of it." She shrugged. "But I suppose when it came to the actual doing, he couldn't muster the strength."

I stared. "You knew Lucifer Bollman?"

She smiled a little. "Only too well. I was his secretary for three years. From 1916 to 1919. That is how I found out about Marina's blackmailing him."

Blackmail! That was the explanation of the letters beginning, "Herewith bank draft—." Yet I might have known. From what I had read of old Lucifer, he was not exactly the type to toss cheques for twenty-five thousand around promiscuously. I could imagine how the old pinch-penny must have writhed at the sums Marina had milked him for. Two hundred and fifteen thousand, the savings account book showed. A small fortune. And God knew how much more she had had from him during her heyday when she had lived so lavishly that her income from singing engagements could not have begun to cover the bills.

I thought of the Lucifer diamond, the "ransom" she had mentioned so coyly. Could it have been that, tired of playing for comparatively small stakes, she had decided to marry the aging wheat-king? That would explain his building the massive old rookery we were now in. Perhaps he had written her of his plans, describing the place. That would have been enough for Marina. Never one to hide her radiance behind a barrel, even one as ostentatious as Lucifer's Pride, she had backed out, settling for the diamond.

Light dawned. At this late date I began to feel that I was actually getting acquainted with Marina Grazie.

Ambrosia was watching my mental struggles quizzically. I think she must have guessed what was going through my mind.

"Don't tell me you were taken in by that 'sentimental pilgrimage' story of hers, Anthony? But then you didn't know her well enough. Marina always covered her unpleasantness with a cloak of superficial sentiment. Lady Bountiful was one of her most effective roles."

Her voice hardened. "Her real reason for coming here was to gloat over old dead Lucifer and the neat way she had escaped the trap he had set for her."

I saw it all now. I had been brought along to play the part of her admiring audience. Suddenly I remembered her outraged anger when, during her sentimental peroration in the library, someone had said, "Madame is a fool." No, she wouldn't like that. It meant that someone was getting out of hand. So she had nipped the rebellion in the bud by ordering them out into the hall. The cold and discomfort would soon whip them back into line.

"But what," I asked, "did she have on Bollman?"

She shrugged. "You've read the clippings. Can't you put two and two together? You can't laugh off a murder charge."

Murder charge? Clipping? I thought back. "There was only one item concerned with murder," I said. "You're not asking me to believe that Bollman was the man who killed that cattleman?"

"Why not? It happens to be true."

I simply couldn't believe it. It was incredible. For another thought had occurred to me. If Lucifer Bollman had paid blackmail to Marina, then—then—

Sandy yelped. "By God! Marina Grazie was that woman named Glory. She would know about it because it happened in her room. And it was Glory who escaped with Bollman before the police came."

"Of course," Ambrosia said imperturbably. "I thought you had figured that out. Marina helped him get away and then bled him in return for her help. It was he who sent her abroad to study, who financed her career in the beginning."

Dazed, I ran my fingers through my hair. Marina! Running a house called "Glory's"! I couldn't understand it. And said so.

"Ran it!" Ambrosia scoffed. "She owned it. It was profitable, she told me once. But Lucifer Bollman was a gold mine."

I gave up. Nothing, I felt, could surprise me after that. I said feebly: "If you were working as Bollman's secretary how did you happen to join Marina's household?"

A shadow crossed her face. "Mr. Bollman took me to New York with him in 1919. While we were there he suddenly decided to—to dispense with my services. I had no money, no place to go. I knew no one—except Marina, who was singing at the Metropolitan by that time. You see, I had learned of her hold on Mr. Bollman and I thought—I decided—"

"You decided to play Marina's own game?"

Her sallow cheeks reddened. "Well, why not? I was no longer young. I was desperate. And so I went to her and told her the facts. She took me on as combination secretary and whipping-boy."

"Whipping-boy?"

"Yes. Just that. It was part of my job to bear her ill-temper, her rages, her fits of sadism. It was part of the job of anyone who accepted Marina's bounty."

"Why didn't you leave her when you found how unpleasant it was?"

She lifted her hands, dropped them hopelessly in her lap. "Why didn't Beale? Julian? Elena? Because we couldn't. And she knew we couldn't. She made it impossible to escape."

I couldn't understand it. "But how?" I asked.

"I don't know what her hold over Beale and Julian was. You have seen her papers; perhaps you do. I know two reasons why Elena stayed. And I know why I did."

"I still don't see how she could keep four human beings in virtual slavery," I said. "After all, this is the twentieth century."

Suddenly she looked very tired. "For others, perhaps, Anthony. But not for Marina. She was pure *quatrocento*. She should have been a Borgia."

She stood up, pressed one hand against the mantel.

"And now I come to the favor I want to ask of you." She touched the packet on the floor with the toe of her slipper.

I thought, "Hold your hats, boys; here we go!" Flippant, yes. But necessary. For in spite of myself I discovered I was moved by her words. I had to put a stop to that. I picked up the papers and shoved them in my pocket.

"Yes, Ambrosia?" I said.

She ignored my calculated gesture. "I know you are planning to give these papers to the police. But before you do, I want you to give me that birth certificate."

"Why should I, Ambrosia?"

"Because"—she looked straight into my eyes—"you are not cruel and inhuman, Anthony. And because if you stop and think you will realize that if the police see it, Elena will find out about it. And you, being you, would not want that to happen."

"You mean she doesn't know—"

She shook her head. "Elena is very young, Anthony. There is much she doesn't know. Ever since she came to live with Marina I have tried to protect her. Marina gave her no affection. I gave her all I could. She thinks her father and mother are dead."

"I see," I said slowly. "But I'll have to think it over. I can't make up my mind in an instant."

"Very well." She moved to the door like an angular wraith. "I'll ask you again in the morning. You will think about it?"

"Yes."

Her fingers closed over the knob. "Remember that it would only be raking up a scandal that would ruin Elena's life and accomplish nothing. Lucifer Bollman is dead. Marina is dead. You will see that I am right."

What was that she had said? Bollman?

"Ambrosia! Do you mean—"

She turned. The grey eyes, infinitely weary, regarded me. "Lucifer Bollman was Elena's father," she said dispassionately.

The door opened.

I swallowed. "And Rachel Marsh? That was—"

Once more the eyes swept over me. "Marina and Bollman are both dead," she repeated. "Let them remain so, Anthony."

27

Sleep was impossible.

At Sandy's insistence, I finally spread myself out on the bed and tried to follow my usual procedure for drifting off—going through, note by note, the score of Massenet's *Thais*, to my way of thinking the dullest opera ever written. (I once forced myself to memorize it as an exercise in discipline.)

Nothing happened. Thais, whom I always pictured as Maria Jeritza, because she had sung the role the only time I was ever unfortunate enough to hear it, kept getting herself confused with Marina Grazie. The courtesan's chamber in Alexandria looked disturbingly like the library at Lucifer's Pride, and the silver statue of Eros on its pedestal became Marina's purple angel-bottle perched on the piano.

That last was the final straw. I couldn't see why I kept thinking of that bottle.

I know now that my subconscious was attempting to thrust the obvious into my mind. I know, too, that if I had put in a little good hard concentration on why I was remembering it I might have taken a long step toward solving the riddle right then and there.

At the time, though, I merely thought I was losing my mind, kicked both Eros and the angel-bottle out, and thought, "I will go to sleep . . . I will go to sleep . . ."

But I couldn't.

I kept worrying about the answer I should have to give Ambrosia when morning came.

I had tried to get some help from Sandy. What did he think I should do?

Punching up his pillow, he had burrowed his head into it with a luxurious groan. "Whatever you decide is O.K. with me," was his contribution.

"But do you think Ambrosia could have done those murders?" I persisted.

"Anyone of 'em *could* have done 'em. Even old Maggie Tait." He flopped over with his back to me. "You can't get me into it that way, Tony. You're the one that wanted to be the detective. Pleasant dreams."

Pleasant dreams, hell!

I began on *Thais* again. This time I couldn't even get the right notes. The page from *Rigoletto* kept intruding itself into the Massenet score. That was bad enough. But when Thais began singing her invocation to love, holding not the statue of Eros but a boutonniere of yarn flowers with the Lucifer diamond, like a gigantic dewdrop, in the center, I couldn't stand it any more.

I got up, pulled on the rest of my clothes, and sneaked out of the room. Perhaps I could think better down in the library. Certainly I couldn't think worse.

The corridor was as quiet as a tomb. And as dark. I wished I had remembered Tait's flashlight, but it couldn't be helped now. I groped my way blindly to the stairway, hearing far above me the fierce fingers of the wind scrabbling at the panes of the skylight. Whenever a tired board creaked under me my heart thudded. If I hadn't had so much on my mind I'd have been scared to death.

It was like a mausoleum on the first floor. A slit of light shone from under the library door. The candles were still burning around the opera singer and the operatic yegg.

I expected to find the room deserted. Instead I was surprised to see a figure sitting before the fire, moodily staring into the crimson and gold flames. It was Beale Thorndyke.

"Hullo, Graine," he greeted me. "Come down to keep a deathwatch?" There was neither surprise nor resentment in his voice. He was merely being polite.

I went over to the chesterfields, suddenly curious as to whether I could find any resemblance between the dead woman and her daughter. Looking down into Marina's face, I had to confess I could see little. Elena's features were delicate, chiseled, cameo-like. Marina's, even allowing for the disparity in years and weight, were gross and sensual. The thick, flaring nostrils and full lips, the broad cheekbones, the heavy-lidded eyes—they were as different from the girl's as—to coin a cliché—night from day.

More puzzled than ever, I pulled up a chair beside Thorndyke and sat down before the fire. Presently I offered him a cigarette. We lighted up and smoked in silence.

"I've been talking to Ambrosia," I said after a while. "She told me some very interesting things."

"So?"

Obviously he wanted to talk about as much as Sandy had. But I wanted to. And I meant to.

"I've seen the papers, too."

"So?"

"Are you as uninterested in them now as Ambrosia is?"

"Not knowing how she feels about it, I couldn't say."

This, I thought, could go on forever. I decided to blast. I said, "But you are mildly concerned about Dr. Scott Newell, aren't you?"

His fingers were steady as he flicked the cigarette away. Only the sudden pulsing of the vein in his temple indicated that my shot in the dark had hit the bull's-eye.

"Dr. Scott Newell was a fool," he said in his clipped voice. "A fool and a weakling." He turned to me. "And you can go back now and tell Julian I've had enough blackmail for one lifetime."

I raised an eyebrow. "I haven't seen Julian since I left you all down here."

His mirthless laugh called me a liar as neatly as if he had said the word.

"That's as may be. But if you should happen to see him when you go back upstairs, you might tell him I have no intention of jumping out of the frying-pan into the fire. Marina's death freed me. I'm not letting Julian Porter put any chains back on me. Tell him that I'm going to tell Elena the truth tomorrow and let her decide for herself."

The truth? What truth? Did that remark about Marina's death and freedom mean what it seemed to mean? Was he telling me in so many words that he had killed Marina?

He must have read my mind.

"No, Graine, I'm not confessing to murder. I'm merely saying that tomorrow I'm going to tell Elena all about a young coward named Scott Newell and then I'm going to ask her to marry me. Is that clear?"

It was. Marina's hold over him was also clear.

I said, "It seems to me you've taken a long time to reach that decision."

He said nothing.

"Why didn't you tell Marina to go to hell? You made a mistake once. So what? Lots of other people have too, but they've managed to survive. Would you really have married her?"

He was silent for a long while. Studying the flame. Then he began to talk. As if he were thinking aloud. As if he were carrying on with a soliloquy I had interrupted.

"I don't know," he said. "That's what I've been sitting here thinking about. Now that she's dead, it seems to me I wouldn't have. And yet . . . if she were alive, I suppose . . . I don't know. You couldn't understand unless you'd lived around Marina. No one could. Not unless you'd ever had her talons fastened in you."

He got up and began pacing the floor, pouring out his monolog.

"She picked me up when I was down and out. In Havana, that was. She bought me a drink and I told her about my—about what had happened. We had a lot more. Too many. . . . And that's how I became Dr. Beale Thorndyke, personal physician to a great opera star."

He uttered a bitter laugh.

"Oh, yes, I pulled myself together . . . cut out drinking entirely. I was grateful. I thought it was my second chance. There was only one thing wrong with it. I wasn't a physician. I could have been, but Marina didn't want that. Little things, yes. I dosed her with laxatives and sprayed her throat when she thought she was taking cold. Once I even set Julian's leg when he broke it trying to play polo. But that was all."

He paused, looking down at me with tortured, unseeing eyes.

"Marina didn't want a physician. All she wanted was another gigolo. That's what I was. That's all I've ever been. Julian, too. That's all we both were. That's all she wanted."

The eyes suddenly focused, as if seeing me for the first time. "She was a bitch, Graine. No one will ever know how I loathed her."

I didn't know what to say. Yet after Ambrosia's story, this shouldn't have surprised me too much. If I had used my eyes and my imagination, I might have guessed the truth long ago.

I felt I ought to say something. Again I asked, "But why didn't you leave her if you hated her so?"

It was as if I had thrown a switch and signaled all-clear ahead. He turned away and once more began his restless pacing.

"Don't think I didn't try to. At first. But I still remembered my disgrace. I was a coward. I couldn't face things. Afterwards I . . . it was as if I didn't have any will left. Ask Ambrosia. Ask Julian. Even Elena. There was something about Marina. Once she got hold of you she sucked you dry, beat and stamped on your pride until you had nothing left . . . no initiative . . . no anything. And so you simply followed along . . . obeying . . . taking whatever she chose to deal out to you . . ."

Of itself it was difficult to believe. Added to Ambrosia's story it became credible. Puppets have no life of their own. They move only when the strings are pulled.

A note of raw agony came into Thorndyke's voice. It sank to a whisper.

"And then, as if things weren't bad enough, I had to fall in love with Elena. I gathered up what little manhood I had and went to Marina . . . told her I wanted to marry Elena. At first she wouldn't believe me. When I insisted, she flew into a rage that congealed the blood in my veins. But I was desperate. I told her I was going to tell Elena the truth about myself. For a minute I thought I had got the upper hand. She didn't say anything . . . just looked at me."

Sweat stood out on his forehead. All his reserve was gone. To give him a moment to pull himself together I said, "Why didn't you? If Elena loved you she would have forgiven you, I should think. And if you told her the truth, Marina's hold over you would be gone."

The laugh he gave was almost a sob.

"You didn't know Marina. But you've seen the papers. You've seen the certificate . . ."

I gasped.

Thorndyke kicked a chair. It fell over with a crash. "She said the day I asked Elena to marry me she would tell her everything."

The vindictive, raging despair in his voice was so violent that I wondered Marina didn't cower in death. I could understand Thorndyke's feelings, the feelings he must have had at that moment. For instead of breaking loose from her, he had only bound himself up tighter. He had only given her another weapon to hold over him.

Suddenly Thorndyke turned to face her where she lay.

"But she's dead now, Graine," he cried. The triumph in his voice was almost obscene. "She's dead now and rotting in hell, I hope. And we're free of her."

Free? I wondered. "How about Julian?" I said.

His hand clenched. "Just let Julian try to stand in my way. Just let him try!"

28

I AWOKE AT SEVEN-THIRTY after as troubled a three-hour nap as I'd wish my worst enemy. A dirty, grey half-light pushed through the slit between the drawn draperies at the window. The wind still howled.

Sandy was up and out of the room. When he had risen I didn't know, but the replenished pile of firewood on the hearth was a monument to his early morning industry. I had heard nothing of his comings and goings. Either he had been remarkably quiet at his chores or I had slept more soundly than I thought.

The idea of getting up depressed me. It would be cold every place. And the bed was warm. Besides, some of the others might also be up and about, and my disinclination to meet any of them amounted to a positive passion.

So, postponing the inevitable as long as possible, I relaxed and thought.

First of all, there was Thorndyke, and the tragic, stupid, pathetic story of Dr. Scott Newell. Oh, yes, he had told me the whole thing. Later on. When he had calmed down a bit. He had seemed eager to pour it out to someone—probably to hear how it would sound to Elena. I, feeling somewhat like the Father-Confessor to a hag-ridden young monk, let him pour.

Newell—or Thorndyke, as you may choose to call him—had emerged from medical school as guileless and eager as a young Parsifal, crammed to the gullet with Hippocratic ideals and burning with naive zeal to be of service to mankind. How he managed to retain it all through his years of study I don't know. I've known a few medical students and interns in my short life and I defy you to find a more sophisticated, disillusioned, earthy crew on God's green earth. How Thorndyke escaped the infection is neither here nor there, however. The fact remains that he did. It also explains to a certain extent his reactions when disaster overtook him.

His internship behind him, he had landed a post as assistant resident physician in a hospital in a smallish town in Maryland. It was a good post. The hospital, one of the numerous benisons of the ubiquitous PWA, was new and beautifully equipped. The patients liked their young doctor. He had been completely happy.

When influenza broke out in the town he had plunged into the battle with banner high, on duty for twenty-four hours out of twenty-four with only catnaps snatched at stray intervals. At the peak of the epidemic he had been on his feet for fifty-six hours without rest. When at last he was relieved he had been, as he put it, "too tired to go to sleep." And so in a desperate effort to relax his nerves he had bunged into a bottle of bourbon.

"I guess I wasn't used to the stuff," he told me at that point. "Anyway, it hit me like a Big Bertha. I went out like a light."

Half an hour later he had been called to perform an emergency operation on a postman who had skidded on an icy street and given himself concussion of the brain.

"But didn't you realize what condition you were in?" I asked, dumbfounded.

"Vaguely," he answered. "I was rather like a fire-horse when the alarm sounds, I guess. There was a job to be done and no one but me to do it. Besides, I had never failed myself before. I thought that once I was in the operating room everything would clear up."

That time, though, his luck had deserted him. Even as he told me of it, his face grew pale as paper. He mopped his damp forehead.

"I botched the operation," he said simply. "The man died. The anesthetist felt it her duty to explain to the hospital authorities. The bottle was found in my room, half empty. And I was out. Wrecked." He gave a deep sigh. "You know the rest."

That had been four years ago. "The rest," I knew, meant Marina.

There was, though, this much to be said for her: she had picked up a disreputable wreck from a Havana waterfront dive and remoulded it into at least the semblance of a self-respecting man. The trouble was that in the process she had excised the integrity and pride and fundamental manhood of the man as efficiently as a chef bones a fowl.

Lying there in bed that morning, I felt that if ever a man had provocation to murder, Beale Thorndyke was he.

But had he? Had he done it?

I could see that Marina was the stumbling-block to Thorndyke's happiness since that now depended on Elena. With Marina out of the way, the coast would be clear. Had he in desperation removed the obstacle? And then finding himself confronted by another in the form of Caruso Horston, had he removed it also?

What was the answer? I didn't know.

My thoughts turned to that indomitable spinster, Ambrosia Swisshome. What of her?

The case against her seemed less conclusive, since as far as I knew there was no motive except hatred for Marina. But remembering her grim, relentless face as she said, "If anyone ever deserved to die horribly, violently, it was Marina," I felt I shouldn't minimize the goading force of that hatred. Pushed too far, inflamed too greatly, it could, I was certain, be as capable and efficient as Thorndyke's cold loathing.

There was, too, Ambrosia's affection for Elena. If she knew of Marina's threat to reveal everything to the girl, might not that same affection force her to go to any lengths for Elena's protection? I thought it might.

As far as the mechanics of the thing were concerned, Ambrosia could, as I had pointed out in the kitchen, have handled it all very satisfactorily. She was strong enough to have driven the needle into Marina's brain. Taken unawares in the dark, Caruso Horston would have been—I can't resist the pun—a pushover.

Yes, the spinster could have done it. But why? I had the feeling that somewhere along the line I had either lost or missed a link.

Then suddenly I knew what it was.

Marina was a blackmailer. She blackmailed everyone. Consequently she must have blackmailed Ambrosia, for if the spinster remained with her, hating her as she did, it was logical that there was some whip held over her head, too.

What was it?

Only then did I realize that during her talk with me Ambrosia had touched on everything but the reason why she had remained with Marina.

I flung back the covers and got into my clothes. Before I gave up any of Marina's documents I was going to have another talk with Ambrosia Swisshome.

29

SANDY CAME IN as I was tying my shoe-laces. He had, he informed me, been stoking the fire in the library and helping Maggie Tait get things going in the kitchen.

"She's a winsome old battle-axe," he said, sprawling on the bed with his customary languor. "She even persuaded me to go outside in this hellish weather and gather icicles off the window sills for her."

"Icicles!" I almost snapped a lace. "In God's name, what for?"

He crossed his legs and waved a nonchalant foot in my face.

"Tait's indigestion," he chortled. "What with two corpses and a murderer running around the place, the Tait stomach isn't what it should be. When it aches, it wants hot water. *Voila!*"

"But I still don't see . . ."

He sighed. "All tenors are morons! Look, I draw a blue print. There is no water in Lucifer's Pride. Tait must have hot water. Icicles can be made into hot water. Catch on?"

"You fool," I grumbled. "You'll catch your death going out in this sub-zero weather."

After I'd said it I must confess I choked a little over that. For I had had that same thought when I had opened the door of the library—was it only yesterday?—and found Marina dead on the piano bench.

I decided not to think about that. So while I put on my vest and coat I told him about Beale Thorndyke. Not in detail. Just a *précis*. As I talked the foot that had been waggling so jauntily became quiet. By the time I had finished, he was sitting up.

"That sounds bad, Tony." His cadaverous face was grave. "Do you suppose Porter really does know enough to try to carry on where Madame left off?"

"I haven't any idea," I said grimly. "But I've got a feeling we're teetering on the edge of a volcano." I gave the knot of my tie a vicious twist. "This isn't going to be a simple day to live through."

I had no idea how close the eruption was. It just seemed that things couldn't go on like this forever, heaving and boiling under the surface. Sooner or later the crust would break. I had no intense desire to be around when it did.

As for my second prediction, I should set myself up in business as a male Cassandra. I'll never forget that day as long as I live.

It began immediately.

In fact, at that moment there came a knock at the door. I looked up in dismay. Of course, it was Ambrosia for her answer. And I wasn't ready with it yet.

As far as I could see, I was no further along than I had been when I talked to her. But at least I could ask her some questions.

So I called, "Come in."

And in walked, not Ambrosia, but Julian Porter. In one of his nastier moods.

"I will have Marina's property, Mr. Graine," he said planting himself insolently in front of me and holding out his hand. "I will have those papers at once, if you please."

Sandy emitted an amazed whistle. I couldn't even do that. I had never liked the fellow from the first time I saw him. "A well fattened stoat," I think I said to Nero. I had seen nothing since to make me change my mind. But this! For sheer, unadulterated gall it took all prizes.

The slumberous Latin eyes regarded me unblinkingly. "Do you hand them over peaceably, Mr. Graine?"

Whereupon I erupted.

"Listen, you. If you've got any idea of making trouble, understand right now I'm just aching to take up where Beale Thorndyke left off yesterday. You won't get off with a half-hearted mouse and a bloody nose this time, either. The complete job of rearrangement

I'd like to do on that unpleasant puss of yours would make the Grand Coulee look like the excavation for a WPA privy. What do you mean stamping in here and giving me orders as if you were God Almighty? Peaceably, huh! If anyone's giving orders around here, it's me. Now you sit down there on that bed and speak up when you're spoken to. And remember I'm just looking for an excuse to take a poke at you."

I gave him a shove that sent him flat—on the bed.

"Now will you behave, Mr. Juan Portales, dope peddler and stool-pigeon extraordinary to the Mexican government?"

I hadn't felt in such good form since I had told Nero off over the phone in Portland. In fact, I surprised even Sandy, who knows me better than anyone else. He simply folded up and began to fan himself in weak admiration.

Porter—bless his little heart!—ran the complete range of Hollywood emotions from pugnacity through startled surprise to resigned acquiescence. He stayed seated.

"So you know about it," he said softly.

I didn't really. But after my success with the Scott Newell clipping, I had a feeling there must be some reason for Marina's keeping the one in Spanish.

"Yes, I know about it. What I'm wondering is, do your ertswhile playmates south of the border know about it?"

"They are all behind the bars." He actually licked his lips with satisfaction. "You cannot threaten me in that way."

I thought quickly. I remembered Scott Newell-Beale Thorndyke and the way he had been practically abducted from Havana. Could Marina have tried the same trick twice? It was worth the test.

I said, "Perhaps not. But how about the immigration officials? Those boys often take an interest in illegal entry into this country? Am I right?"

The last question had been unnecessary. His face had told me I had struck gold. For just one instant live terror flamed up behind the surfaces of those melting, liquid eyes. Then he looked down, studied one carefully manicured hand.

"You are only trying to frighten me, Mr. Graine," he said.

"Frighten you, hell. We can check up on that easily enough when we get back to Portland. And by God, I'll do it unless—" I paused suggestively.

"Yes, Mr. Graine?" He snapped me up with just a little too much eagerness.

I knew I had him. The rat would do anything to save his skin.

"—Unless you choose to tell me what I want to know. Under those conditions I might—just might possibly forget that I can use a telephone."

Blackmail? Of course. I always say, use your adversary's weapon. It does away with misunderstanding. You know where you stand.

He swallowed the bait whole. "What is it that you wish to know?"

"Suppose we begin at the beginning." Just to reassure myself I patted the pocket where Marina's papers reposed. "How did you come to join up with Marina? Where did she pick you up?"

He smiled. A lazy, retrospective smile.

"Pick up? I do not quite like those words. But"— he sighed— "you are right, Mr. Graine. When I ran from the police I had the good fortune to find refuge in a taxicab outside the Opera House. It was my greater good fortune that the taxicab was waiting for Marina. When she came out I told her the truth and begged sanctuary. She—she was graciousness itself. She hid me at her hotel and brought me with her to this country. I—I have been with her ever since."

"She took you on, knowing you were a drug peddler? Wanted by the police?"

His laugh was silken. "Why not, Mr. Graine? Women do not find me unattractive. Certainly Marina did not. At least, I do not think she ever regretted her bargain." He spread his hands. "For I was faithful—in my way. And Marina was always like—how is it?— clay in a man's hands."

Once I saw Angna Enters in a sketch called "Odalisque." In her inimitable way she created an atmosphere of fascinating obscenity. The theatre swam with the fleshy, perverted air of the harem.

Sickish-sweet slime seemed to ooze all over the place. All it needed was the musical accompaniment of the last few pages of Richard Strauss's *Salome* score to complete the perfect presentation of passive lust.

Listening to Julian Porter gave me the same reaction.

"Somehow," I said, "Marina did not strike me as being exactly putty in anyone's hands?"

"That depends on who the someone was." White teeth flashed. "Marina was a woman of passion. She was forever seeking, searching out new fields. When she was disappointed in her—shall we say?—researches, she could be as ruthless as—as I am." He laughed again. "She used to tell me of some of her less successful experiments. There was one I recall which will show you how she could be. Would it interest you?"

Dumb, I nodded. It had the same obscure, vile attraction as watching a peep-show.

He licked his lips again. "It was, I recall, a young tenor. Marina found him in New York just before she sailed on her European tour in 1936. She told me he was young, fresh, *naïf*. So she took him with her, promising him study with a well-known Italian *maestro* and a debut with her in *Rigoletto* in Dresden.

"But the young man proved a disappointment. Marina was, as one says, a connoisseur. After a few months of him she turned to a young, dark-haired baritone who was more experienced. The tenor, however, would not be thrust off. He wished his debut, you understand. But Marina was decided on his going. So what did she do? I ask you."

His dark eyes, amused, regarded Sandy and me. I said weakly, "I couldn't guess. What did she do?"

"Most subtle," he said with satisfaction. "They were, you understand, in Dresden by this time. With great effort Marina obtained pamphlets against the government and placed them in his room. One night the Gestapo knock at the door and pouf! the troublesome young man disappears. Marina never told us any more about him or what happened to him, but it's easily enough imagined. I don't know how the police came to know of those hidden pamphlets, but Marina once showed me a letter of gratitude written to her by a very high-placed official."

He was silent for a moment, contemplating Marina's gentle thoroughness. Then he sighed.

"In some things, however, poor Marina was unfortunate. The new favorite, the baritone, you understand, married an English girl of the chorus shortly after. Marina was heartbroken. Right after that she came to Mexico City. I consoled her."

The fingernail he clicked rang out like a castanet.

"I tell you this story to show you that she could be ruthless if she wished. She must have her own way. I myself, I had admiration for her. She knew it. That is why I was closer to her than any of the others. Because I understood her. She told me many things she did not share with them. I knew her secrets like no one else."

Sandy, I observed, had picked up the revolver and was twiddling dangerously with the trigger. When I reached over and twitched it out of his hand, he gave a very fair imitation of a man retching.

Julian watched the by-play unmoved. When I settled back, he said, "Now that I have answered your questions, you will give me Marina's papers?"

"What," I said, trying not to think of how much I'd like to wring his sleek neck, "makes you think you should have them any more than any of the others?"

"But I have told you," he said reproachfully. "Marina shared her secrets with me. I know all that is in them. She would want me to have them."

"But whether I do is another matter. Besides, I'm not through with my questions." I had had another thought. "What do you know about a piece of wrapping paper which reads, 'God help you, Marina Grazie,' and is signed 'Caro Nome'?"

"It is a souvenir," he said sullenly. "She kept it to remind her not to make any more mistakes like the one with the young tenor."

"But why 'Caro Nome'?"

"I do not know," he said impatiently. "Except that she called him that. Now will you please give me the papers?"

I decided to test a theory. "All of them, Porter? You wouldn't be willing to settle for one in particular?"

He knew what I meant. His eyes flickered, then went brazen. "Well, why should you not know? Soon everyone will know it. For I am going to marry Elena. Yes, I want that one paper very much. And I intend to have it."

"If you're so certain of marrying the girl, why do you want the paper?"

He sucked in his lip. "There are, you understand, complications."

"I see. Meaning Beale Thorndyke?"

"Thorndyke! Pouf! I shall handle him."

"That's your opinion," I said. "What if Elena won't marry you? I happen to know she loves the doctor."

His face clouded, then brightened. "That is not true. You yourself saw us in the hall last night. What of that?"

I had forgotten that embrace at the foot of the stairs. For a moment I wavered. Yet my reason told me it was impossible that a girl like Elena Grazie could be attracted to a snake like Porter. There must be some explanation even if I couldn't see it.

"Yes, I saw it," I said. "But I'm not convinced. Any more than I'm convinced that you love Elena. After all, she isn't your type, Porter. Come on. Why are you so set on marrying her?"

Again his eyes flickered. Then he shrugged.

"A man must live. When Elena inherits Marina's fortune she will be a wealthy woman. I am weary of living on an allowance."

It was out at last. And he had played right into my hand. For evidently there was one secret Marina had not shared with her foreign gigolo. I dropped my bomb.

"You will be interested, then, to learn that Marina's will leaves everything to Elena only on condition that she does not marry. And how do you like that?"

He eyed me reproachfully.

"Did you plan to surprise me with that?" he said. "You were wrong, if you did. I have thought much about it. Ever since I first knew of it. And I have made my plans. Such a condition would never hold in a court of law. It is against all reason. I have already engaged a lawyer to break the will as soon as Elena is my wife."

I should have known better than to try to outwit a ferret. I concealed my chagrin as best I could. After all, other bombs have been duds. They still dig them up on long-quiet battlefields.

I had only one more bit of ammunition. I let fire. "Even if you could, as you say, 'handle' Beale Thorndyke, aren't you forgetting one other person?"

"You mean Ambrosia Swisshome?"

"I mean Ambrosia Swisshome. I got the impression from a talk with her that she'd go the limit to keep you from marrying Marina's daughter."

"Daughter?" He stared at me. "What do you mean?"

"Oh, don't pull that, Porter," I said impatiently. "I told you I know the whole story. Elena isn't Marina's niece any more than I am. She's Rachel Marsh's daughter and Rachel Marsh was Marina Grazie."

He studied his fingernails with devotion. "Ambrosia told you that?"

"How else would I know?" I exploded. "She's asked me for the certificate and after talking to you, I think I'll give it to her."

He stood up. I couldn't help noticing that he was the only male among us who had managed to keep his clothes unwrinkled after living in them for twenty-four hours. The rest of us looked like walking invitations to a pressing-service. He was as elegantly groomed as if he had only that moment finished dressing.

"I am going," he announced, "to have a few words with Ambrosia. After that, I think she will come and ask you to give the document to me. You will excuse me."

His confidence was too complete. I found that it annoyed—and worried me considerably. I said caustically, "And just how do you think you can persuade Ambrosia?"

He shrugged his beautifully padded shoulders. "It will not be difficult," he answered. "You see, my friends, Ambrosia has not been entirely frank with you. True enough, Elena is the daughter of Rachel Marsh. But Marina's name never was that."

"No?" I said. "Then suppose you tell me who Rachel Marsh was."

"Not was, Mr. Graine. *Is*," he corrected me gently. "Rachel Marsh is Ambrosia's real name."

30

WHEN HE WAS GONE, Sandy said plaintively, "Shades of Madame X! Aren't the mad Marches to be let off anything?"

I didn't quote Michael Arlen, but if there had been a few straws lying around I'd have plucked at them aimlessly. Ambrosia Swisshome Elena's mother! I couldn't get it through my head. Yet as sanity slowly returned, I saw that if I had used half the brains God gave a good strong plough-horse I might have seen the fact.

It explained Ambrosia's willingness to submit for years to Marina's tyranny. The mere fact that she was fond of the girl would not, I saw now, be sufficient reason for knuckling under. But if the girl were her own child, even the particular brand of hell that Marina dished out could not have forced her away. Yes, undoubtedly that was the whip Marina had held over her. And if I knew Ambrosia, she would have died—or murdered—before allowing Elena to learn the truth.

Other things, viewed properly, might have pointed the way for me.

The birth certificate gave September 23, 1919 as the date of Elena's birth. Ambrosia had told me she had been Bollman's secretary until 1919. That year Bollman had taken her to New York City where he had suddenly decided to dispense with her services. In other words, had kicked her out. It seemed logical to me that having discovered that he had gotten his secretary in trouble he would put the width of the country between her and his home town of Seattle.

There was Marina, too. Why had she been so willing to take on the deserted, friendless woman? Not through fear, certainly, that she knew too much about the blackmail. Ambrosia had no proof to offer even if she did attempt to kick up a row. Anyway, what would a row have profited her? No, Marina would not, I felt, have been influenced by Ambrosia's knowledge of the blackmail. It must, therefore, have been the child. With Lucifer Bollman's illegitimate offspring close at hand, the hold she had on him was strengthened just that much. I could hear her assuring herself, "You can't have too many weapons on hand."

And so she had taken in the discarded secretary, played the role of Aunt to explain the child's presence in a husbandless household. Ambrosia had thrust her head into the noose willingly, accepting anything to be near her daughter.

It also explained the lack of resemblance between Marina and Elena. That a mother and daughter should be dissimilar is not surprising; I've seen some who looked as much alike as I resemble Abraham Lincoln. Yet you can always find something, even if it is only a sudden flash of expression, if you look closely enough. There was much in common between Ambrosia and Elena. In fact, now that I thought of it, they were much alike if one allowed for the lines that bitterness and humiliation had etched into Ambrosia's face, the patina of restraint and distorted emotion that had hardened into a cast-iron mask.

"Do you believe it?" Sandy roused me from my meditations.

I nodded. A sinking feeling came into the pit of my stomach, as an inkling of what might lie ahead for that unhappy crowd occurred to me. I wished for the hundredth time that I were far away, that I had never become involved with Marina Grazie and her psychoneurotic household.

"What're you going to do about the certificate?" he went on. "You're not going to let that slimy lug get his hands on it?"

Right then I made my decision.

"We're going to find Ambrosia. I'm going to tell her I know the truth. Then I'm going to give her the thing and stay there until she burns it."

"Even if she murdered Marina? And Horston?"

I considered. "Even so, I think I want to help her. Yes, I know I do. But I don't think she did it."

"Then you've got a candidate all picked out?"

"Not exactly." I hesitated. "But when you stop to think of it, it does seem strange that Porter has a lawyer all ready to break the will . . ."

"Meaning?"

"Meaning that he wouldn't go to that length unless he were pretty sure something were going to—uh, remove Marina."

"Now you're talking." He grinned with approval. "That something was himself. I'll bet on it."

I stood up. "It's one thing to bet, another to win. But I'm going to try to prove it. Come on, my bucko. Let's find Ambrosia." I pulled him to his feet. "And let's hope we don't run into Elena. I haven't much desire to see her right at this moment."

So of course she was the first person we ran into.

We went down the corridor, circled the rotunda, and knocked on Ambrosia's door. There was no answer. I knocked again.

"She's gone downstairs," Sandy wheezed. "If she's as hungry as I am she's probably scraping out tin cans at this point."

A door opened. Elena's voice said, "Mr. Graine, I—I wish you'd come in here a moment. There's something I want to ask you."

Sandy gouged me in the ribs. "I'll go on downstairs and see how the ineffable Maggie is getting along with the food problem."

"You, too, Mr. Sands," the girl said. "It is nothing you do not know already. I wish you would."

He shrugged. "Lead on, Macduff."

I did. We went into her room.

The fire crackled cheerily. Two chairs were drawn up before it. The girl sat down in one, motioned me to the other. "Mr. Sands, will you just pull up a packing-case," she invited with a little smile.

"Don't worry about me, Miss Grazie," he grinned back. "I'm a confirmed bed-sprawler." He stretched himself out.

I regarded the girl, amazed to find out that I had for so long overlooked just how attractive Ambrosia Swisshome's daughter was. The firelight cast ruddy beams on her page-boy blonde hair. The delicately moulded face was infinitely appealing with its great violet eyes, the thin slightly uptilted nose, the curved smoothness of her red lips. I didn't blame Beale Thorndyke for going off the deep end over her; I could understand Ambrosia's sacrifices to protect the child. If I hadn't had so much on my mind I could have fallen for her myself at that moment.

I wouldn't, however, allow myself to think of that. The haunting loveliness of her face reminded me too forcefully of the danger that was gathering over her head. It was as if she felt it, too. There was urgency in her eyes. Her slender white fingers laced and unlaced themselves in her lap.

"I want to apologize for the rudeness we've shown you since we've been here, Mr. Graine," she began. The crimson lips quivered slightly. "I think you know by this time that our household has not been exactly a—a gay and carefree one. If we seemed to shut you out, it was only to protect what—what little pride we had left."

Ambrosia had used almost those same words before. Mother and daughter—they even thought alike, reacted alike.

"It's nothing," I said awkwardly. "As you say, I understand now."

She looked down at her hands, still nervously active.

"Mr. Graine, I realize I have no right to ask this, but—" Suddenly she turned the full flood of her eyes upon me. "Will you tell me what it is that Beale—Dr. Thorndyke is afraid of? Oh, I know there is something. Everyone was afraid of Marina. Ambrosia tried to keep things from me, but I do have eyes. That fear was in all of them. I don't know what it was, but I sensed it."

My curiosity came to the fore again. "But you joined as hectically as the others in the search for your aunt's jewel-case. What were you looking for?"

"Auntie always called that box her treasure-chest. I knew there were things in it, and it was Beale I was worried about. I thought if I could just get whatever was in the box that concerned him and destroy it, he might be—free."

"Free?"

Color flooded her cheeks but she lifted her little chin defiantly.

"Free to love me, free to marry me," she said stoutly. "It is probably shameless of me to say it like that. But it is the way I feel. I know he loves me. He has told me so. But he was going to marry Auntie. What was it, Mr. Graine? Can you tell me? I'm so bewildered and unhappy and . . . now . . . with Julian . . ."

I sat up with a jerk. Had I waited too long? Had Porter already seen the girl? Had he gone straight to her from my room?

"What about him?" I demanded. "What's he been doing?"

"Oh, nothing definite," she said hastily. "It is more his—his attitude. His confidence. He behaves the same way Auntie—used to. It's just as if he—he had taken up right where she left off. I—I can't make it any clearer than that."

I felt a little better. At least, he hadn't talked to her yet. I still had a little time.

"But hasn't he said anything?"

Her head drooped. She drew a quavering breath.

"I might as well tell you the whole story, Mr. Graine," she said softly. "You see, a few months ago Julian asked me to marry him. I didn't give him any definite answer, but Auntie heard about it. I told Ambrosia and I imagine she went to Auntie with the story. Auntie was simply furious. She called me in to her room right away and told me all about Julian . . . his trouble in Mexico City, what he had been, and all that. I was horrified . . . which was exactly what Auntie wanted . . . to keep me from marrying him . . . ever . . . As though I would!

"I was in love with Beale. And he loved me. Right after that he asked me to marry him. When I told him that he must ask Auntie about it first he . . . he got very pale but said he . . . he would."

Her eyes filled with tears.

"The next day he told me he had changed his mind. He was going to marry Auntie instead."

She was silent for a long moment. I felt I knew the agony she was going through, and if I could have, I would have stopped the thing. But I wanted to help. Genuinely. In order to do that I had to know everything. I waited.

At last she went on:

"I don't think I ever was really fond of Auntie. She wasn't the sort of person you could really love. But I had felt that I owed her gratitude for what she had done for me. Now even that was gone. I hated her. I know that sounds awful, but I couldn't help feeling that she was behind this sudden change in Beale.

"Then Julian began again. I couldn't bear him. And I told him so. He just laughed and said I'd get over it. Beale tried to be friends with me but . . . but that was even worse. Julian got violently jealous every time he came near me. At the airport in Portland Beale started to help me out and Julian almost made a scene." She broke off. "But you were there. You saw it. You know."

So that was the explanation. I couldn't help reflecting on the riotous glee of the reporters if they had unearthed that little tidbit in time for the afternoon papers.

"And then there was the fight upstairs yesterday afternoon," she went on. Her head was so low I couldn't see her face. "You see, Mr. Graine, we all knew that Auntie was dead. Before you told us.

"And right in front of the others Beale asked me to marry him again. Julian went into a rage. He said I could never marry anyone but him. And . . . and then they went off to that other room. . . .

"Later on Beale told me that Julian was right. Everything was still the same . . . except that he wouldn't have to marry Auntie now."

She darted me a quick glance.

"You saw us in the storeroom last night. We were . . . saying goodbye. I didn't know why, but Beale insisted. And then . . . downstairs . . . Julian took me in his arms and . . . and . . . Oh, Mr. Graine, you've got to help me. I'm going crazy with worry. You've got to tell me what it is that Beale is . . . is afraid of. I've got to know. I can't stand it much longer."

What would you have done? With that girl's white, pleading face looking at you? I knew I had no right to reveal Beale's secret. It had been told me in confidence. I pulled myself up. Had it? Thorndyke had thought I knew everything from reading the clipping in the packet. But even so, it was his affair.

I still think, however, that I did the right thing. Sandy's encouraging nod was all. I needed.

So I told her the story of Dr. Scott Newell. Oh, I softened it up a bit here, toned it down a bit there. Especially in the latter part when Marina came into the picture. Beale himself had said he intended telling Elena. I consoled myself with the thought that I was merely anticipating him by an hour or so.

When I finished, still more than a little worried over my interference in someone else's affairs—as though I hadn't been doing it for twenty-four hours!—Elena's face lighted up like a small sun. She was radiant.

"But that's nothing!" she exclaimed. "That wouldn't have made any difference to me. Nothing would have."

I thought it wise to interject a note of caution. "Perhaps not that. Don't forget, however, that we have murder on our hands now."

She stared at me. "But Beale wouldn't commit murder!"

I hazarded a shot. "You say that positively enough now. But wasn't there a time when you thought he had done it? Confess now. Didn't you? And besides," I added as gently as I could, "he had everything to gain by your aunt's death."

Her hand went to her heart, toyed with the bunch of yarn flowers. A tiny frown creased her forehead, then disappeared. She returned my gaze confidently.

"I'm sorry about that flower business," she said. "You did see these downstairs, Mr. Graine. They must have fallen off when I—I realized she really was dead. And you're right about the other, too." She reflected. "But not entirely right, either. You see, I couldn't make up my mind. I thought it was either—Beale—or Ambrosia."

"Ambrosia?" I exclaimed, as if the idea had never occurred to me before. "What made you think she might have done it?"

A tender note came into her voice. A note of genuine affection. "Ambrosia knew about Beale and me. And she liked him. Oh, she quarreled with him at times, but she was fond of him in her way. She told me once that he would never have to marry Marina. Even if—even if—" She broke off.

I thought: Even if she had to take matters into her own hands. Yes, Ambrosia's love would go that far. "And now?" I asked.

Her eyes lighted up. "It doesn't make any difference. I don't care."

"Beale might. Did you know your aunt has left you her estate with the provision that you never marry?" She hesitated only for an instant.

"I don't want her money. All I want is to be with Beale . . . always."

"But there's the possibility of murder, Elena," I insisted. "You must think of that."

"He didn't murder anyone. He wouldn't. He couldn't." She stood up, her body tense with the force of her conviction. "I know it."

"You can't know it," I said. "Wishes aren't facts."

The golden head lifted with determination. "Then the facts have to be found. When they are, you'll see it wasn't Beale who did it."

"Ambrosia then? Don't you care about her?"

Her eyes grew troubled. "You know I do. But I wasn't thinking of Ambrosia, either. There's one other person who might have wished Auntie dead." She paused. "You're forgetting Julian."

I wasn't forgetting Julian. Far from it. Nor was I forgetting Elena herself. She had as much as the others to gain from Marina's death. Looking at her, I confess I found it difficult to conceive of her having done the thing. But, I told myself, rationalizing, other murderesses have been young and vibrant and lovely.

I started to say, not that, but that I hoped it would be Julian. I didn't get the words out.

The door was opened at that moment. Stony-faced, Beale Thorndyke stood there.

"Elena!" His voice was like jags of granite. "Julian wants you to come to breakfast."

I looked away from the shattered ruin of her face, the sudden obliteration of the radiance I had seen there.

She faltered, "Julian . . . wants . . . me?"

"Yes," came the clipped response. "I'll take you down to him."

31

I GOT OUT OF THAT ROOM as fast as I could.

There are some things I can't take. The sight of Elena's face was one of them. It was enough to tear your heart out. Too, Beale Thorndyke's frozen look was enough to make you want to go out and take a dose of arsenic in sympathy. So I, as I say, got out.

On the way downstairs Sandy said, "What's up now?"

My mind was made up. If I could throw a monkey-wrench into Julian Porter's works I was going to move heaven and earth to do it. I knew he was at the bottom of all this. Only he could have killed what I had seen in Beale's face early that morning. Only he could have been bastard enough to send Thorndyke up for Elena.

"I'm going to give this certificate to Ambrosia before I'm a minute older," I told Sandy. "And furthermore I want to do it before Julian gets hold of her. If I have anything to say about it he's not going to do to her what he's done to Beale."

I knew, of course, as Ambrosia and Beale must also, that destroying the certificate could only postpone the show-down. Julian could easily obtain a copy of it in New York. The only salvation was that that would require time. Meanwhile, something might turn up.

Something. Anything . . .

We reached the library just in time to forestall one of the "anythings."

Julian was kneeling on the hearth, stuffing boards into the fire. He turned to us, smiling a little sardonically.

"Breakfast is not quite ready, Mrs. Tait tells me," he said. "Would you mind letting us know when we may eat? Ambrosia and I have a few words to say to each other. In private."

Only then did I see that he was not alone. Ambrosia was standing over by the piano. One hand grasped the angel-bottle like a bludgeon. On her face was such a look of concentrated loathing and hatred that I felt more than a little frightened. At sight of me she put the bottle quietly back on the piano, but her face did not change.

I turned back to Julian. It was all I could do to keep from shoving my fist against that grin of his.

"Get out of here, Porter," I said. "I'm the one that's going to talk to Miss Swisshome, and I'm going to do it right now."

He stood up. "You cannot order me, Mr. Graine. I—"

"The hell I can't! Sandy! The bum's rush!"

We each grabbed an arm and a handful of the seat of his pants. Before he had time to open his mouth he was out in the corridor. I pushed Sandy out after him.

"Don't let him stick his nose in here till I give the word," I instructed. "Keep him out in the kitchen. Tie him up if you have to, but don't let me see him."

At the foot of the stairs Elena and Beale Thorndyke were watching in amazement. I slammed the door on Julian's Spanish-English welter of profanity.

Ambrosia had sunk down in a chair. She sat there rigid. Her sunken eyes looked straight ahead. She was like a sleepwalker.

I went over to her and shook her gently by one shoulder.

"What's been happening down here, Ambrosia? What did he say to you?"

Her lips moved. "Why didn't you let me do it, Anthony? I would have killed him. The angel-bottle . . . while he knelt there by the fire. I knew just where I would strike. It would have been so simple . . . so simple . . ." The words trailed off. She shivered.

I shook her again. This time I took both hands to the job. This was serious. The woman sounded as if she were out of her mind.

"Ambrosia, listen to me. I'm going to give you the certificate. Look. Here it is. I want you to have it. We'll put it in the fire right now."

I pushed the document into her fingers. "There it is. There's what you wanted."

She looked down at it, up into my face, back again to the folded, flat whiteness. Her manner reminded me of a woman I had seen once years before when I was taken on a tour of the State Hospital back home. The woman had sat on a bed with an open magazine on her lap, her eyes directed on the page. And there she sat, staring with a horrible, unseeing intentness. Half an hour later I passed through the same ward. She had not moved.

But if I had thought Ambrosia was anything like that mental wreck, I had another think coming. A moment later the blank eyes came slowly to life. The mouth twisted; the thin, faded lips quivered. I thought, "Oh, God, she's going to cry." And I dreaded it. I had had enough of scenes. I wanted no more of them.

For an instant it was touch and go with her. Then the lips regained their firmness. Without unfolding it, she held the paper up. "Is—is this it?" she asked, seemingly not daring to believe.

I assured her it was, adding, "Burn it. Now."

Her hand shook so that the paper rattled. Then she leaned forward and laid the thing on the flames. In silence we watched it crinkle, char, flare up.

When it was blackened nothingness she gave a sigh so full of relief that I felt that even if I went to the electric chair for what I had done I was well repaid. She touched me with her hand and said simply, "Thank you, Anthony."

I don't know how to explain it but right then I got a little choked up. Those three words did things to me. They expressed all the overwhelming relief, all the banished mental agony, all the released emotional tension that had forced her to the verge of insanity. I have never admired a woman more in my life than I did Ambrosia at that moment.

I walked over to where Marina lay. I looked down at the cold, dead face. I thought nothing. I simply looked down at her.

Then Ambrosia was beside me, her hand on my arm.

"I think Julian has lost his mind," she said. "He talked like an insane man. And yet so calm . . . so confident. He told me I must make you give him the certificate."

I had to say it. "You know that the certificate is really unimportant, don't you, Ambrosia? He can get another where that one came from."

Her breathing made the candles flicker.

"Yes, I know," she said presently. "But at least he cannot prove anything until then. We have . . . a little more time. Perhaps . . . perhaps something . . ."

The candle-flames bent flat in a sudden draft. The door had opened. I turned. Maggie Tait, her one good eye alert, stood there.

"Mr. Graine, you oughta go upstairs, I think," she said. "Mr. Sands says to let 'em be. But Miss Grazie's cryin' her eyes out. Maybe it'll clear the air, like Mr. Sands says, but that Mr. Porter don't look none too safe to me. I think you oughta go up and see what they're doin'."

"They?" I shouted. "Great balls of fire, what's happened now? Who are *they?*"

"Why, Mr. Porter an' the doctor. They got in another fight out'n the kitchen. I tried t'make 'em stop it so they went upstairs. I think you better go."

32

I WENT OUT OF THE ROOM and up those stairs like a bat out of hell. Things were happening too thick and fast for me, and I was getting fed up. No one, not even Sandy, could be trusted to behave like a human being for two consecutive seconds. I had only asked him to keep Julian under control for a minute. And what had he done? I felt like the *raisonneur* in a Pinero play who spends his whole time dashing about madly straightening out the difficulties of the other characters.

The final straw was to find the two gladiators drawn up for battle in my room. My room, mind you. I stormed in:

"The last time you two went primitive was enough. There isn't going to be any more. Beat it, Porter. I want to talk to Thorndyke."

Neither moved. They simply stood there, facing each other, waiting, alert and cautious, for the first false move. Over his shoulder, Beale said, "It's too late for talking. We're going to finish this here and now."

"Come home with your shield or on it, eh, Thorndyke?" I jeered. "Very Spartan of you, but I say it's stopping right now. Porter, are you going to get out of here or do I have to throw you out again?"

Slowly the slumberous eyes turned on me. In their depths I could read his opinion of me. It was not flattering. Nor soothing.

"That," he said slowly, "is the second time you have given an order to leave the room, Mr. Graine. I do not like it."

"I didn't ask you what you liked. I told you to go. I meant it. Thorndyke, get out of that shadow-boxer pose of yours. You both look like a third-rate imitation of a Golden Gloves bout."

That did it. The ridicule struck home. Thorndyke dropped his hands and whirled.

"God damn you, Graine, why can't you keep your nose out of things? This is my affair. I'm going to handle it."

I was satisfied. The electricity in the room was short-circuited, even if I had had to play the penny in the socket. I walked over to the bed and sat down.

"Why not let the police handle it for you?" I suggested.

"Police?" Thorndyke said it, but they both stared.

I looked at Porter. "Do you want to get out or shall I let you have it right here?"

He glared. "You know nothing against me that the police could not know," he blustered. But he was bluffing. I saw the flicker of fear shoot up in his eyes.

"No? Aside from any little question of illegal entry—you can take that up with the authorities later—you might be interested to know that I think you murdered Marina."

The effect of my words surprised me. Not that he reacted to them, but that they drew out the response they did. He practically frothed at the mouth.

"That is not true," he cried, waving his hands. "I did not kill Marina. I was her friend. I would not do such a thing."

"But you would hire a lawyer to start breaking her will as soon as he gets word that she is dead?"

"You twist my words," he shrieked. "I did not know she would die now. It is only that he is ready . . . was ready whenever it happens . . . happened. Marina was alive the last time I saw her. I saw her through the window. She was alive, I tell you."

I stiffened. "You saw her through the window? You lied when you said you went straight to the garage and came straight back?"

He wrung his hands. "You—I don't know what I am saying. No. Yes—I did. I did see her through the window. But I did not go into the room. You cannot make me say I did."

"Nobody's trying to make you say anything. You're doing all the talking. And, brother, you're saying plenty."

"I have said nothing except that I went to the window," he said frantically. "That is not wrong, is it?"

I appeared to consider. "No, not that. But I'll bet you anything you want to bet that you did more than that. I'll bet you climbed in that window. I'll bet that Horston followed you from the garage, saw you kill Marina, and then tried to—"

"No! I did not do it," he screamed. "You are trying to trap me. I did not do it. You cannot prove it."

Well, he had me there. "Maybe not at the moment, but, by God, I'll get proof. I'll get it if I have to tear the place to pieces to do it." I stood up. "Now get out of here before I lose my temper."

He got. Calmed a little by my admission, he managed to pull himself together. With a sickly smile that was meant to be contemptuous, he swaggered out of the room. In the corridor he hesitated. Then his footsteps sounded on the staircase.

I turned to Thorndyke who had been watching in stricken silence.

"Now, suppose you sit down, Dr. Thorndyke, and tell me what was behind that great renunciation scene at Elena's door. I'm curious."

He came to life, grasped my arm. "Were you telling the truth, Graine?" he demanded. "Is that right about Julian?"

"I've asked you a question." I shook him off. "How about it?"

The story I finally got out of him was just about what I had imagined.

Julian, breathing fire, had come down to the kitchen for a talk, but seeing Paris and the Taits wandering about, had insisted on Thorndyke's accompanying him to the library. There he had issued his ultimatum: Thorndyke was to have nothing more to do with Elena or he, Julian, would tell her immediately about the certificate.

"I tried to talk him out of it," Thorndyke said, "but he acted like a madman. You couldn't reason with him. I didn't know what to do. So finally I thought if I humored him, played along with him for a while, I could . . . well, something might happen . . ."

That was the third time I had heard that. If wishes had anything to do with action, I had the feeling that Julian Porter would never live to confront the police, much less the immigration officials.

"When I brought Elena down," he went on, "we saw you and Sands putting him out of the library. He was mad as hell, as you can imagine, but Sands kept a grip on him. Out in the kitchen, though, he became more offensive than ever. From the way he talked you'd have thought he was already married to Elena and I was an unwanted guest who had forced himself in on them.

"I took it for a while. But a man can stand just so much. Then when he ordered me to stay on the other side of the room from Elena I couldn't take it any longer." He drew a deep breath. "I invited him to come upstairs . . . and . . . well, that's all."

"Didn't Sandy try to stop you?"

"He may have. I wouldn't know. We weren't paying attention to anyone besides ourselves. But what about Porter? Did he really do it? Do you know anything you haven't told me?"

I shook my head, regretfully. "That was bluff. But at least we found out that he did go to the window and look in."

"Couldn't he have climbed in as you said?"

I explained my idea about Marina's silence and the fact that she couldn't have helped seeing anyone entering the room through the window. But I wasn't really thinking about it. Something else had occurred to me.

"When I was talking to Elena upstairs she said that you all knew Marina was dead before I told you. Is that right?"

He nodded. "I thought you'd gathered that long ago."

"I had. I just wanted you to admit it. The fact is, you were all in the room at various times during the wood-carrying, weren't you?"

"I wasn't," he said promptly. "As for the others I know only that Ambrosia told me she hadn't been in. And—" He broke off.

"Oh, I know about Elena's boutonniere," I said impatiently. "She told me herself she had been in. You found the flowers and gave them back to her, didn't you? When you all ran down there?"

"Yes, but Elena had nothing to do with it, I swear. Once I thought perhaps she had, but I know now it isn't true."

I smiled. "Once she thought you'd done it. So I guess that evens you up. Anyway, we're not trying to pin the thing on Elena. It may be a pretty poor way to go about detection but I'm trying to see how Julian could have done it. Either he's lying about—"

He gave an exclamation. "Graine! He's lying. He told you Marina was alive the last time he saw her. Through the window. But he must have seen her once more. He must have."

His excitement infected me. I found myself jittering. "How do you know?"

"Because he was the one who told Ambrosia and me upstairs that Marina was dead. I told Elena myself. And Paris didn't know about it at all until you broke the news. Don't you see, Graine? He must have been in. He must be lying."

I grabbed his arm. "Are you sure? You're not just imagining it because we both want it that way?"

"You can ask Ambrosia," he said vehemently. "We were together when he told us."

I began to pace the room. If there were only some way to get around that stumbling-block! For Marina would have made some sort of outcry. But she hadn't. The Taits and Sandy had heard nothing. And yet . . .

I stopped with a gasp. Tait's indigestion! I saw Mrs. Tait almost dropping a glass of boiling water. Could it—was there a loophole?

I made for the door, shouting, "Come on, Thorndyke. I've got an idea."

We made it to the kitchen in nothing flat. As I pounded into the room Maggie Tait gave a scream and cowered behind her husband and Paris. Ambrosia, sitting at the kitchen table, looked up in stunned amazement.

I tore over to Mrs. Tait and yanked her out into the open. I found I was so jittery I could hardly talk. But I managed it.

"Nobody's going to hurt you, Mrs. Tait. I just want to ask a simple question. Now listen carefully and think before you answer: did you have a kettle of hot water on the stove here yesterday afternoon?"

She gulped. And nodded.

"Where did you get the water? There isn't any in the house."

"Tait an' me got some icicles outside." She clawed at my hand to free her arm. "Same as Mr. Sandy done fer us this mornin'. Ain't nothin' wrong with that, I guess. This's a free country."

I dropped her skinny arm. I could have killed her. "Why didn't you say so before? Why didn't you tell me?"

"A person kin fergit," she said, massaging her arm. "It clean slipped my mind. Tait here didn't remember it neither."

I looked at Tait. "Is this true? You did go out?"

He scratched his head. "Never thought of it till this minute. 'Member it all now. Mr. Sandy was asleep there with his feet in t'oven when Maggie an' me went out. Must've took us five minutes er so. Icicles uz hard to find. Seems like the wind blew most of 'em away."

Five minutes! And Sandy was asleep! That was the final bit. It all fitted together. I could have grabbed Ambrosia and bussed her soundly.

"By God, I've done it!" I could hardly contain myself. "I've found the loophole. Now where is Julian Porter?"

Maggie Tait was looking at me dubiously, edging away. "He went out with Miss Grazie an' your friend Mr.—"

The rest of the sentence was drowned in a scream—a scream that came from the library. It was Elena Grazie's voice. She screamed again.

There was the sound of a shot.

33

My mother always said that in all her life whenever she received either a telegram or a long distance telephone call she experienced a sensation which made her think that her stomach had been turned inside out. I had always wondered what that must be like.

That morning in Lucifer's Pride I found out.

Although it was Elena who had screamed, my first thought was of Sandy. When the six of us stood there in the kitchen, stunned to paralysis by those three awful sounds, I knew as certainly as if I had been in the library and seen it happen that Julian Porter had shot my friend. Only after that did I think of Elena.

Beale Thorndyke anticipated me there. The blood drained from his face; reeling as if he had been clubbed over the head, he uttered the one word, "Elena!" and plunged blindly toward the door. The rest of us followed him, streaming out of the kitchen like bees shaken from a hive.

The library door was open. Light from the room laid a rectangle on the dusty floor of the hall. In the center of this glow, bracing herself against the frame of the library door with one outflung arm, stood Elena. Over and over she was sobbing the words, "He's dead ... He's dead ..."

That much I saw before Beale reached her and swept her into his arms.

I pushed past the lovers and into the library. What I saw stopped me in my tracks.

Sprawled out on the hearth, a gaping hole in his face just above the bridge of his nose, lay Julian. A gush of crimson covered one cheek like a bloody veil, dripped down to the floor. Kneeling beside him, Paris's revolver dangling from limp fingers was Sandy. He looked like a ghost.

I couldn't move. I stood there. My mind was a complete blank. Not a thought. Not an idea.

Slowly Sandy turned his head, and his eyes turned me sick. They were living bleakness, dumb circles of shocked horror.

"He's dead, Tony," came the merest shred of a whisper. "My God, Tony, I've killed him. I've killed him!" The revolver dropped from his hand, thudded to the floor. He buried his face in his hands. His shoulders shook.

I got him into a chair and realizing that his hands were cold as ice, I tried to leave him to put some wood on the fire. But he wouldn't let me go. His fingers clung to me. I thought if there were only some whiskey, anything, around the place I might be able to bring some color back into the ghastly whiteness of his face. But there was none. Even the angel-bottle was empty.

I rubbed his hands. "Sandy, listen to me. You can't let go like this. Sandy! Come out of it. Tell me what happened."

Beale and Elena had come in. The girl was sobbing brokenly in Ambrosia's arms. Beale, his head silhouetted against the flames as he bent over, was examining Julian's body.

A fit of shivering seized Sandy. He was like a man with the ague. I motioned Paris over to put more wood on the fire. The blaze leaped up.

Sandy stared at it. "He's dead, Tony," came that monotone again. "I killed him. I shot him. We were fighting over the gun. It went off in my hands." His face twisted. "God, if you had seen his face, Tony, when the—when the—"

"Steady, fellow. Steady. Pull yourself together."

"Tony, it was awful. His eyes . . . the blood . . ." Again that godawful spasm of shivering wrenched him. I was helpless.

Thorndyke had by that time finished his examination. I left Sandy and walked over with him to the door, out of hearing of the others. I looked the question I couldn't ask.

He shrugged. "Dead instantly. Right between the eyes." He seemed ready to keel over himself. "Did I hear Sandy say they were struggling for the gun?"

I nodded.

"That would explain the powder burns," he said.

"The muzzle must have been pushed right against the bridge of his nose. It's a mess."

I glanced around numbly. "Do you suppose Elena could tell us what happened? I've got to know. This is getting me down, Thorndyke."

Ambrosia had the girl over on the piano bench, her arms around her, soothing, comforting her. It seemed inhuman to question her then but for Sandy's sake, if for nothing else, I felt I had to know the straight of it.

The gaunt, grey woman stiffened as we approached, sensing what we had in mind. Her arms tightened around the girl's slender figure. "Can't it wait, Beale?" Her voice was pleading. "This has been a terrible shock. I don't think the child could stand—"

"Yes!" Elena sat up, pushed back the hair from her reddened, swollen eyes. "I want to tell you now. I want to get it over with . . . now."

Ambrosia started to protest, but the girl silenced her with a gesture. Then falteringly, she told the story.

Sandy had taken her into the library as Mrs. Tait complained that with everyone under foot she couldn't get together what little food there was. By that time Elena had succeeded in restraining her tears, although, she said, she was still so worried about what was going on upstairs that she could hardly think. In a desperate effort to distract her Sandy had told a long, complicated joke. She couldn't remember now what it was all about, but she had laughed politely when he came to what she thought was the point.

At that moment Julian had walked in, still smarting from his encounter with me upstairs. Taking a leaf from my book, he had ordered Sandy out of the room. When Sandy had refused to go, he had insisted, saying he had something very important to tell Elena, something that had better be said in private.

Suspecting what it was, Sandy had stoutly refused to budge. Indeed, he had gone further than that. Drawing Paris's revolver from his pocket where it had been ever since Ambrosia's visit to our room, he had politely informed Julian that he would blow his head off if he opened his mouth to say one word to Elena.

It was stalemate for a moment, I gathered, for Julian had not dared to speak with that threat staring him in the face.

When she reached that part of the story, Elena started to tremble. Her eyes filled with frightened tears.

"I don't know exactly what happened just then," she continued with an effort. "Mr. Sands must have looked away for an instant or something. But the first thing I knew Julian had jumped forward and reached for the gun. They wrestled with each other. I was so frightened I could hardly breathe. I think I screamed then. I . . . I don't remember . . ."

She paused, staring across at Julian's body. It was as if she were seeing the whole thing again. After a moment she went on:

"The revolver went up . . . and up. It was in both their hands. I couldn't see which one really had hold of it. I thought I was going to faint. I screamed again. By that time the gun was pointing right against Julian's head . . ." She closed her eyes. "Then there was a shot. I saw Julian slump down . . . all limp and . . . and I turned . . . and ran out into the hall . . ."

She buried her head against Ambrosia again. Beale took her hand and held it tight. I looked at him. "It was an accident then?" I brought out.

He sighed. "Obviously."

I was so relieved I felt like slumping down myself. All I could think of was that Sandy was blameless, and that the reign of terror at Lucifer's Pride was ended.

Julian was dead.

A third ghost had gone to join old Bollman's.

Even as I was thinking that, Sandy came out of his stupor. "I didn't mean to, Tony," he cried suddenly. "It was an accident. I was trying to keep him from telling Elena—"

In one jump I reached him and clapped my hand over his mouth.

"I know, Sandy," I said hurriedly. "Elena's told us what happened. It's all right. Everything's all right."

The bewilderment died out of his eyes. He nodded slowly. I took my hand away from his mouth. I sat down weakly.

"In a way it was execution, Sandy," I told him.

"Execution?"

I nodded. "Julian was the murderer. I'm sure of it. Why didn't you tell me you fell asleep out there in the kitchen and couldn't hear Marina cry out?"

"Asleep?" He sounded dazed.

"If you hadn't mentioned going after icicles this morning I never would have found out that the Taits went out to gather them yesterday afternoon."

"Asleep?" he repeated. "I didn't know I had been, Tony. I was awfully cold, I remember. I didn't know the Taits had gone out."

I squeezed his arm. "It's all right, fella. Don't worry about it."

The room was silent for a while. Outside the wind still howled and screamed. I realized suddenly that we had become so accustomed to it that only now and then were we aware of its ceaseless wailing.

I stretched my legs out to the fire. "If only we could have gotten some sort of confession from Julian before he died," I remarked, thinking aloud. "He didn't say anything, did he?"

He shook his head.

Another thought came to me. "I wonder," I said, "what he did with the diamond. If I'd only insisted on—"

Sandy jerked upright. "Tony!" he gasped. "While we were fighting there . . . in his vest pocket . . . a hard knob . . . pressing against my ribs. . . ."

Thorndyke and I reached Julian's body at the same moment. I lifted back the coat, slipped my fingers into the waistcoat pocket.

When I took them out I was holding the Lucifer diamond.

34

PEACE HAD DESCENDED on Lucifer's Pride.

Trying to describe the atmosphere, I can think only of that breathlessly beautiful calm following the nocturnal street brawl scene in the second act of *Die Meistersinger*. The screaming, rioting burghers with their bludgeons and broken heads have scurried away; the night-gowned women in their bed-caps and braids have taken their empty pitchers and pans back into their houses. One by one the lights in the windows are extinguished. The full moon streams down on the deserted streets.

So it was at Lucifer's Pride.

After the excitement over the discovery of the diamond had ebbed away, Mrs. Tait reminded us of food. Obediently we went out to the kitchen where she had set out what miserable scraps remained from dinner the night before. We looked at the table, turned away, and drifted back to the library. No one had any desire to eat. Reaction had set in and a pall of lethargy hung over us. No one said anything. There really was nothing to say.

I sat there before the fire and tried to realize that only a little more than twenty-four hours had passed since the telephone had jangled in my room and Marina's voice had said, "I am wishing to invite you to make an excursion with me."

Twenty-four hours!

It seemed like a lifetime. So much had happened. Marina's song was ended. A burglar named Caruso Horston would never again collect pictures of opera stars. Julian Porter lay in a corner with a bullet-hole in his too handsome face.

Now it was over. The bloody business at Lucifer's Pride was at an end.

I closed my eyes and tried to rest. But I couldn't. Thoughts sprayed over my mind like warm jets from a half-open shower: a bellboy delivered a note to a great prima donna . . . two crimson words scrawled themselves on a mirror in a dusty dressing-room . . . the angel of the Annunciation, wings pointed above its head, gleamed purple in the firelight . . . a page of music ripped from a score danced before my eyes. I thought of them all. Thought, too, of a note that read, "God help you, Marina Grazie."

In a far corner of the room sat Ambrosia Swisshome, holding her knitting. Her face was haggard and drawn, but there was peace, serenity in her eyes. It was as if she were saying to herself, "My secret is safe now. I have nothing more to fear."

On a divan near the fireplace Elena sat with Beale Thorndyke, her hands linked with his. She looked radiant, happy for the first time since I had laid eyes on her. Beale, too, was different. A new confidence showed in the lift of his firm jaw, the half-smile that played on his thin lips. Neither spoke. Between them words were unnecessary.

Out in the kitchen Maggie Tait was singing a gospel-hymn as she worked. Paris and Tait were out there, too.

Beside me Sandy was writing on a long strip of wrapping paper he had salvaged from the trash-pile in the kitchen. When I had asked him what he intended to do with it, he had answered:

"You'll be a celebrity when we get back, Tony. I'm going to write out the whole story for Nero. Publicity is still being used, my boy. Will the reporters eat this up!"

Eat it up . . . Nero, I remembered, had said that at the airport the morning Marina's plane had descended out of the dingy sky.

And now Marina was dead . . . had died with a sheet of paper crumpled between her fingers . . . watched over by the purple angel of the Annunciation.

Murder Ends the Song

I stirred impatiently. There it was again. Why did I keep thinking of that damned angel-bottle? It was getting on my nerves.

Suddenly I made up my mind. I went over to the piano, picked up the bottle and started out of the room. Sandy followed me out into the hall.

"What goes on, Tony? You're as nervous as a cat. You're not sick, are you?" He looked curiously at the bottle. "What the hell's the idea of dragging that thing around?"

I shook my head. "I'm not sick. I guess I'm just worried."

"Worried? What've you got to worry about? Everything's just dandy now." He paused. "Or isn't it?"

I told him what I'd been thinking. "Do you realize," I wound up, "that not one of the incidents that first interested me in this affair have a single thing to do with Marina's death? That is, if Julian really was the murderer. The note, the words on the mirror—for a while it was nothing but *Caro Nome* all over the place. Then we picked on Julian—and nothing fits."

He stared at me. "What are you getting at?"

I hesitated, then blurted out my fear. "Sandy, what if we've fastened these murders on the wrong person?"

"The wrong—! Tony, you're nuts."

How could I put into words that vague, intangible doubt that kept recurring?

"Perhaps I am," I said. "But there's too much left over. Too many things left unexplained. I—I'm just not satisfied. You asked me why I have this bottle. I can't tell you. I only know that the damn thing's driving me screwy. I can't get it out of my mind. And that sheet of the *Caro Nome* . . ."

"What about it?"

"I can't get over the feeling that it was intended to mean something. I'd swear Marina was trying to leave some message when she tore it from the score."

He looked at me soberly. "You know what I think?"

I said I didn't.

"I think you're punch-drunk. How long's it been since you've had any sleep?"

Sleep? I couldn't remember. I smiled wearily.

"I think I'll go up and try to get some now. You go on back to your story." I started up the stairs. "And make it good enough to convince me I've got the right answer."

The fire had died to embers in the bedroom. I piled wood on it. Then I pulled a packing-case over by the bed and ranged my souvenirs on it: the angel bottle, the sheet from my notebook with a reproduction of the scrawl from the mirror, the page from the *Rigoletto* score, the note the bellboy had handed Marina at the hotel, and the dog-eared message that had come from Marina's box.

When they were placed so that I could see them from the pillow, I got myself a sheet of blank paper—it was the stiffish backing from Marina's will—and a pencil and stretched myself out on the bed à la Sandy.

I don't know much about crime and its detection. I'd never come in contact with either before. One thing, however, seemed logical. According to my way of thinking, when a murder case has been solved and the murderer's identity has become known, the sum total of all the clues and facts must point unerringly to the murderer and the murderer only. I can't quite feature a police inspector saying, "Nine of these facts point to our man but the tenth one has no connection with him. Therefore since we know we have our man, we'll simply overlook that tenth item."

That's what I should call bad business.

And that is what I had meant when I told Sandy that there were too many unexplained tag-ends, too many stray facts left over. If Julian was our murderer, then as far as I could see, not one of the objects on the packing-case beside my bed had any relation to him. My opinion, right or wrong, was that they ought to have, since the *Caro Nome* business bulked so impressively, so ubiquitously. Unless they were all false alarms, red herrings scattered aimlessly about, they should have some bearing directly on Julian. If they did, I wanted to know what it was. If they didn't, I wanted to know why not.

For two hours I lay there on the bed, staring at my collection, removing my gaze from it only long enough to write a question on my sheet of paper from time to time. I let my thoughts ramble where they would, without any attempt at order, seeking out only those bits which seemed to me to be unexplained.

I suppose I could lapse here into the stream of consciousness and diagram my mental meanderings in every minute detail. But I shan't. Anyway, it was not my thoughts but the questions evolved from them that were important. They indicate, I think, where I traveled in my imagination.

Just as the answers to them pointed inevitably to one person . . . for one person, and one person only, could have been concerned in *all* the answers.

Here is what I wrote:

1. To have written the note that was delivered to Marina at the hotel, the murderer must have been at the hotel-desk that morning to leave the note and the tip for the bell-boy. Who was there?

2. To have scrawled the message on Marina's mirror at the Auditorium and overturned the glass of blood, the murderer must have been in the building. Who was there?

3. Paris said Horston told him that the murderer jerked the diamond from Marina's neck but did not search long for the key to the box. Who would have been so apparently indifferent to the contents of the box?

4. All the boiling ferment *chez* Grazie had been brewing down south. Why did the murder not occur until Marina's arrival in the northwest?

5. If the other *Caro Nome* notes meant anything, surely the "God help you, Marina Grazie" one must also. How could it?

6. Why did the murderer use one of Ambrosia's knitting-needles?

7. If Julian was not the murderer, how did he come to have the Lucifer diamond?

8. Had Marina really had a purpose in mind when she tore out that page from the *Rigoletto* score? If so, what was it?

9. The angel-bottle—

Again and again I kept coming back to that confounded bottle. It hypnotized me. Why did I keep thinking of it?

In a desperate effort to unearth some reason I forced myself to concentrate on the various times I had come in contact with it. The last time I had noticed it was right after Julian's death when I had wanted a drink to revive Sandy and had remembered that the bottle was empty. Before that, I had seen Ambrosia grasping it while Julian knelt at the fire. Sandy and I had had a drink from it after we had found Marina's body and Sandy had remarked, "Well, sherry's better than nothing." Before that, Marina had invited me to have a drink with her, saying, "The others have all had some."

That was all. I was positive.

And yet—

At that moment the answer crashed down on me. It was right there. It had been there all the time. Yet it was incredible. Unbelievable. Was I losing my mind?

I snatched up the questions I had written, went over them one by one. Then I dropped the page and stared across the room.

Even the eighth one was answered. Marina *had* left a message behind her. "*Gualtier Maldè, nome di lui si amato* . . . I know his name, Walter Maldè . . ." The message was there.

With fingers that shook so that I could barely write, I added two more questions to my list:

10. Which of us had not, to my knowledge, tasted Marina's amontillado at her invitation and yet knew that the purple-glass angel contained sherry?

11. Was there anyone else who could have entered the library while the Taits were gathering the icicles?

As I finished writing that last word Sandy burst into the room, burbling with excitement.

"Tony, the wind!" he croaked. "The wind's died down. The storm is over."

I looked at him with dazed eyes. "Sandy, I've been a fool. Julian didn't commit those murders. I know now who did."

"You know?"

I nodded. "I should have known early this morning . . . when Julian told his story about the Dresden debut and the concentration camp."

He tossed me the long sheet of wrapping paper I had seen him working on downstairs. It was covered with writing now. He grinned.

"Tell me about it later," he said. "I'm going down to see if they've started a boat across the river for us. While I'm gone I wish you'd check over this story for Nero. See if there are any corrections to be made."

He turned and strode out of the room.

35

I MADE NO ATTEMPT TO STOP HIM.

When the door had closed behind him I looked down at the paper he had given me.

There was no salutation. It simply began.

> This isn't meant to be any *Apologia pro sua vita*. I'd be a goddam fool to try that. Just call it my *Nunc Dimittis* and let it go at that.
>
> I was going to write this and give it to you after we got back to Portland, Tony. It was to have been a beautiful document, worthy of posterity. But I haven't time now. As soon as I saw you pick up the angel bottle I knew it wouldn't be long. You've got brains, Tony. You'll put two and two together. You'll know it was me, but I wonder if you'll figure out why I did it. It all depends on whether you remember that story Julian Porter told us. The one about the young tenor. Remember?
>
> Yes, I was that ass. I could have been great, I think. I had the makings—voice, youth, ambition, a fair amount of looks, and determination. I lacked only one thing. That was brains.
>
> There's no point to re-hashing the whole thing. Julian gave you the story as it happened. The details are unimportant. They only show me up for the

fool I was. And it isn't pleasant to look back and see how stupid you've been.

From the day I sailed with Marina to the day I came to in the camp at Dachau I lived in a haze. You told me once that you'd learned very early that no one ever gets anything for nothing in this life. That's smart. And true. I had to learn it the hard way. And I do mean hard.

The whole business sounds screwy enough to have come out of an Oppenheim novel. I almost have to laugh right now as I sit here writing. Communist pamphlets and concentration camps! But it wasn't funny then. And it wasn't funny when during a little session with some of the investigators a rubber hose caught me across the Adams-apple. During my first year in prison I had no voice at all. I didn't think I'd ever be able to speak again. By the end of the second year I could whisper a couple of words. When they let me go after my third year, believe it or not, I could actually croak out a few sentences.

But sing? Don't make me laugh. You know what I sound like now. That's the best I'll ever be able to do.

When I got out of that hell-hole they shoved me on a cargo-boat and shipped me out of the country. I didn't even have time to find out if Marina was still over there. I felt badly about that. You see, I wanted to see her. To have a little chat with her. I wanted it very much indeed. Understand?

During those three years I'd done a lot of thinking. Mostly about Marina. Of course, I didn't know Beale and Ambrosia then, so I thought I had a monopoly on hatred. I used to spend hours in that cell of mine planning what I'd do when I got my hands on Marina Grazie. I sometimes think it was the only thing that kept me alive.

When I finally got to New York I was down and out. Naturally. I had had a siege of pneumonia on the boat coming over. Sleeping in Central Park didn't help that along any. But it was the only thing I could do. And I could always keep my mind busy figuring out some way to get to California—where Marina was living.

One day I picked up a *Times* and saw that someone named Anthony Graine had arrived back in this country and was joining the Monte Calvo Company for a tour. The item went on to say that Marina Grazie would join the company in Portland for guest appearances.

So I forced myself on you. Luckily for me, my hands hadn't been broken, even if my voice had. They'd been stamped on plenty of times but they were still in one piece, so to speak. You happened to need an accompanist and you took me on. Sorry for me, I guess. But if you hadn't done it, I'd have managed some other way. You see, I had a feeling that one day soon I'd meet Marina face to face.

It was so simple. You all went upstairs to get wood and right after that the Taits, who thought I was asleep, started out for icicles. When they began to bundle themselves into their coats and boots I knew that a just providence was presenting me with a tailor-made opportunity. As soon as they left I slipped into the library.

I wish you could have seen her when I walked into the room and she turned around from the piano and saw me. She started to scream, but I stopped her mouth with my hand. Then I pushed her head forward till it rested on the music-rack and her fat neck was stretched out straight. I had intended to strangle her but Ambrosia's knitting-needles were temptingly at hand. I grabbed one and jabbed down, right where the dyed hair grew to a point at the base of her skull.

She never moved.

Then I went around the piano and drank a toast to her from the angel-bottle. I knew that before long you'd remember that slip I made. For how would I know it was sherry in that purple bottle unless I had had some?

The phonograph was another break. Bollman had apparently collected Marina's records and I put on *Caro Nome* hoping the batteries would be good for a few minutes at least.

I got back to the kitchen before the Taits returned. I thought I'd gotten away clean. So when Horston got hold of me that night and told me he'd seen me from the window I was floored. I promised to meet him later on after everyone was asleep and turn the diamond over to him. When I met him—well, everything happened just as you figured it.

Julian was my wedding-gift to Beale and Elena. After all, I was in it so deep that one more wouldn't make any difference. I went into that room determined to kill him. He played into my hands by grabbing the gun. Elena told the truth. It did look like an accident. I haven't any regrets over him. He was a rat and a dirty one. Just like Marina. They were two of a kind.

How did he happen to have the diamond? I put it in his pocket myself. It seemed the perfect solution. And it almost worked.

Just one more thing and then I'm through.

You were right about the sheet of the *Rigoletto* score. I'll have to give the old girl credit for some fast thinking. For by tearing out that page, even while I was holding her down, she did try to tell you who had killed her. Remember the words, "*Gualtier Maldè, nome di lui si amato!*"

Come, come, Tony. Have you called me Sandy so long that you've forgotten my name is Walter—*Gualtier?*

But that's enough of this. Time's getting short.

I'm sorry I had to use you like this, Tony. You've been swell to me. A fellow couldn't ask for a finer friend than you've been. The only repayment I can make is in opera-singer's coin. I'm giving you this. Don't hesitate to use it. It'll make swell publicity for you. That's why I'm writing it.

Goodbye, Tony. . . .

I went down to the library, pushed the curtain back from one of the windows. The afternoon light was grey and wan. Snow was falling quietly. The wind had died away. Across the river two rowboats were pushing out from the shore.

Nearer at hand, from the front door of Lucifer's Pride, across the narrow, snow-covered yard, across the little roadway, straight toward the river ran a trail of footprints . . . footprints that ended at the brink of the precipice. . . .

It is Canio in *Pagliacci* who says, "*La commedia e finita*" . . . "The comedy is ended."

I pulled the curtains together . . . turned away . . . blindly. . . .

The Author
(1941)

Paging Robert Ripley's *Believe It or Not!* Here is a man who went to Notre Dame and did *not* play football. While Rockne's adept artists were tossing the pigskin Alfred Meyers was getting his sheepskin in journalism and was singing in the glee club.

After his graduation he followed the well-worn path of the Western college graduate to New York, attended every play in town, and one day, much to his surprise, found himself in the chorus of a Shubert operetta. During a long run in Philadelphia he sold his first short story—and the Metropolitan Opera Company lost a prospect. For he promptly deserted music as a career and returned to Notre Dame to take his master's degree in English and to teach courses in freshman composition.

But Mr. Meyers' musical inclinations would not play second fiddle, as the saying goes, to literature. Shortly he found himself back in his home town of La Grande, Oregon, working off and on in his father's bank and singing in any chorus that would use his talents. In the fall of 1937 he went to San Francisco, singing in the chorus of the San Francisco Opera during the winter and in Billy Rose's Coast edition of the Aquacade at the San Francisco fair. Somehow, he did not let that display of correct aquatic curves keep his mind off *Murder Ends the Song* which was written during this period.

Besides this novel he has turned out numerous short stories and one play which was produced at Reed College and won the prize of the Portland Civic Theatre's contest for Oregon authors.

Although this novel is told in the first person, it is to be distinctly understood that Mr. Meyers is not the singing sleuth who solved the mystery of the frayed canary's by no means premature death. That tenor detective had only three aversions—boiled cabbage, scrambled brains, and coloratura sopranos—while Mr. Meyers confesses he dislikes Italian primitives, Dorothy Lamour's singing, Picasso, Mickey Rooney, imitation swing and amateur productions of Gilbert and Sullivan.

Coachwhip Publications
CoachwhipBooks.com

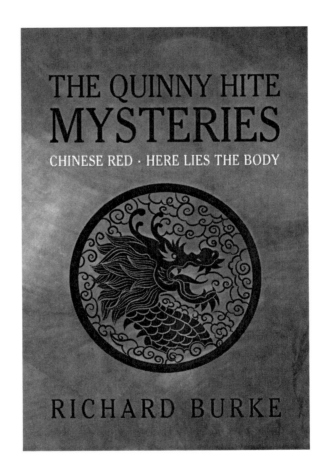

The Quinny Hite Mysteries, by Richard Burke
Chinese Red / Here Lies the Body ISBN 1-61646-247-7
The Fourth Star / Sinister Street ISBN 1-61646-248-5

Coachwhip Publications

Now Available

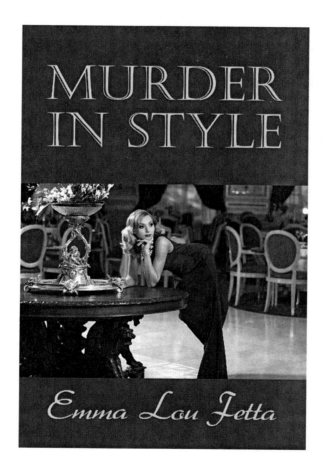

Murder in Style, by Emma Lou Fetta
Introduction by Curtis Evans
ISBN 978-1-61646-232-1

COACHWHIP PUBLICATIONS
COACHWHIPBOOKS.COM

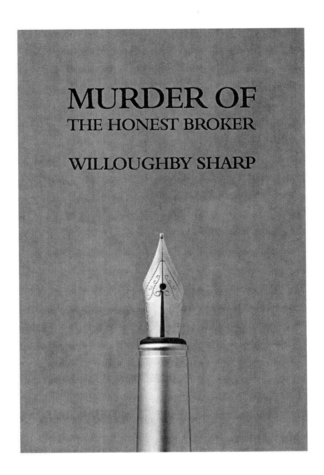

Murder of the Honest Broker, by Willoughby Sharp
Introduction by Curtis Evans
ISBN 978-1-61646-211-6

Coachwhip Publications
Now Available

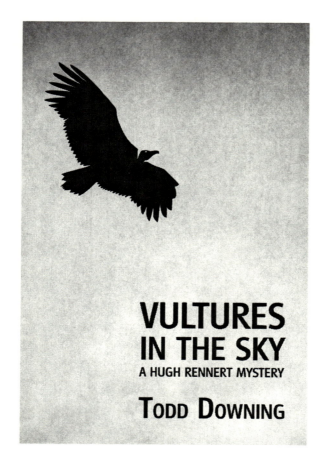

Vultures in the Sky, by Todd Downing
Introduction by Curtis Evans
ISBN 978-1-61646-149-2

Coachwhip Publications
CoachwhipBooks.com

There is No Return, by Anita Blackmon
Introduction by Curtis Evans
ISBN 978-1-61646-223-9

CPSIA information can be obtained at www.ICGtesting.com
Printed in the USA
LVOW07s0138171115

462775LV00002B/54/P